"Thomas creates a detailed, transcendental world full of both beauty and brutality. There are too many monsters to count, and yet we still dare to hope. My favorite work of his to date."                —Mercedes M. Yardley,
Bram Stoker Award–winning author

"Reading *Incarnate* is a visceral experience—weird cosmic horror at its purest. Brutal and unforgiving, Thomas's novel is epic in its scope and ideas. The creature horror is mind-blowing—endlessly unique and fascinating in its variety. In his skilled hands, even the wildest beast is human and capable of redemption. I truly don't know how else to describe this meditative, monstrous, delicate, icicle-sharp novel. You'll just have to taste it for yourself."                —Sam Rebelein,
Bram Stoker Award–nominated author of *Edenville*

"A numinous slow burn . . . from one of horror's best, *Incarnate* is a sumptuous and sinister exploration of human sin."          —Lee Murray,
Bram Stoker Award–winning author of *Grotesque: Monster Stories*

"Richard Thomas is a major name in the horror genre, and his latest book once again proves why. This is a strange, profound, and powerful tale about good and evil, and it's one that will stick with you long after you've turned the final page."                —Gwendolyn Kiste,
Lambda Literary and Bram Stoker Award–winning author
of *Reluctant Immortals* and *The Haunting of Velkwood*

"Thomas is one of the best when it comes to the art of visceral horror. *Incarnate* is as cold and immaculate as winter in the deep Arctic."
—Laird Barron, author of *Not a Speck of Light*

"A mournful meditation on the solitude of sin and the connective cosmic web that binds both man and monster together. Richard Thomas writes of our fall from grace with such transcendent eloquence, such astute empathy for the wicked and divine, it's enough to rekindle a reader's faith in the power of horror literature."                —Clay McLeod Chapman,
author of *What Kind of Mother and Ghost Eaters*

# INCARNATE

A NOVEL

## RICHARD THOMAS

Podium

This book contains highly sensitive and mature subject matters including graphic sexual content, depictions of suicide, animal abuse, and violence. Reader discretion is advised.

Cover design by Christina Mrozik

ISBN: 978-1-0394-5320-3

Published in 2024 by Podium Publishing
www.podiumaudio.com
**Podium**

*This novel is dedicated to Lisa, Ricky, and Tyler.*
*None of this would be possible without your love and support.*

# INCARNATE

She was continually shocked by the fact that the others seemed to forget the obvious: that the mountains, like most beautiful things in this world, were deadly.

—Alma Katsu, *The Hunger*

# SEBASTIAN

As I stare across the never-ending whiteness that is my arctic prison, I realize that while I seek isolation at times, the work requires me to interact with the locals—we each have something that the other party needs. And out here in the frigid wilderness, the night creeps in, expanding across several months, making my life, and duty, that much more difficult. I'm not getting any younger, and the cabin I live in, while ringed with several layers of protection, is not going to keep me safe from my work.

Not forever.

I have to seek out my neighbors. This tricky relationship we have—my way of helping them to cross over, them giving me what I need to keep the shadows at bay. To the naked eye, I am an elderly man, at the edge of town, constantly chopping wood, planting strange bushes and flowers when the ground isn't frozen, a smile and a wave as hunters pass by with their kills. Inside this ancient flesh, I'm something else entirely. Soon, the village will be buried, the passes closed by chest-high snowdrifts, roads erased, nothing entering, and no way out. It's a good time to regroup, to heal, and prepare for the long night, as the woods will come calling soon enough.

My name is Sebastian Pana, and I'm growing tired, but there is much to do as winter approaches, never truly going away, always lurking, my life held in my shaky, freezing hands every time I step outside. There are so many ways to die here—the cold, the wet, the animals hungry at the edge of your vision, the isolation, starvation, drink, the traditions, and loneliness as well. I have few friends, and that is on purpose, but I am still human, for the most part. I long for companionship, as much as I seek out warmth and enveloping peace. When I push out into the endless void, it is with a bright light, on the end of a long, sharp stick.

The veil is weakening, and they're pushing through. I fear it won't be long now.

ACT ONE

# THE SIN-EATER

An elk mother, cornered, will slash with her hooves and tear
with her mouth and even offer the hope of her own
hamstrings, and if none of that works, she'll rise again years
and years later, because it's never over, it's always just
beginning again.

—Stephen Graham Jones, *The Only Good Indians*

# CHAPTER ONE

# ARRIVING

The darkness is expanding—sixty days of night looming on the horizon—so I step out onto my porch and take a deep breath, the cold air burning my nostrils and making my lungs ache. There is so much to do, so much pain to repurpose into the void. I rub my hands together to warm them, already dressed in layers—long thermal underwear over boxers, two pairs of wool socks—with more to come. The morning is brisk, hoarfrost sparkling across the snow-covered ground, but I know I can't stand here for long. I inhale again—juniper, salt, a whiff of fish, my own musk—and take in my humble abode, knowing that the season is upon us, preparing for what will come. It is both invigorating and daunting.

My neighbors give me a wide berth, the odd man on the hill, at the foot of the mountain. I am far enough away for them to feel safe, but close enough that they can walk to me with their offerings and requests. I've been here for years, but not as long as some say. When they pass my cabin, they talk of the boy who used to live here, and then the man who took his place, now an elderly curmudgeon holding down the fort. If they did the math, it wouldn't add up. The boy, the father, the grandfather—we are one in the same. Not three separate individuals, but one soul, aging at a rapid pace. It all comes at a price, this calling. The trek I took north, away from friends and family, all assuming me dead now, this dot on a map my destination, the tear in reality my post.

When I got here, there was little work, the village struggling, most residents hunting and fishing to survive, sometimes working with local scientists doing research, sometimes traveling to larger cities for factory jobs, or down to the water—the cannery, and various boats providing sustenance. Some make a living guiding tourists in search of big game. We all live off the land in one way or another, taking so much, and giving back so little.

There were empty apartments, dilapidated houses, and abandoned warehouses everywhere—so many places to curl up, freeze, and die. This was not my first rodeo, other places across the land having similar pockets of darkness and vulnerability. And for a while I'd toil there until the wounds healed and my work was no longer necessary. It's true, that parable—it's the wolf you feed that survives.

Walking the town that first time—a hot cup of coffee at the local diner, a warm glass of amber at the one bar in town—I felt the waves of desperation wash over me, the sickness, and the despair. No telling which came first—the dying chicken or the rotten egg—but it doesn't really matter, does it? Was the diseased moth drawn to the flickering flame, or did the flame create chaos, burning everything that surrounded it?

The cabin.

It was a place that held my gaze, but only for a moment, because what I was looking for was something else entirely. The reason I was here. And as the darkness began to spill over the gray, frozen ground, the black spruce and lodgepole pines lining the base of the mountains, the distant bay shimmering on the horizon, I found a path that wound off the main road, behind the cabin, and into the woods. No footprints, an immaculate ribbon of white. I turned my head this way and that, looking for somebody to stop me, looking for any sign of life, but there was none. Everyone was inside—you don't stand out in the cold here, unless you have a death wish. So I walked toward the edge of the forest, the virgin layer of snow crunching beneath the soles of my boots, and the grand archway that held the trailhead in place, an electricity filling the air, my skin suddenly warm and flushed, a single drop of sweat running down my left temple.

I stood at the opening to the neglected trail, looking as deeply as I could down the path and up into the slow incline that would certainly continue up the hill, rising slowly into the mountains. Across the sky, now pitch black, there flowed a curtain of lights, the Aurora Borealis, drifting and floating as if great amorphous eagles, rising and falling on thermal streams, charged particles sputtering and crackling as they swayed back and forth. In the distance something howled, most likely a wolf or coyote. I thought about where I might bed tonight. I thought about sharp teeth and weak flesh. I thought about hunger, and desire, and vengeance. I listened to the promises the lights made to me, the deal we were about to broker, and the history of this land spilled out across the wavering streaks, as they changed from yellow to green, with just a splash of red. We would palaver for some time, the lights and I, warnings made, uncertainties broached, a smile creeping across my face as we came to an agreement.

I nodded my head and took a few steps back, as the lights faded into the night, and a ripple formed at the opening to the trail. It was subtle, a glimmer of gold thread, an oily smear that started at the top of the archway, the slender trees bent over, holding each other in the cold, empty space, running all the way to the ground. It was starting already. Though the long night hadn't officially begun yet, still a few days away, the tear was already forming. And from that rip there emanated a rush of heat, as if a long, hot breath had been slowly exhaled—rotten eggs, meat gone sour—a ripeness that made my nose wrinkle and bile rise up in my throat. And wheezing through the slender gash was a screech and bellow filled with anger and remorse, some great venting created out of anguish and hunger, an eagle cry over a grizzly's roar that ended as quickly as it had begun. A ripple of goose bumps ran over my skin, and I backed away from the breach.

I had to get started. There wasn't much time.

And so I took the cabin—bought it outright for a song and a dance—and quickly got to work.

The cabin.

It wasn't much, but it had potential—proximity, simplicity, and away from prying eyes. It would do.

They told me it had been built by hand—by one of the locals, a man who hunted and fished like so many do here, a place to build a fire, lay his head, and be left alone with his thoughts. The logs were cut from the towering spruce that filled the space around us—sawed and hewn, notched and stacked. Tedious hours were spent with a hammer and chisel, chinking the gaps between them with oakum and tarred cloth to keep out the unrelenting cold. The low stone wall that surrounded the base of it must have taken him days to find, carry, and stack—providing a solid structure around the bottom of the cabin, for warmth, and security, and strength. The vines and other greenery that ran up the walls, the roof covered in sphagnum moss, swallowing the cabin—it drew me in, and I felt that I could work here, that I could commune, and heal, and absolve.

Stepping inside, out of the meagre warmth of the low sun, it was one main room, with a large stone fireplace to the right, a torn leather chair, and a faded cloth couch filling most of the space, with simple wooden end tables and lamps with shades that looked like leather, or perhaps deerskin. The metal shade frames held the silhouettes of wolves and caribou and bears. Stale alcohol and cigarette smoke lingered from its last occupant, blending oddly with the sweet aroma of cut wood in the cold, stagnant air. The table was simple—one huge, round stump of oak, sanded and varnished to a shiny hue. It must have weighed a ton. I almost tried to lift it up to see if there were roots sinking into the floor and earth below it.

At the other end of the space was what would have to be my kitchen—a small counter with a steel sink and a faded blue propane refrigerator that felt out of place, from another time— rounded edges and shiny chrome, standing out like a jewel that had been dropped in the dirt. Inside it were jars of expired herring, ketchup, mustard, and soy sauce. There was a full-sized bed tucked back in the corner, and a singular door that opened into a tiny bathroom. It was more than I needed.

The man had killed himself, they told me. So I stood in the doorway, soaking up the space, speaking to the spirits that lingered, asking them what they might need, offering up what I could—blessings and forgiveness—as I eased over to the fire-place, dry kindling and dusty logs still in place. With a box of matches I had found in a kitchen drawer, I opened the damper, dragging the wooden stick across the rough, black edge of the box, and lit the fire to break the chill. I walked around the space, inhaling and exhaling, but not taking a bite. There wasn't much here for me, but I chewed on what I could find, and then spat into the warming room a gray mottled moth, with rings of yellow, that looked like eyes. It fluttered and danced in a circle before landing on my outstretched hand.

It was all that was left of him.

Lingering, uncertain, and unhappy.

He had been a lonely man, seeking peace in his isolation, and instead finding a lifetime of regret and remorse. This was not the plan he had in mind, and as the weeks unfolded, the lake slowly freezing from the shore outward, the wild game quickly disappearing, he found that there wasn't much left for him here. Or anywhere else it seems. The endless nights and constant snowfall have driven many a man to empty his last bottle and stare into the narrow darkness of his rifle.

Turns out it's pretty easy to undress, walk out into the cold, and freeze to death. I turn my eyes to the two windows over the kitchen sink, gazing out into the land behind the house, through the intricate patterns of frostwork on the glass, and the woods beyond it. He walked until he couldn't feel anything anymore, floating along on legs deadened by the cold, and then, in a moment of panic, he turned around, changed his mind, and tried to make his way back down the mountain, down the trail, to his warm cabin, and the promise of a new day.

He didn't make it.

I stare at a patch of grass out back, the shape of the weeds and faded flowers now making sense to me. A simple man, with a sad little life, that amounted to nothing in the end.

The moth fluttered on my fingertip and took off into the air.

Maybe it would stay.

Maybe it would wander out the door.

Either way, it wouldn't be here long.

I took a deep breath, and a blueprint appeared in my mind.


Knowing I only had a few days to fortify my homestead before the long night arrived for good, I did what I could to strengthen my abode.

I brought a few things with me, but the rest I would have to acquire in town.

It started with the fresh herbs, and a slow circling of the cabin. It burned and smoked, the windows open, the door wide, my mind seeking out the presences that still lingered, the last remnants of death and loss—the man, his few friends, the neighbor who had found him, the handful of women who had spent time with him, the lost souls that had lived here briefly after he was gone—all of it had to be cleansed, and escorted out, to make room for other speculations. It didn't take long to walk this cabin, inch by inch, foot by foot.

And then I was outside, examining the perimeter of the structure, taking notes as I went—stones to be put back in place, logs to be nailed down, cracks filled. There was a ring of bushes that ran around the entire property, part of what drew me to this space. I walked the circle and touched the shrubs, seeing the work that the man had put into this property. The holly was tucked up tight from one bush to the next, red berries popping out like dots of blood. The circle was complete, but for the opening that let me in. A stone path led from the front door straight forward and through the opening in the bushes and down the front yard all the way to the dirt and gravel road that meandered into town. And then farther out from the bushes were evergreens—juniper, and spruce, and pine.

It was a good start, and it would help, but I had to do more.

It started with the salt. There were a few tools in a tiny shed behind the house, including a variety of shovels for clearing wet, heavy snow from the cabin roof to keep it from collapsing, and so I took my supplies and began digging a shallow trench just inside the ring of bushes, all the way around the house. The ground wasn't quite frozen yet, but it would be soon. In the bright sunlight I worked up a sweat chipping at the surface ice with a pickaxe, digging deeper into the soil beneath with the shovel, my arms burning, my back aching as I went. By the time I was done, the sun had gotten much lower in the sky, and my feet throbbed in my work boots, my jeans dusted with dirt, my blue flannel draped over the bushes, only a black t-shirt between myself and the elements. The moment I stopped digging, the cold rushed in, as it always did, and I took a moment to survey my work.

It would do.

Walking backward, I took the fifty-pound bag of salt and started to fill in the trench, sprinkling a solid line all the way around the property, completing the circle as hawks circled overhead, marking my progress. To the ring I added a number of herbs, flowers, and seeds—dill, rosemary, lavender, fennel, and rue. If you were standing in my kitchen, you might just think I liked to cook, my herb garden now filling the space above the sink and under the window. You might notice the purple flowering bushes, and spiky plants, and think I had a green thumb.

When I finished, and looked up, the sun was gone, and I was suddenly cold. It was not dangerously cold yet, but it would be soon. It would be easy to get caught out, and I shivered as I hunted down my flannel, eager to get back inside to the fire that burned brightly, a plume of smoke rising from the chimney like gray tendrils.

Later, when the moon hung overhead, and the animals gathered at the edge of the woods, watching and waiting, I would return with water, trucking buckets from the nearby river where I kept a hole chopped all winter, one bucket after another, and slowly filled the trench, the ground certainly frozen now, as the temperatures had dropped, the sun long gone, dipping down below freezing, and into the teens, the wind whipping in over the water, and up the hill, cementing this moat that I had built around my house.

It would hold the salt, so that it wouldn't blow away. It would complete the circle, as the herbs and flowers blended together. It would close a loop that I was desperate to finish, so that I might sleep, my muscles aching, my mind reeling, as the auroras danced over the horizon and the tear slowly widened.

Every location is unique. I've spent time in the crippling heat of the desert. I've spent time in the crushing blanket of humid swamplands. I've spent time in thick woods that felt ancient and undisturbed. They all have something to offer, and different ways of taking. Here, in the cold, the far north, the brutal winds and interminable winter, there are unique challenges to this work. So during that first week, as I prepared for my first meal, I wandered the landscape to see what I might find—allies, enemies, resources, and traps.

I would not be disappointed.

With that first long night approaching, and the cabin secure, I decided to take a walk to explore my immediate surroundings. I bundled up in jeans and long underwear, two pairs of socks, my work boots, a thick turtleneck, a heavy sweater, knit hat, insulated gloves, and a parka over the top. I would learn about cold and rain, about ice and sleet, how to layer better, but that would take time, and I'd make mistakes. Everyone does; frostbite was inevitable here. It only took a tiny gap in the clothing, an inch of exposed flesh. The pins and needles came first, then the numbness before it started to burn and swell. It would turn a waxy white, stiff, and still cold to the touch, even after you were warm again inside the safety of your cabin. A day later, the blisters would form, ugly and angry, without relief. If it got down deep enough, the flesh turned black as coal and hard as old ice, as the skin slowly died. It only took losing one finger, or one toe, to not make that mistake twice.

Or so I've been told.

With the woods to my back, it seemed the obvious place to start. So, I started my hike with the sun high overhead, passing through the archway that led into the encroaching forest, the rift hardly a flicker in the brightness of day.

The path was well trodden, and I wondered what might draw the locals up into the woods, into the hills and the craggy mountain that lurked with such a heavy presence. The farther I hiked up the trail the quieter it got. The chirps and calls, the fluttering and rustling, faded into the background. The skittering of small woodland creatures disappeared as the forest grew thicker and darker around me. I had assumed that once I started to climb the mountain proper that it would all thin out and start to die off—the thinner the air, the higher I went, the colder it got. But not yet. For now, the bushes, and shrubs, and foliage closed in tight. It was both comforting and claustrophobic.

It took a while for me to notice its presence, so focused I was on maintaining my footing on the icy slope, pushing my way through the snow-laden spruce boughs. My pulse throbbed in my neck the higher I hiked, and the more I started to sweat. I unzipped my coat and stopped at a gap in the trail, a natural overlook that exposed the rocky beaches and the shimmer of the bay below, and the ocean beyond it.

I smelled it first, something ripe and musky, a blend of damp hay, dirty dishrag, and wet dog. In the distance branches snapped, and dense foliage brushed up against something, a gentle *whooshing* sound, and then a heavy trembling in the earth. My eyes darted from the water to the trail, up and down, back to the woods, trying to gaze as deep into the greenery as the forest would let me. The pine and spruce swayed in the breeze, creaking and bending, as they moved. Birds cawed overhead, a rustling of black wings fading as they flew away.

I considered going back, but I'd hardly gotten started, and so I continued on, up the trail, higher and higher, the incline gradually steepening.

I passed a downed hemlock tree, snapped in two, a black scar running down one side. It had fallen across the path, blocking my progress, so I paused for a moment to consider moving it.

It was way too heavy, and as I tried to lift it, estimating the weight, I noticed three scrapes, long drags of exposed wood and missing bark.

I could duck under and keep going, or I could turn back. The wind picked up, and heavy clouds drifted over me, a storm sliding down the mountain, out of nowhere it seemed, as the temperature dropped, chilling my skin.

The day was moving quickly, faster than I thought, some bit of time lost out here, perhaps, in my thoughts, under the spell of nature, and so I started to head back down.

After a few minutes I noticed a pile of scat in the center of the trail. It had not been there before, on my way up. This was not a rabbit, not a coyote. It was something else entirely. The lumpy pile steamed in the cold air, pieces of white stuck in the slimy, glistening pile of dark matter. Bones, teeth, something sinuous, fur, hair—I didn't like any of it. It seemed unnatural, not of this place. This wasn't a bear or a lynx. This was something else entirely.

Suddenly I wanted to be down off the mountain. In my hurry to prepare the cabin, I must have missed something. Just because the tear was small now, didn't mean that this was the first time it had ripped. I had made a mistake. I assumed I had been called here at the inception, the tipping point, the first time this point had manifested.

I was wrong.

I had been slow getting here.

I was late.

And in that moment, I smiled, and laughed, thinking about how embarrassing it would look to run screaming down the hill, scared of a fallen tree, a pile of crap, and some strange noises, and smells, emanating from the woods.

"Take it easy, Sebastian," I whispered to myself.

And then I saw it.

It faded into focus, not twenty feet from me, hidden in the brown of tree bark, blended in with the dirt and dead leaves, two massive horns branching up into the sky. A moment ago they were merely that—branches, two red glowing eyes just berries, a snort and heavy breath filling the air with copper, sour anger, and decaying teeth.

I ran.

I ran down the hill, trying not to trip, bulky in so many layers, my boots catching roots and embedded rocks, not looking back, but listening. Oh how I listened, my ears straining to stay behind me, reaching back into the forest to try and understand if it was going to come after me, or stay where it was. Perhaps it had just eaten, maybe it was tired, or just territorial. It certainly hadn't been following me, stalking me, as I wandered about the woods and trails.

Something to the left caught my eye, and I hesitated to look, needing to stay focused on the path, but I glimpsed the red, the glistening white, and kept my gaze on the broken limbs of a doe. Its head wrenched into a twisted knot of fur and muscle, eviscerated and lying in the leaves, guts strewn about as if being searched for something elicit, some gem or drug or buried secret—intestines loping out in long strands, the broken legs sticking up at odd angles, its eyes open wide, tongue lolling, a long dead cry and bleat buried in its throat.

And then I was tripping and stumbling, hands held out in front of me, the archway at the end of the forest in sight, the rip winking, the gold filament reflecting the sun, and I barreled through the opening, head turning back to see what must certainly be upon me by now.

I was suddenly falling onto the dying grass, onto my face, arms outstretched, turning over, my mouth open and ready to scream—and there was nothing. Just the snowy silence and the first drops of freezing rain, clouds rolling in to blot out the sun. I heard voices down the hill—fishermen, hammers banging, a loud lid slamming shut, the honk of a horn, and laughter, a tarp rippling in the wind, being tied down no doubt, and my breath—heavy and fast accompanying a pain that rifled through my chest.

I wasn't alone out here.

I thought I had more time, that it hadn't started yet.

But it was already happening here, it seemed.

It was time to eat, I feared.

But I had no banquet to attend.

I would have to improvise, and fast.

It had already come through.

And there might be others.

CHAPTER TWO

# THE LONG NIGHT
# RETURNS

Standing on the porch as the winter sun creeps along the horizon, a shiver runs over my flesh. I knead my back, running my fingers over a long scar that traverses my spine. I massage my hands for warmth, but also to appease my aching digits, some of them bent and swollen, the tip of one finger missing entirely. I rub my eyes and stars appear, a stitch in my side as I inhale, a sharp pain in my rib cage, the bones and muscles still knitting themselves back together. They may never fully heal. Running my hand over my scalp, my gray hair long and thick, I can feel the pressure in the air starting to form, a headache looming, tension rippling across my skin like a dull shock of electricity. Side-stepping the strange grass and yellow flowers that bloom in the shape of a man, I don't have to walk to the back of the cabin to know that the tear is forming. I can feel it in my bones. I see that singular line of golden filament in my mind's eye every time I go to sleep. It glimmers and sparkles in the dark, eager to expand, ready to open up and spill out whatever horrors clamor at the rift.

There will be wood to chop today; that always needs to happen. You can never have enough stockpiled, because surrendering to the cold out here is certain death. Electricity is more of a concept, a philosophy, this far north—lines going down, sagging under the weight of icy build-up before losing the battle against the winter winds. So whether you have a fireplace, like I do, or a pot belly stove, you need to have a plan B, or you'll never make it through. I will gather and chop and split until my arms are too weak to heave the ax, and then I'll rest and do it all again. There is wood stacked on one side of the cabin from the ground all the way to the roof. It's a good sweat, this work, and I know under the gaze of my neighbors that they wonder how the old man on the hill has such energy, how he doesn't break into pieces at the exertion. They see my wrinkled skin, my gray hair, the sorrow in my eyes, the slight stoop in my stance, and it doesn't jive with my actions. So, I try to stay in the shadows, out of sight, so that my exertions don't reveal my truth. They already think I'm something else, and those that have come to me—bringing me their dead or inviting me to their homes, taking succor in my presence—they're already believers. I hire local boys to help—and that quiets some of the rumors. They move stones, they help split wood, they dig and paint and stock supplies in the light of day, where all can see. And then they go home safe and sound—no ancient spells cast in their presence, no lingering hand on their shoulder or back, nothing that might scream witch, or warlock, or demon.

I turn to the large block of ice that sits on my front porch. It seems the offerings are coming in a few days early this year. There is nothing quite like iceberg water, carved out of the massive floating mountains of ice. This is a nice one, several feet square, like a small refrigerator, or a safe, squatting here like a translucent toad. It is white, and clear, with a dash of blue running through it. It sparkles in the sunlight, but it won't melt. We're almost at the polar night, the temperatures dropping, already below freezing. The ice pick jammed into the middle is a nice touch. If I didn't know any better, I might take that gesture the wrong way, as a kind of threat. But it's not the community here that I fear. I have a shotgun, a rifle, and a handgun, something I didn't address many years ago, the first time something came through.

It should have been an obvious decision on my part—hunting and fishing an important part of life up here—but back then, I was still learning. I thought the rules were set, carved in stone. And I was wrong. And it almost cost me my life. Enter the woods one time, unprepared—leaving behind water, not dressing for the elements, forgetting to check the weather first—and it can be a painful reckoning. Not being able to defend yourself? Or at least slow your enemy down? That's suicide. Sometimes a rifle is all I need, enough to hurt them, scare them off, and give me a bit of time. If they're smaller, or younger, or vulnerable in some way—I can take them down. But most of the time I'm running, one glance telling me that I don't stand a chance—leathery skin, muscled legs, thick armor, sharp talons, elongated incisors—it always changes, and each time I have to learn anew.

I don't know what this circuit will hold, how this season will unfold, but it seems to be getting worse. And that's a problem. I think about who I know in town, how my connections have grown over the years, what I've learned from past mistakes.

Two days and the darkness will be complete.

I've heard the engines running, the car doors slamming, the footsteps up and down the road. They know it's coming too, and so they're preparing their dead. They're checking in on the sick, the elderly, the suicidal, with a gaze up the hill toward me. They will seek me out soon enough. And I will welcome them with open arms, but I may have to go looking as well. Their kindness may not be enough. They are good people, for the most part, victims of nature and nurture and proximity. Their worries are unfounded, their transgressions minor.

What I need won't come to me.

What I need doesn't want to be absolved.

Tonight, I have dinner with a friend, but tomorrow, or the day after—sometime soon, as the tear won't wait. I learned that the hard way. I may have to go hunting, soon.

And that's always a dangerous task.

When Kallik shows up, he's full of questions. He has a school project that is due tomorrow, a slight whiff of panic running over his flesh as he barrages me with inquiries. He's a good kid, tall and skinny, long black hair pulled back into a ponytail, piercing blue eyes that never cease to hold my gaze.

But there is work to be done, as the ground solidifies, and I tell him to pepper me with questions as we try to salvage the last of my garden out back. All that remains are the root crops—carrots, turnips, beets, onions, and rutabagas. So, we shovel and pick and dig, the sad, bent, dull vegetables not amounting to much. But I'll take what the earth gives me. Later, we'll process and can what we harvested here, and place these bent, but not broken, items on the pantry shelves alongside the beans, rhubarb, and zucchini. The symbolism is not lost on me. They will help to fill the space alongside strawberry and raspberry jams, applesauce, and sacks of barley. When the roads close, and we're iced in, we'll make do with what we have. Plan A turns to plan B turns to plan C.

Kallik and I sit by the fireplace and sort through a box of photographs I have—the internet down at his house, probably across the entire town, no set of encyclopedias for him to reference. I tell him stories and cite newspapers, inventing reporters and articles that will never be checked. He's a curious lad, having only known the long winters, the cool summers, and the endless landscape. His whole life he has been surrounded by mountains, lakes, trees, and snow, never having traveled south, unable to experience other climates, cultures, or communities. So I tell him stories, as he furiously scribbles in a notebook, a gleam in his eye, the unavoidable draughts whipping through the cabin, dry wood crackling and sparking in the fire.

I tell Kallik about my time in central Missouri, living in a small town, at the edge of a massive cave system. I talk about the limestone outcroppings that buffer the highways, and the veins of white that marbled the gray stone. What he doesn't know is that if you rub the stone, if you polish it, or cut it for counters or slabs, it gives off a smell like sulfur, like rotten eggs. I discuss the caves that appear everywhere, not just the massive ones like Meramec Caverns—with the six-foot-tall structure of onyx called the Wine Table, originally grown underwater—but also smaller ones that can be explored by yourself, stalactites and stalagmites pushing up from the earth and descending from the ceiling. What I don't talk about is the rip I found after descending into a small cavern on the edge of a Boy Scout camp as a child, the glimmering tear my first foray into what would become my darker aspirations. I don't tell him about the bigotry and hatred that manifested in the small town that surrounded the camp—the cave emanating a black, smoky essence that corrupted the land, the people, and the crops. When I left, it was in a battered Jeep, the hot, humid summer air like a suffocating blanket, one rainbow flag on the edge of the village, the air, and my lungs filling with crisp hope, the tear silenced after years of pain and suffering.

I tell Kallik about my time in Arizona, and the painted desert that stretched for over one hundred twenty miles. I describe the sand and dirt running all the way to the horizon, and the stripes of color that filled the hills, dips, and valleys. I tell him about the stratified layers of siltstone, mudstone, and shale, and how one time when I walked down into the bumpy landscape

I had a moment of uncertainty, something strange unfolding in the dry heat. The land went quiet, not a single sound to be heard for miles—not a plane overhead, not the voice of a fellow traveler, not the slam of a car door, or the laughter of a child. Total silence. And in that moment, I explained, I felt three things happen simultaneously: the sensation that I had died, and that this was some version of heaven, no context upon which to put my current existence; a feeling that the matrix had broken, and I'd found some sort of glitch; and the certainty that I was in the presence of something holy and spiritual, basking in the heat and glory, a blessing placed upon me. I didn't mention the well I found, a hole at the edge of a petrified forest where the rocks I dropped never hit bottom, a smell working its way up and out of the depths that reeked of fermented fruit, mossy wood, and something sour underneath it all. I stood at that opening and dropped rock after rock, never hearing a *plink* or *bloop*, a tiny glimmer of gold suspended in the air, gradually expanding over time, circling and circling like water down a drain. I didn't tell him about the hatred that was directed at the Native American Indians who lived in the area, the ways that the police, and engineers, and entitled business owners dispensed their violence toward the Apache, Navajo, and Hopi that clung to their land with increasingly fewer resources. When I left, a bit older and wiser, a pipeline had been redirected, acres had been returned, and offices were being held by those who belonged there in the first place. In a faded Corolla, I drove west, a stack of frybread on the seat next to me, my skin tan and glistening from the sun that held court overhead.

I tell Kallik about my time in Chicago, as I circled back to further my education, the city skyline filled with metal, glass, and stone. I try to describe the way the city was filled with life—the populace filling the streets and el trains like a hive of buzzing bees. I talk about the way the buildings were so tall that the first time I truly looked up at them I almost fell over, the way they filled the sky, bending at strange angles. I talk about how one neighborhood would ease into another from Polish to gay to cops to artists to Ukrainian to Black to Cubs. I tried to explain how a person could bike from prairie-style architecture and painted ladies through housing projects surrounded by rusted fencing on to skyscrapers and lofts with red brick facades ending with tan beaches and rippling lakefront—all in about twenty minutes. I don't tell him about the alley behind a warehouse on the west side, and the way the throbbing gold amoeba held my gaze on a wall made out of concrete blocks. I don't tell him about the diner around the corner and the meal my classmates shared, the first time I accidentally supped at the sins of my brothers and sisters. I leave out the scene of my kneeling in that alley, vomiting out one cicada after another, a pool of ants running out of my nose, slick with snot, and one final purge landing on the ground, in the form of a stag beetle, clicking its pincers, a purple iridescence reflecting light. When they circled each other in a tornado of wind and detritus, to form something else entirely, I could only gasp, saliva stringing from my mouth to a puddle of liquid below me. They coalesced into an eight-legged creature, a stack of black eyes scattered on its head, translucent wings buzzing in a shaky dance, before flying off into the tear. When I leave Chicago, it is with a weary gaze over my shoulder, whatever cosmic duct tape I managed to apply to that alleyway a temporary solution at best.

No, I don't tell him everything.

I give him three photos to use for his paper, one from each location—the luminescent dripping cave walls of the Meramec Caverns; the ever-expanding Grand Canyon with the green Colorado River bisecting it; and the glowing Chicago downtown skyscrapers on the shores of Lake Michigan. I give him three objects—a piece of limestone from Missouri, a chunk of petrified wood from Arizona, and a tiny metal sculpture of what I still call the Sears Tower, from Chicago.

When he leaves, the sun has set, his mother certainly worrying, a few steps away from sauntering up the street to retrieve him, a lecture brewing on her lips, no doubt. The boy has been a sponge, eyes wide at every turn, a smile plastered across his face. I have taken him on a journey that he probably thought would never happen, not in this lifetime, and it has sparked something in the boy.

I chew on the essence he has left behind, blowing a pink bubble, that drifts out of my mouth, fluffy wings flapping as a tiny pink snout sniffs the air, emanating squeaks and chirps.

I may be on to something here.

I can't do this forever.


My dinner companion waits.

I head down the road to Yara's house, bundled up, in layers that I can remove. We have been friends for a long time now, and she accepts me for what I am. It is a safe place where I can not only eat without fear of sabotage, but can confess my worries and ask for her advice.

I do not eat out in public. It is too dangerous now that I have a reputation, now that the community knows what I am. Or at least, *suspects* what I am. Most are happy to have me because they know about the darkness, they have lost brothers to the bottle, they have had parents give in to the bite of a bullet, they have witnessed their coworkers take the long walk into the deep night, knowing they would never return. But not everyone is so accepting of my presence. I have enemies here as well.

On my stroll down main street, I use a cane, a gift from a man down on the south side of the village. I prefer to think of it as my walking stick. The carving at the top is of the head of a raven, its wings folded in tight, extending down the shaft. The wood is spruce, as the trees are common up here, lining the roads and filling the mountain sides.

"Sebastian!" somebody yells, and I glance to my left.

"Hello, Dominic. Are you staying warm?"

"Always, brother, always," he says, wandering over.

He is the sole proprietor of the only gas station in town, and therefore, a minor god. Not only for fuel—and his ability to repair everything from a Ford pickup and a Toyota Camry, to lawnmowers, snowblowers, and ice augers—but for whatever bit of the lower forty-eight he can find—Coke and Cheetos, Marlboros and Skoal, aspirin and Tums, *Playboy* and *Penthouse*.

I never worry about Dominic. He is a stout fellow with a heavy beard and long, wavy hair. He is a bear of a man, swarthy and thick, hairy from head to toe, his dirty gray sweatshirt pushed up, forearms like brown moss.

"Do you want in on the pool this year?" he asks.

"Sure, how much?"

"Twenty bucks. It's already up to two hundred, and we still have a day or two before the darkness fully descends."

I hand him the money.

"The twenty-second," I say.

"Bit early don't you think?" he asks, looking up at the sky, a flutter of snow starting to drift down upon us. "If the roads close that early . . ."

"I can feel it in my bones, Dominic. It's going to be a rough one."

He chews on his bottom lip, taking the money and stuffing it into his jeans pocket. He turns back to the brown Nova he was working on, the hood up, and then back to me.

"Shit," he says. "I have to make a call. I'm going to double my order. You sure about this?" he asks.

Before I can open my mouth, two dogs come tumbling out from between the gas station and the house next to it. They are a pile of snapping teeth, flying fur, and manic snarls. I don't recognize them, so they may be wild, or feral, gray and brown fur flying, teeth clicking, as yelps and spatters of blood spray the air.

We don't see the child until she wanders into our line of sight from the edge of our vision. She is in a pink snowsuit, her eyes wide, cheeks flush, her mother a house or two over, rooting around in the trunk of her car.

"Doggies!" she says, as the animals roll and bite and wrestle in the dirt.

I only glance at Dominic for a second, but he knows what I'm thinking. As I dash for the girl, dropping my cane, moving faster than an elderly man should, he runs for the gas station and the rifle I know he keeps behind the counter.

I'm moving too slow, the dogs rolling to the left, and then the right, popping up, then attacking again, teeth imbedded in the thick fur of a neck, whining and snarling as the child stumbles closer.

And then they lurch to the side, and she's covered in fur, the pink gone, nothing but gray and brown and stamping feet, jaws opening and closing, a tearing sound filling the air as fluff from her coat spills onto the ground.

I'm too late.

I stutter to a stop, looking for a way to jump in, waiting for a pause, a gap, where they might separate and give me a chance.

And then the gunshot echoes, once, twice, a ringing in my ears, as the ground and a thin layer of snow are spattered in red, bone fragments and flesh spreading out in two cones of gristle and wet matter.

Dominic stands with the rifle in his hands, a serious look crossing his face, as sweat beads on his forehead.

I run to the pile of dogs and girl, and fling their carcasses to the side, afraid of what I might find.

I pull the girl out and up, her eyes wide in shock, a scream building in her, as her hands open and close into tiny little fists. I count the fingers, and they are all there. I wipe the smear of blood off her face, and it's only that—a smear.

The mother comes running, screaming, "Oh my God, my baby," and I hand the child to her as Dominic walks closer.

"I think she's okay," I mutter. "I don't see any cuts or tears. I think they just bit into her coat and the snowsuit."

She holds the child to her, patting her down, searching for damage, as the cry finally erupts like a siren. She walks away a gibbering mess of *thank you* and *oh my God*, counting her blessings, no doubt, as she stumbles home.

"I'm going to go call a guy," Dominic says.

"Good idea," I respond.


I arrive at Yara's place with a heart that threatens to beat out my chest, but it's slowly calming down, as the cold night air tries to cool me off. Taking a deep breath, I unzip my coat and take off my hat, steam rising off of my sweaty brow. I will try to leave the violence of the incident behind me.

She opens the door in a cloud of ice crystals, spilling light and heat into the dark street, her skin pink and flushed, as a smile expands on her face.

"Sebastian! So good to see you."

And then she truly sees me and her face turns.

"You okay? What happened?"

"Nature. You know how it is. Little girl almost mauled to death in the street."

She nods her head. "She okay?"

"Yes, not a scratch, somehow. But it could have gone horribly wrong."

"Usually does," she says.

I shake my head and force a grim smile.

"Come on in out of the cold. You need anything?"

"A stiff drink and whatever you're serving," I say.

We sit at the 1950s Formica kitchen table, in aqua and white, with chrome running around the edge. The matching chairs, with the pop of aqua on the back of the seat, and the pristine white seats, feel like we've traveled back in time to a simpler and less threatening era. A snifter of bourbon sits in front of me, some red wine in a tall curved glass for her, and we catch up on the local gossip.

I tell her more about the dogs, and she nods her head, understanding that out here the world can turn in a moment— bear or ice or gun or hate. Her cheeks are still rosy, an almost permanent look for her, her dark eyes glistening as we talk, filled with so much history, and loss, and concern. Yara is the kind of neighbor who checks up on people when she doesn't see them at the community center for bingo. She will drop off a jar of preserves or a plate of chocolate cupcakes or an extra bowl of stew when she hears that somebody is struggling. Where I never worry about Dominic, I worry about Yara all the time. She never puts herself first, just her and her mother here, an ex-husband down south, who left years ago, unable to take the cold and isolation. She has roots that go deep, back for several generations. Leaving for her would be like severing an arm.

I know when I stop by that she will scrutinize me—she always studies my hands and wrists, looking for signs of sorrow, abuse, or merely incompetence. She holds my gaze to make sure that it is steady—not bloodshot and yellow, or weepy. When we hugged each other at the door, we were both running diagnostics—too skinny or too fat, inhaling soap and deodorant, but looking deeper for sickness and disease. It's how we are, how we've always been. And when we part from that hug, we hold each other at arm's length, and smile in approval. One less person to worry about. One less bit of weight to carry.

"So what are we having for dinner?" I ask. "Please tell me it's chili. It smells amazing."

At the inquiry she stands and moves to the stove.

"You are correct, sir," she says, stirring the pot. "I hope that's okay?" She beams as she turns to face me.

"Perfect. Is your mother going to join us?" I ask.

She turns back to the pot, her red flannel shirt rolled up to her elbows, faded blue jeans capped off by a pair of fluffy pink socks.

"No, she's not feeling well."

"Oh, that's a shame. Give her my best, will you?"

She nods her head and keeps stirring.

"So, tell me what's in it," I say.

"I start with ground beef, but if I have it, and I almost always do, I add chunks of caribou or venison. You'll have to taste it and tell me which you think it is."

I grin, anticipating the bounty we are about to receive.

"Onions of course. I prefer red, as they're sweeter."

"Definitely."

"And then several kinds of peppers," she says, stirring the pot and lowering the heat. She puts the lid on and comes back to sit at the table. "I always start with red or green bell peppers. And then I add whatever else I can find. One jalapeño for sure, and then something smoky like ancho peppers—or maybe chipotle."

"Very nice. And how do you feel about beans?"

She smiles. "I'm a three-bean girl. I know, I know . . . some people don't like them at all, but you know we have beans up here—one of the few things that grows—and it makes for a heartier dish, I think. I like a mix of black beans, kidney beans, and pinto beans. Or fava beans if I have them from the garden."

I nod.

"Tomatoes, of course, diced and canned, most likely—I like the ones with garlic and Italian spices. Gives it more depth."

"Yep."

"The dried spices and powders I usually just buy in a kit, since they tend to go flat if I have to buy large quantities of chili powder, cayenne, garlic powder, salt, and pepper. I mean, I have some of that on hand, but it's easier to just buy it premade. And then I add some other stuff," she says shyly, blushing a little.

"Some other stuff?" I ask, one eyebrow going up.

"Secret stuff," she says, smiling.

"Do tell," I say.

She pauses for a moment, eyeing me, and then continues.

"Okay, but keep this to yourself, okay? It's the only way I'll hold on to my Chili Queen title. I add some Tabasco, the chipotle one. I shake in a bit of Sriracha, for the sweetness the chili sauce gives it. If I have coffee sitting around, I pour in whatever is left in the pot. And then a single square of dark chocolate."

I'm practically salivating at this point.

"And my secret ingredient? One tablespoon of peanut butter."

"What?"

"Trust me," she says.

"Can we eat now?" I say.

"Yes," she says smiling, and then her face turns, as if remembering something. "I've made macaroni noodles too, if you want it chili mac style. And there's bannock by the stove."

She places bowls on the counter with spoons, shredded cheddar cheese, and sour cream.

"I have to go to the bathroom; go ahead and get started," she says as she scuttles out of the kitchen.

I'm starving and fix a bowl, the spices and warmth drifting up to me, filling me with peace. I sit down with my bowl and the bread and tuck in.

It starts out sweet—the tomatoes there, of course—but the beef, and I'm guessing venison, provide texture, and I chew. The beans are hearty—a comforting presence in my mouth, the liquid layered in smoke, spice, and garlic. The peppers blend in with the onions, so soft, but an occasional punch rises up out of the chili as I get a bite of jalapeño.

And then I swallow. And something is wrong.

I take another bite, cheese melting, the sour cream a nice bit of relief on the top of it all, and it tastes fine, and then it shifts.

Under the spices, and meat, and vegetables, and beans is something sour. Something bitter. My tongue tingles, and my eyes start to water.

"Yara, no," I whisper.

Once I've started, I cannot stop. Those are the rules. Otherwise it is incomplete. In order to cleanse the soul, it must all be eaten.

I look up to see Yara creep back into the room. She is crying, tears running down her face.

"I'm so sorry, Sebastian."

"Why didn't you just ask me?"

"It's too early. I knew you'd say no. She died this morning. She couldn't hold on until the long night began. She tried so hard, Sebastian. She was a good woman. I pray that my instincts are correct."

"There's no turning back now," I say.

She nods quietly. "I knew she wouldn't hold on for long. I can feel her fading already. I'm so sorry."

The betrayal, it stings, my stomach rolling, as I know what I have to do now. I wasn't expecting to work tonight, the darkness still hours away. But for Yara, I'll finish. I have to.

I spoon the chili in, trying to savor the smoke and heat, but the bitter aftertaste, it ruins every bite. I spoon and swallow, spoon and swallow, spoon and swallow, as Yara stands there wringing her hands, her eyes bloodshot now, her skin pale and shallow.

"I have to go," I say, standing up quickly. "I don't have much time."

"Sebastian, please . . ." she says.

I grab my coat, slide on my boots, and fling open the door. It's too early, there is nowhere for this to go but out into the world. I stumble forward into the shadows, trying to figure out how long I have. The streetlights push a hazy glow into the fluttering snow, and I work my way north, knowing the rip is closed, but hoping I can get as far up the hill and into the mountains as possible.

As I pass my cabin, I fling the cane toward my front yard and break out in a slow jog, the moon overhead helping to show the way, as the stars come out to witness this premature birth.

Through the archway, and up the hill, I feel it surging, and drop to my knees. A string of black smoke wafts out of my mouth, as a long slender form starts to crawl out of my gaping maw. My eyes water as it slides and pulls and slowly works its way out of me, trying not to bite down, struggling to breathe. And in the glow of the moon, the serpent finally weaves its muscled form out of me—a diamond pattern running down its length, crisscrossed threads of silver, a flicker of its tongue, and an angry hiss permeating the night. As it slithers into the underbrush—ten feet, twenty feet, thirty feet long—the last of it to disappear are three razor sharp needles sticking out of its tail.

Grandma wasn't a saint, it turns out.

But it could have been so much worse.

# CHAPTER THREE

# FINAL PREPARATIONS

When I wake it is with a heavy heart. I know that Yara had no choice, that she feared the eternal damnation of her mother's soul, but it doesn't change the fact that she held this secret close to her chest, lured me in with the promise of a good meal and friendly conversation, only to betray me with her actions. I thank whatever gods watch over me that her mother was a good person, her sins and transgressions minor, by comparison. When I think of what might have been unleashed on this poor, unsuspecting community it makes my skin crawl.

Outside, the gusting wind slams against the cabin, causing the timbers to shift and crack, spitting sleet rattling against the windowpanes, the dull embers from the fireplace pushing a soft glow into the room. Taking a deep breath, my desire is to pull the covers over my head, but the darkness is almost here, this the last full day of light for several months. I have prepared the house, I have stacked the wood, I have filled the pantry. My rifle is cleaned and loaded, leaning against the wall beside my bed. Not that my perimeter has ever been breached. But there is a first time for everything. And I don't like the way things are going.

What comfort might I provide to survive this long night? What last efforts can I expel today before the feasting and suffering commences? What does the land have left to offer? I aim to find out.

I will forage one last time. I will fill my bowls and jars with herbs, flowers, and berries. The tea I will blend might be that one simple act on any given day that holds back the night, pushes the cold away, keeping my spirits high for one more day. It's a gradual process, one hesitant step after another, that will keep me from imploding, help me to protect my neighbors, as I send whatever beasts I conjure into the tear that taints this land.

I will put on a pot of coffee, I will add a few logs to the fire, I will take a hot shower, scrubbing my aging skin from head to toe, and then I will head out as the light descends for the final time, soaking up what rays I can, before it disappears entirely.

I think of Yara, and then push away the image of her flushed face, tears running down her cheeks. We do what we have to out here, to survive. I don't begrudge her that. But once a trust has been broken, it's hard to repair.

When I open the front door there is an offering.

So it begins.

It is a piece of carved ivory, in the shape of a fish. Most likely salmon or trout. I pick it up, as the cold air rushes in, the sunlight dappling the ocean below, ice and snow sparkling across the skeletal branches and lush evergreen. Without thinking, I pop it into my mouth and hold it there, running my tongue across the ridges of the scales. I will hunt well today, a burlap sack over one shoulder, my rifle over the other. This blessing will guide me to flora and fauna alike. It does not care about the end result, merely that the hunt will be successful and the rituals followed.

I turn and go back into the house, placing the soapstone fish on a shelf alongside the others—bears, and wolves, and hawks, and whales, and seals. Some in white ivory, others in various stones, a few carved from wood. One is inlaid with mother-of-pearl. One is carved out of something black—I don't like to touch that one—obsidian I assume.

This fish might be from Yara, a peace offering.

Or from a neighbor with a dying elder.

I sit down on the couch for a moment, tightening my boot laces, cuffing my jeans, buttoning up my flannel shirt, as I prepare to brave the elements once again.

I think about Dominic and how I know he will be burying the dogs today, shovel blade clanking as it bounces off the frozen ground. He will honor these creatures, and their deaths, thank whatever spirits linger, knowing that at one time these animals were pups, sucking at their mother's teat, looking for warmth, and comfort, and inclusion. He will think of the little girl, as I am thinking of her now—that bundle of pink, the fluffs of stuffing flying into the air, the smear of blood across her cheek. He will close his eyes, as I close mine now, inhaling pine and frost, and woodsmoke and death. He will picture the animal spirits ascending, a drift of warm colors floating on the wind, muttering whatever names and images come to mind—Akela, Amarok, Tikaani—blessing their torn hides, their broken skulls, as he shovels the crumbling, frozen dirt over their bodies. He will stand in the pet cemetery that resides up the hill behind his humble abode and remember his own pets, as well as those that belonged to his neighbors—Chinook, Nanook, Miska, Klee Kai. And he will wonder what went wrong with these two. He will stop at one gravestone in particular and spend a few moments tossing a ball, hiking a trail, petting the concrete stone as it slowly changes into thick fur. And then he will go inside and try to shake off the cold, one eye on the woods out the window, the other gazing inward, evaluating his own chances of survival.

I head north, up into the hills, looking for a clearing where I know there are still a few flowers. I scout the edge of the trail for any pop of color, gathering what I can—the pink flowers of the wild rose, which will add a soft perfume to the teas, the prized and juicy cloudberries with their golden-yellow ripe fruit. I spot rosehips, in a huddled mass, just off the trail, so I pluck as many red berries as I can find. And then just beyond that, a nettle bush, where I carefully grab as many dark green leaves as I can using my gloves to avoid their toxic hairs and inflammatory rash.

Under a low hanging branch of old bull pine that has broken off and fallen to the earth, I spy a patch of pale green tentacles—usnea lichen. Locals call it witch's hair, or old man's beard, and I stare at the strange growth, and its oceanic qualities, as if a great coral reef once existed here, the waters slowly receding over time. Legendary for its medicinal properties, I feel gratitude at the bounty I've just found.

Beyond that I can see a clearing, and along the way I pass a shock of violet, stopping to harvest as much larkspur as there remains to be taken. I thank the forest for providing, and continue deeper. At the edge of the clearing is a wild patch of mint, and so I drop to my knees to take my time, tearing off a leaf and chewing on it, as I pluck every leaf from the bushy patch of greenery.

Eventually I make my way into the clearing, where I spy a few more pops of color—the yellow centers of the chamomile flanked by white petals and the faded fuchsia of the fireweed still in bloom. When that is done, all that is left are the green leaves of the birch tree, a patch of wild tarragon and chickweed. On my way back to the trail is a patch of elder flowers, and I end my harvest there.

Tromping back to the trail, when I think there is nothing left for the forest to offer up, I find a black clump of chaga mushrooms, as large as a grapefruit, on the side of a birch tree. I pause to take out my knife, carving away until the golden amber hue of its inner meat is revealed. It's a hearty mushroom, but I'm careful to leave behind at least a third, so it will continue to live. I pat the birch and thank it for the delicacy, making sure I haven't damaged it as well.

Symbiosis, after all.

Tonight, it will freeze, and tomorrow, this will all be dead—most of it, anyway. Or maybe the day after. But I won't come back as the temperatures drop, this hike risky on a normal day, let alone in complete darkness, as the rain turns to ice and then snow, the cold becoming deadly, the wind chill suicidal.

My back aches, my knees ringed with dirt and grass stains, but the sun hangs overhead, and so I take a moment to turn my face up to it, soaking in what few rays are left. And in that moment of vulnerability, there is a rustle from the woods surrounding this clearing. In an instant, I am transported back to the first time I came here, that first creature in the woods, and the mistakes I made preparing myself for the long night that awaited me.

The trees, the bushes, the salt, the fortified cabin—it was my last defense. I spent that first summer digging and planting, moving stones and securing walls, and chalking symbols and phrases over the doorway and onto the floor. I consulted with locals, listening to every elderly resident I could find, and then I purchased their carvings, their crosses, their tapestries woven out of hemp. I honored the animals I caught—with phrases and names, by utilizing every aspect of the fallen, by burying what was left. I made gloves out of fur, and boots out of hides, and lucky trinkets out of feet.

But I didn't forget the horned beast that lingered in the woods. Every time I went out to hunt or gather, or to just stroll the lake shore or the trails that ran up into the woods, I would find evidence of its existence.

Why didn't it come closer?

I would find claw marks on trees—from its meaty paws, or shedding antlers, I didn't know. There was scat and fur, and once, the ripe smell of urine. But I didn't see it again, not for a long time, hoping it had moved on, or somehow died of the elements.

There was a new trail of trampled bushes and broken tree limbs that started where I found the first scat, going deeper into the forest, across the boggy muskegs, and over creeks, through dense clearings, all the way up to a rocky outcropping that seemed to hold a cave. But that was where I stopped. To enter that cave would be suicide. If it was hiding there, then it had the advantage of knowing the layout.

But my curiosity got the better of me, and so one day, with a flashlight in hand, I approached the opening, the smell of rotting meat, musky flesh, and mossy dampness filling the cave. I turned on the flashlight, and it cast a long beam, deep into the darkness, but not all the way to the back wall. I saw a smattering of smaller bones, likely from rabbits, squirrels, foxes, and coyotes. They covered the ground of the cave like gray ashes, the crisscrossed femurs and spines broken up by the occasional skull. And toward the back, there were larger bones, which I can only assume were human.

I thought for a moment about the rumors and stories that now came rushing up to me—the boy from the trailer park on the east side, the drunken hunter who caused so much trouble in the bar that night, the girl who would tell everyone within earshot that her man was no longer hitting her and they'd sorted it all out. They all disappeared. Gone to see grandma or an uncle over break. Back to the city when the hunt didn't go as planned. Finally leaving him to pursue greener pastures, where a smart mouth didn't end up with a fat lip.

Maybe all of it was true.

Maybe none of it was true.

A crack of thunder split the quiet, and I turned back away from the cave as a storm rolled in, a shock of lightning spiking the sky. The clouds overhead cast shadows over the field, the woods, the cave, and in the rapidly expanding shadows, the creature stood.

I dropped my flashlight and reached for the rifle that was slung over my shoulder, but I was too slow. It lunged.

Its horns slashed and rammed my upper body, knocking me to the ground as it grunted, a white cloud of condensation spraying from its mouth and nostrils. The clacking of its teeth snapped, missing my exposed neck as I fell to the ground, land-ing on my gun. Before I could turn over it slashed at my back, cutting through the waterproof nylon jacket, the lined interior, my flannel shirt, and my t-shirt underneath—deep into my flesh.

I screamed into the pattering of rain, a hot trickle running down my spine.

Rolling over, I faced upward with the rifle in my hand, and fired wildly toward the red, beady eyes that glared out of the dark cave.

The creature roared as I stumbled down the trail and through the clearing as fast as my legs could move.

Behind me, there was the rush of bushes and branches part-ing, the grunting and heavy footsteps pursuing as the rain fell harder and the cold descended with weight and permanence.

As it grew darker, I knew that staying on the path, on the main trails, would only reveal my location, and so I crashed into the high grasses and heavy bushes, off the trail, and toward the creek. I hoped to lose the beast, knowing full well that it was probably futile.

A tree fell in the distance, the heavy thud shaking the ground, as I ran into the creek, following the low water south, water splashing, every leap just waiting to find a slippery rock, the water spirits asking for a broken ankle, a shattered wrist, any offering to offset the rape and pillage of the forest.

In the distance I could see my cabin, a pale glow coming from the windows, a plume of smoke rising up out of the chimney and it telescoped away, every step feeling as though it was growing smaller and smaller, blood slicking my back, running down my ass crack, my thighs slick with tacky liquid.

It was a straight line now, from where I was in the creek to my house, but something told me to turn, to run the tree line, to maneuver between birch and pine and pin oak. Slaloming in and out like a skier, I felt a great rush of air as something tapped my shoulder and then crashed into a massive black spruce, shaking the tree so hard that needles and pinecones showered the forest floor.

I dashed for my house, straight line be damned.

I ran across the backyard, the dead grass and thin layer of snow hard as rock. A stitch in my side ached as I struggled to find my breath, a sheen of sweat breaking out across my flesh. As I hit the stone path and ran through the opening in the bushes across the moat of salt water ice, I paused to look over my shoulder.

There was no sign of the beast.

I looked left and right, and then quickly walked backward toward the front door.

It would take one hundred twenty stitches to close the long scars that ran up and down my spine. I would get sick with a nasty infection, and fever of one hundred four degrees. I would hallucinate rainbow eagles dipping down from the skies, sprinkling flowers and fish bones into my welcoming arms. And at night, when I slept, shadows visited me, what I thought were my concerned neighbors. Yara would tell me later that she was the only one inside the house, the rest of the community afraid to step inside—curse or disease or mark of the devil, they didn't say. I would revisit those visions of the long, tall shadows, on the nights when the cold and wind howled as if dying. No answer ever came.

The next day I would find bloody hoofprints on the stone path just outside the perimeter of my land. It didn't cross, it stayed outside, but I pictured it huffing and snorting, its red eyes glimmering with hatred and hunger.

Maybe I scared it away.

But most likely, I only pissed it off.


Back in the clearing, I turn my head left and right. It has been so long, there is no way it could still be alive all these years later. And then I spy a hole dug in the ground, dark against the white snow, dirt sprayed out in every direction like a dog had just buried a bone. Inside this pit is a massive pair of curved horns, twisting and turning, sharp at the tips, with clots of skull and hair at the base. On the other side of the pile of large bones is an elongated skull, detached from the horns, cracks on the top where they once resided. I stare at this familiar snout, the row of teeth exposed in the top of the skull, the bottom row missing, the jawbone off to the side. I squat and look closer, the rib cage nearly as big as a refrigerator, femurs and tibias as long as broom handles, a pelvis that could hold a watermelon. Many of the bones are broken. And as I lean in a bit closer, there are scratches and teeth marks, as if something even larger than this monstrosity once sat here, picking the bones clean, pulling every bit of fat and muscle off with a long raking of its teeth.

I close my eyes and take a deep breath. Finding these bones is a relief—I know the beast is no longer out there, but something even worse may have taken its place. I open my eyes and try to reason with this ossuary. I picture a giant woolly mammoth taken down by a pack of hungry wolves—circling and circling, nipping at its heels, trying to trip it up, find an exposed bit of flesh, tearing away fur, seeking soft flesh, as one after another is stomped to death, or impaled on its curved horns. I envision a cackle of hyenas yipping and dancing around an injured ante-lope, darting in and out, mad tongues lolling, as their yellow gaze glistens with insanity. I picture the aggressive fisher gather-ing its brethren in a cacophony of brown fur to hunt an aging mountain lion, jaws salivating as they weave in and out of the forest, here one minute and gone the next—striking without an ounce of fear.

It's possible.

Anything is possible.

I stand and stretch my back, feeling as old as I look.

It's too dangerous to try and release one apex predator to pit one against the other. All that would buy me is a different danger at my back. Or maybe two, working in unison. No, I have to stick to the plan and deal with the rift. When the evil is expunged, the land can start to heal. And when the land starts to heal, it will take care of its own, one way or another.

But I watch the woods as I head back home, listening as far as my hearing can manage, for a grunt or a growl or a rustle. I turn an eye to the sky, catching the shadow of a hawk gliding overhead, making sure its wings aren't any longer than they should be. I let my gaze traverse the creek as I cross the water, one step at a time, a flash of silver in the running liquid, but nothing more.

I can expect the unexpected, or I can focus on what I know is coming.

The rest will have to sort itself out.

# CHAPTER FOUR

# NIGHTFALL

The darkness engulfs our community like a grizzly bear coming out of hibernation—with a sense of urgency, hunger, and history. It never forgets. Overnight, the snow fell wet and heavy for hours on end before turning to sleet—ice pellets spitting and slicing the air, picking at my cabin like a woodpecker searching for worms. Before today, winter had been relatively mild, a few inches here and there, the sun breaking through the clouds to melt it all away—if only for a few hours. I thought perhaps we might have a few days, maybe even weeks. But there is no going back now—we are blanketed with whiteness, knee deep and drifting higher in the raging gale, showing no sign of letting up.

I may win the pool after all.

I place another log on the fire and stare out the window, the only sounds the baying of the wind and ice chips pelting the homestead, a crackle and snap from the fire behind me. I can sense the tear, a thread of glimmer barely visible amidst the swirling snow, but a rip materializing nonetheless. Through the frosted glass, I watch the blood-red mercury of the outside thermometer plummet—twenty degrees, ten degrees, slipping down into negative digits. The windchill will make this even more dangerous. A snow devil whirls across the yard, and a thin layer of ice forms across the surface of the water down the hill. It's not fit for man nor beast, but both will roam the streets out of necessity—be it companionship, hunger, or vengeance.

In my mind's eye I cast a gaze to the mountain top, to the house that squats there, light emanating from the fortress, a man inside laughing in the darkness. His presence comes and goes, but it is always here. His role in all of this may be important.

There is work to be done.

I dress slowly, one layer after another—more contemporary clothing to start—thermal underwear bottoms, a merino tur-tleneck, and then wool socks, followed by snow pants over that to keep out the moisture and the wind, a fleece sweater, and a knit hat. Though I'm only going outside to get more wood—a few feet—I add a ski mask and beaver mitts and pull on a pair of mukluks gifted to me by Yara. My first winter here, she made these for me out of reindeer hide, and I slide them on with a bit-tersweet twinge of emotion. Over the top of it all is the warmest piece of clothing I own—a traditional parka made from car-ibou. It is lined at the cuffs and edges with rabbit fur, a soft, white fluff offsetting the thicker, longer wolverine fur around the hood to wick the moisture of my breath away from my face. On the inside of the jacket a long zipper runs up the seam, but facing outward are handmade bone and ivory buttons, rectan-gular shapes that are rounded at the edges, inserted through looping eyelets. It is long—almost down to my knees—and it's worth quite a bit of money. It has saved my life on more than one occasion.

The last thing I did the day before was screw in sheets of plywood all the way around the front to create a cold porch. It protects the firewood I have stacked up to the roofline, keep-ing the wind and snow from rushing in every time I open the front door, adding another layer of protection between myself and the elements, and whatever walks the frozen tundra in the darkness. A simple door on the right side is held in place with hinges and several latches. It's rudimentary, but works. And in the spring, next year, assuming I survive this winter, it's easy to remove, to open up the porch to the elements, letting in the sunshine and fresh air.

As I walk to the wood pile, and the blue tarp that rattles in the wind, eager to bring in some extra logs, I notice that a screw has shaken loose on one of the sheets of plywood, an edge bending in a bit from the harsh wind blowing all around me. I quickly step back inside to grab a screwdriver—the red-handled tool still sitting on a windowsill. As I approach the board, I decide to bend it back a bit, and take a quick peek out, to see if anything is out there.

Down the road is a glow of orange, in a rectangular shape, and I know immediately what this is. They are already burying the dead. The ground is so frozen that hot coals have to be brought out from a fireplace or pot belly stove  and shoveled onto the ground in order to soften it up. A shadowy figure moves quickly, inside and out, layering the coals, and then stepping back into the house, and safety. Later, shovels will come out, and the earth will be hacked at, sharp blades piercing dirt and clay, rocks clanging as the metal strikes, hands reverberating at the resistance. And then the process will be repeated, again and again, until it's deep enough to hold the corpse. I had hoped that I might have a few days before this all started, but it seems that whoever has died, this was as long as they could hang on. At least they had made it this far.

So be it.

I screw the board back into place and turn to the mail slot I have cut out of the plywood, a flap of wood covering the opening from both sides. Below it is a small wooden apple crate, where I receive my mail this time of year. Not that much arrives. But more importantly, it's where my neighbors leave their invitations, their summons, handwritten notes folded and stuffed into envelopes. Sometimes parchment is rolled up into a scroll and tied with a ribbon, family signatures lined across the bottom. Now and then, it is nothing more than a piece of hide with a cattle brand burned into the fur. Once I got a letter with a wax seal holding it shut. Our community is relatively small, and I know most of the families by their names, their symbols, their homes, and their auras. I have dealt with all of them—those struggling to get by and those who flourish on the mountain top, those who are absent of sin, and those who bask in the glory of their dark deeds, looking down on the community from on high.

Inside the box is an envelope made of thick paper, with my name scratched on the front in shaky letters. Sitting next to it is a turtle, carved from soapstone—green, with yellow inlay or paint. I know this family, and I'm surprised to see the offering. We have had our differences over the years, but now in their time of need, they beckon.

It will be a good place to start, something to send through that can hold back the inquiring snout that might appear at any moment—the long, slender talons that will soon appear at the tear, encouraging it to widen as it snuffles at the air, its hot, rancid breath pluming into the eternally frosty night.

I take the letter and carving, along with a few pieces of wood, and head back inside, my eyes watering as the wind rips all along the tree line.


I spend the day purifying myself.

It starts with my mind—pushing aside all negative thoughts, a cup of nettle tea spiked with rosehips, steaming on the living room table, a few drops of honey to sweeten it up. I meditate, eyes closed, legs crossed, elbows on my knees with my hands turned toward the heavens. A white candle burns on the side table, the essence of nag champa filling the air with a sweet blend of amber, rose, and lily of the valley; sandalwood, patchouli, and violet underneath. I picture warm, healing colors—burned umber and mahogany; carrot and tangerine; salmon and rose.

And then I cleanse my body from head to toe—a long, hot shower where the shea butter and coconut milk powder soften my skin, as the healing scent of patchouli and cedarwood keeps me connected to nature, my home, and this community. The poppy seeds scrub and scratch at my skin, painful at first, and then comforting as I let my old skin go, embracing my mottled, rosy flesh.

Long live the new flesh.

My last acts are to purify my soul. Sitting by the fireplace, the warm glow blanketing me with heat, I make amends with any spirits I may have offended or angered, asking them to forgive me, releasing them from toxic renumerations. I renew my vows with the woods, and waters, the desperate lands around me— promising to take only what I need, vowing to plant what seeds and bulbs I can in the spring, honoring every part of whatever animals I might hunt and kill for sustenance and warmth. I commune with the dead that I have helped pass on, asking for their support and guidance in whatever new endeavors I may pursue. Shadows flicker at the edges of the room, creeping in and then dissipating as quickly as they arrive. The fireplace dims, the flames dying down, the candle blowing out, as a single line of smoke drifts up and away from me, rising to the ceiling above.

It is time to go.

I dress again in layers, preparing myself for the elements and the night that waits for me down the road, out in the forest, and in the rippling waters that struggle against the impending freeze.

As I venture out toward my neighbors, a snowy owl hoots three times in quick succession, head twisting this way and that, followed by a harsh screech that pierces the darkness. It preens for a moment, cleaning its gray and white feathers, nipping at parasites and its plumage, searching for something. Then it gracefully leaps into flight from the roof of my cabin, the wind pushing it down, wings expanding and fighting back, soaring up and then diving down, eyes locked on a small gray shape that is scuttling across the white yard.

I take this as a good sign.


When I arrive at the small, battered house down the road from me, I am dusted with snow, the only light on the street the handful of streetlamps that haven't been busted or shot. It's early in the season, but give it time—they'll all be broken soon.

An aging husky shakes its coat and barks at me, the sound of its master bellowing from a door that opens quickly and then shuts, the gray and white dog barking again, before dashing off to the house, scratching at the metal door, where it is let in quickly, as the heavy inner door slams shut with finality.

I walk up three slick concrete steps and knock on the wooden door. It opens immediately, as if he was standing there waiting for me to appear.

And maybe he was.

I glance to my right toward a mound covered with dirt and graying snow. The grave is hardly visible, but I know it's there.

"Sebastian, come inside," a man says, as he turns and walks back into the house.

I enter, closing the door behind me, and begin to shed my layers. A pot belly stove in the corner glows red at the center, the smell of coffee brewing, and something sweet.

"How are you, Jacob?" I ask, knowing the answer.

"Been better."

Jacob is skinny, emaciated almost, sinewy and muscled, wiry in every way. His hair is a mess, sticking up in every direction, oily and brown to match his tepid eyes. He is wearing a dingy gray sweatshirt and blue jeans, moccasins on his feet. When he turns to me, his face wan, eyes bloodshot, I can tell that he's been drinking. His nose is red and splotchy, run through with veins, pockmarked from acne.

"So, it was Martha, then?" I ask.

"It was."

I nod my head.

"Sorry for your loss."

He offers me a frown and a wrinkled brow.

"Thank you. Coffee?" he asks.

"Sure. Cream and sugar please," I say, and he smirks.

Jacob is a man's man. He chuckles at anything feminine—what he considers soft or weak. He drinks his coffee black, his bourbon neat, and I've heard rumors that he doesn't wipe his ass—because that might be seen, somehow, as gay. *Thou doth protest too much, Jacob*, I've thought on more than one occasion. But then I let it go. It wasn't my place to judge.

Ironically, Martha was a homely woman—rather masculine, a tomboy of sorts, the two of them twins in their camouflage hunting jackets, orange hats, Carhartt jeans, and Timberland boots. They kept their hair short, sometimes in a buzz cut, both of them. I never saw Martha in anything remotely pink or flowery—never in a dress or with a touch of makeup. I don't know if either of them cooked, but I guessed it was meat on a grill, when the weather allowed it, with a large quantity of potatoes, in every variety, vegetables few and far between. For entertainment I'd seen them throwing darts at the local watering hole, or shooting pool, drinking a Budweiser or two.

We didn't talk politics or religion anymore, as that had come to blows in the past. He was a bigot and an abuser, one more alcoholic in a long line of angry, entitled bastards—a nasty piece of work. Exactly the kind of person I needed to see.

"What happened, if you don't mind my asking?"

"As a matter of fact, I do," he said, his face scrunched up in resentment.

He sat at the simple kitchen table—a circular top of cheap, scarred wood, that had seen better days, cigarette burns dotting the surface. Four metal folding chairs surrounded it with torn, padded seats, duct tape holding it all together. A faded couch and sagging recliner sat in the living room, in muted colors that might have once been black or dark brown. The rectangular coffee table held copies of *Field & Stream, Guns & Ammo*, and *Playboy*, next to a metal ashtray overflowing with cigarette butts, an American Eagle hunched on the edge of the rim.

"Jacob, I need to know everything. It helps with what I do. You asked me to be here. And I know that turtle didn't come from you. That's Martha's doing, and I'm sure I'm here at her insistence, not yours. So why don't you stop being an asshole for a second and just help me do my job."

Jacob glared at me, and then ran his gnarled hands through his greasy hair. He stood up and poured me a cup of coffee and set it down hard on the table.

"Sugar's in the jar," he said, nodding his head to the ceramic bowl with wildflowers on it, one of the few bits of color in the room. "Cream as well." A few nondairy creamers sat in a simple white bowl next to it, no doubt stolen from the diner the last time they were there.

"It was cancer," he said, unironically picking up a pack of Marlboro Reds off of the table and lighting one.

"That's a hard way to go out," I say.

"Yup. It sucks. Breast cancer," he said. "Wasn't nothing to do with smoking. Just something in the family lineage. She didn't want to have her tits cut off, and fuck radiation—her hair falling out. We worked through it together our own way. It was stage four anyway; Martha hadn't seen a doctor in years. I got some morphine from that Jenkins kid that deals out of the bar. Fucker has a little bit of everything," he snickered.

"Did you push her over the edge or did she go naturally?" I asked.

He opened his mouth with a snarl, but I cut him off.

"I don't *care*, Jacob. I just need to know. Suicide is different than cancer, assisted or otherwise. I need to sus out the poisons and black matter, to truly know what she has done, or not done, so that she might be absolved of her sins and move on to someplace better. That's what you want, right?"

"Fuck. I guess."

I nod and then sit down, fixing my coffee.

A tear forms in his eye, and he looks away from me.

"I didn't help her. And she didn't help herself. She was worried it would taint her soul, whatever that fucking means. So she suffered, and then when it got to be too much, I'd shoot her up, and she'd smile, like a goddamned junkie. We'd watch our shows, and then I'd look over to ask her a question about what time of year salmon spawned, or whether turkeys could fly, and she'd be passed out, that stupid grin on her face."

"I'm sorry, Jacob," I said.

"Sure you are."

A silence filled the air, and we locked eyes for a moment, and then he softened and stood up. He returned with a chocolate cupcake. There was a light brown icing on top, a sprinkle of white crystals dotting it.

"Let's get this shit over with," he said. "This was the last thing she ever baked, and she baked it for you."

I nod my head.

"Thank you for honoring her last requests, Jacob. I'm not going to say you're a good man, because we both know that's not true, but you've at least done this for her. And I can respect that."

Now it's his turn to nod, and I dig in.

It's a chocolate cupcake, sweet and dense, with a gooey center that I wasn't expecting. The icing is a salted caramel and it complements the rich chocolate filling and cake nicely. And then I swallow and everything changes. It turns bitter, and smoky, like burnt paper, or cigarette ash, and I choke to swallow it down. I grab for the coffee and take a sip. My eyes start to water as Jacob stares daggers into me, but I have to continue, so I take another bite. The sweetness is a welcome respite, and then as I swallow again it all turns sour, the caramel tasting burnt, the salt overwhelming my palate. It is melting plastic, spoiled milk, and moldy bread.

"Finish the fucking thing," he says, glaring, and as much as I hate it, I shove the rest of it into my mouth, chew as fast as I can, and choke it down. I grab the coffee and gulp it sloppily, spilling it all over the table and my chest. To leave incomplete would not only taint the process, but it would manifest in my own flesh, staining my soul as well.

"Now get the fuck out of my house," he fumes, and I stand up to leave.

I dress quickly, never looking back, and I'm out the door before he can say another word to me. My stomach lurches, and I walk quickly back home, picking up the pace, as my gut knots, and my throat tightens. She was a horrible woman, and as I gasp to pull in fresh air, the sharp bite of the cold is a welcome distraction.

The tear is hardly open, but I have to get there, and push through whatever comes out of me.

Behind me I hear glass breaking, and the front door slams shut.

*Good riddance to bad rubbish*, I think as I stumble toward the rift.

Visibility drops to zero as the wind picks up and the whiteness swallows me whole. Stumbling blind, hands outstretched into the colorless void, my eyes struggle to stay open against the sting of the driving snow. A miscalculated step sends me down hard, smashing my elbow against the icy ground. I heave myself ungracefully back to my feet, readjusting my twisted parka as a stream of curses is ripped from my mouth by the swirling wind. Pulling my hood down tight, I squint into the flurry until the distant cabin drifts into view like a ghost ship emerging out of the fog. The muted glow of its windows is now my only guide. I push back against the raging squall. The only sounds that fill my ears are the flapping of my clothing and my own heavy breathing. My heart pounds like a stunned rabbit, but I must get closer, or this is all for nothing.

Up the hill, past the cabin, around to the back where I am somewhat sheltered from the gale, the filament of gold runs from the top of the arching trees to the icy ground below. It pulses and ripples through the swirling snow, as the middle expands and pushes outward. Sensing my presence, perhaps, three brown talons tear at the edges, gripping the lip, tucking over and into our dimension.

And then the coughing begins, as I struggle to find my breath. I drop to my knees in a snowdrift and raise my hands to my neck, unable to pull away my coverings, as something sticks in my craw, flinging my snow-encrusted mitts from my hands. I can feel something lodged in my throat, but I'm unable to get it out.

In the woods around me, three sets of eyes appear, a sickly yellow, matted gray and ivory fur nearly invisible in the deluge of white.

I cough again and a bone lands in the snow, coated in blood. I crumple under the pain and howl, the coyotes in the woods answering my response in kind. I can't take off my under-gloves, or I'll lose my fingers, my hands. The only parts of my body that are exposed are my eyes and my lips—the ski mask covering everything, with a thin line where my mouth can exhale, an opening to be violated at will.

I double up again, and vomit more bones—chicken legs, one after another, my throat tearing in the process; metacarpals and phalanges of what must be human hands, spitting out of me like bullets; stringy bits that look like tails. A pile slowly starts to gather as the coyotes creep closer, the bones dancing and rattling as if on a hot pan, or a vibrating bed. And then they start to elongate, growing in size, connecting as some yellow ligaments bind them together.

And then my throat swells, as something else struggles to escape me, a swollen mass forcing its way up my esophagus, thick and musky, blocking any intake of air. Desperate for breath, I clasp my hands together and fall forward onto them, pushing inward and upward beneath my rib cage, feeling something snap inside my chest. My forehead scrapes across the cold, hard ground as the ball of fur, soaked in blood, bursts out of my gaping mouth, a pool of crimson on the pristine, white snow. I roll onto my back, choking for air, frantically praying for some sort of relief as the urge to vomit rises again, my stomach heaving and bucking with every retch.

The coyotes listen to my suffering, pause, and sniff the air, hesitant now.

And then, I sprawl onto my belly, eyes bulging, as another wad of blood-matted fur surges its way into the daylight, sliding out of my mouth like an afterbirth, hot and steaming onto the icy ground. And in a great rush of blood and fur, my legs kicking and thrashing in desperation, I reach into my blocked throat, fingers slick with blood, my jaw straining to the point of cracking, and pull the whole long and bloodied skin of the animal from my excoriated throat.

It's then that I pass out.


When I wake, it is to the sound of the coyotes yelping, teeth snapping and bones breaking, a deep growl and roar filling the night. I open my eyes to a skeletal polar bear standing on its hind legs, muzzle crowned in crimson, blazing red eyes searching the space for more of the pack. Several matted gray and white bodies lie bent and broken on the ground, the rest fleeing into the woods, abandoning whatever plan they might have had.

It's not fully formed—its rib cage is exposed, muscle and ligament stitched together, black claws extended from exposed bones, dirty white fur slowly forming around the flexing digits. It turns away for a moment and I see its spine—huge metal sheets in the shape of diamonds, running up and down its back. It bellows into the night, and then turns back to face me, hot saliva spilling from its mouth, falling to the ground, where it shatters into pieces.

I cough into the storm, spraying a cloud of particles outward in a fan of red snow, that is pulled into the darkness, powdering the bear.

Its head is still a skull, no snout or ears, just a wide-open jaw, with rows of razor-sharp teeth, bloody incisors glistening in the moonlight.

A cry works its way out of the glittering rend, something pushing open the tear, screaming into the snowy darkness. The bear turns its head at the noise and lumbers forward, snuffling and roaring, as the talons disappear. Without a glance backward, the beast pushes into the opening, its head shoving through, massive arms pulling at the tear, as the rest of its fur stitches across its expanding backside. As it pushes open the rip, a wave of heat pulses through, melting the snow in front of me, pushing toward me as if I have opened the door to a massive blast oven. My chapped lips and watering eyes are hit with a wave of heat, and the bear pushes through, disappearing.

For a moment I see colors—red and orange, yellow and tan—a mangled cropping of scraggly bushes and anemic trees. And then the rip slams shut, the beast gone.

I don't have time to dwell on what I've seen. The heat has melted the snow, and now it's freezing again, threatening to stick me to the ground. My fingers and toes are numb, never a good sign, pins and needles across my face, a throbbing ache running across the surface of my flesh.

I swallow a mouthful of blood and moan, the pain of this birth running all the way down to my stomach. My eyes water, and I wipe the moisture from my face, flinging the icy shards into the darkness.

And the season has only just begun.

# CHAPTER FIVE

# TRANSFERENCE

The green lights dance over the horizon, sweeping left and right, as the sky is filled with a gentle swaying, waves of purples blending in, with the occasional spike of red, like an EKG heartbeat, stuttering across the darkness. There is a sound like wind chimes made of crystal—ice breaking in a cacophonous melody, a metal xylophone played with great skeletal fingers. Shadowy figures elongate and then dissipate, reforming in silhouettes, twisting and turning as the wind pushes clouds across the moon. I whistle at the shifting colors, a hard-edge blade slicing the night, a call and response of inquiry, followed by violent movement. I am without form, amorphous, as I float across the blanketed land, icy branches hanging with daggers, a symphony of crystals crashing, a wall of glass that shatters to the earth, turning to dust. The dark waters flow in and out, reflecting the light, as it thickens, slowly freezing, pushing away from the coast and out into the sea. Everything is going quiet, nothing is moving now, as the walls go up, and the doors to the outside world are slammed shut with permanence.

I remain in darkness, but there are voices around me. I am riddled with pain, a prick and stab at my forearm, something sharp piercing my flesh, swallowing broken glass as a slow moan works its way up from my gut. A woman speaks in whispers, like wind seeping between the pines, and then her voice raises, underwater, bubbling up but never breaking the surface. A man mutters in a deep bass, vibrations skittering across my flesh like tiny spiders, a deep thrumming resonating and reverberating. A boy interjects a high-pitched request, and then they overlap, these distant mutterings, my skin on fire, my lips dry as kindling, chipped and rough as my tongue runs across them, tasting copper. A hot spike runs through my veins, and then a coolness washes over me, and I go under.

When I awake the room is dim—a glow of embers from the fireplace, a dark form lying on the sofa—as I strain to lift my eyelids and keep my gaze from blurring. My throat is dry, and when I swallow, there is a dull throb. I try to speak, but there is only a crackling squeak, and nothing comes out.

Yara stirs, and moves quickly to my side.

"Don't try to speak," she says. "Here, sip this water first." And I see a small chunk of ice in a rocks glass, floating like it's a tiny iceberg, submerged in a miniature world.

She holds it to my lips, and I sip and swallow, the cold numbing my throat, a blessing all the way down. Water spills down my chin and onto my bare chest, and I realize that I am naked, bandages wrapped around my chest, as well as my hands and my fingers.

"Better?" she asks.

"Yes," I whisper.

"What happened?" I ask.

"You were hurt. I saw you run past my house, and I followed you. I was worried that something had gone wrong. You would have frozen to death out there by the woods. I got you home. When you kept coughing up blood, I called the doctor. Luckily the phone lines hadn't gone down yet. They're down now. You've been unconscious for quite some time."

"How long?" I croak.

"Eight days," she replies, and as she steps closer, I can see the bags under her eyes, a tear running down her face, hair matted and sticking up, as she wrings her hands.

"Eight days!" I shout, and immediately regret it, tearing at my esophagus, a sticky trickle running down my throat. "The dead, the people . . ." I start.

"It's okay. There was nothing you could do. You almost died. The doctor gave you medicine to keep you under, to help you sleep. He worried there was internal bleeding, but it eventually stopped, nothing more we could do, as we're snowed in, and he's not a surgeon."

I notice an IV drip hanging off of a nail that has been pounded into the wall, leading down to my arm. She walks to it with a syringe in her hand and plunges the needle into the port.

"Wait, there are things I need to do," I beg, but she shakes her head.

"You need to rest. You're no good to us dead. We'll talk tomorrow. They can wait."


The next few days are a blur of Yara and broth, the wind outside whipping up flurries, the snow building up around the house, drifting all the way up to the windows. I am eager to get back to work, the tear rippling in my mind's eye like a filament glowing with electricity. It must have widened; anything could have come through. Unless the bear has held them at bay. But I'm not holding my breath.

On the third day of her ministrations, some twelve days into the long night, there is a break in the storm, and the sun comes out. Everything sparkles and shines, like diamond dust scattered across a bone-white blanket.

The boy, Kallik, stops by, to relieve Yara, his Saturday otherwise filled with family stuck together in a small, cramped house, snapping at each other, finding excuses to step outside into the freezing cold. And he has a valid excuse, a reason for coming here, aside from being a good neighbor.

His dog, Balto, has died. And he's scared.

"I can't ask you to help him," he says. "I know you're recovering, but I don't want him to suffer, and I'm not sure where his soul is, or where it might go."

His gaze darts to the front door, and I know that the husky is outside on the porch, frozen in a ball, curled up as if merely taking a nap. Its double coat of fur atop a thick layer of fat would have kept it warm even in the coldest winters. But it's of no use to it now.

"I know what you do," the boy says. "I've heard the stories, Yara has told me. Everyone knows. You can't live forever, old man," he says and laughs. "Perhaps it's time you took an apprentice."

I shake my head.

"You don't want this, Kallik. It's a hard life. You probably wouldn't stay here. You'll have to turn your back on your family. It's dangerous, as you can see."

"My father works at the fishery, my mother broods in the house all day long, pining for her past, and my big sister, Allia, will run away to the first university that takes her. In many ways, she's already gone. There isn't much here for me, and I see the way the land devours itself, chewing at its own leg, like a rabid dog, caught in a trap."

I take a deep breath.

It's true, I won't live forever.

I decide to test him, to see what he is made of, to try and understand if he can handle the work.

"Have you brought me something to eat?" I ask.

He nods his head and walks over to his backpack, bringing a Tupperware container full of chocolate chip cookies, still fresh and soft, a hint of warmth still present.

"My mother and I made them this morning when we found Balto. He was lying on his dog bed, his food untouched, as still as a painting. He was fourteen years old, and he had a good life. We're isolated, but we're survivors," the boy said.

"And Balto is outside?" I ask.

"Yes. I brought him on my sled. Are you sure you're up to this?"

"I am. This shouldn't be a problem. No nuts in there, right?" I laugh.

"No, no nuts."

"I have a question for you, Kallik. And it's an important one, though I think I know the answer. He was a good boy, wasn't he?" I ask.

And the boy opens his mouth to speak, his lip trembling, his eyes squinting as he fights back the tears.

"He was . . . he was . . ." the boy says and sniffs, swallowing, taking a shaky breath. ". . . yes, he was a good boy, a good dog . . . a *great* dog. He could track with the best of them, he would cuddle up by me and keep me warm, and I swear that he would smile at me when he was happy, his bright blue eyes like some sort of shimmering water spirit, always looking to play. He protected me when we went out hunting—chasing away lynx like they were house cats, barking at black bears, scaring away coyotes. He could bring back grouse from the long grasses and shallow ponds without so much as a tooth mark on them."

"Then this shouldn't be a problem. The darker the spirit, the nastier the meal. What I send into the void is to protect us here, to try and heal the wound, to cauterize the tear so that nothing else can come through. I can't use a knife at a gun fight. I can't send a litter of kittens to battle an alligator. I need soldiers, not saints. You understand?"

He nods his head.

"But it always comes at a price. A price that I have to pay."

The boy lowers his head.

"It's what I do, my calling. Most people are a blend of good and bad, sins offset by kindness, so the birthing is pain merged with closure. Not every sensation is torture, not every aspect of what I create is driven by loss and regret."

The boy goes to get two glasses of ice-cold milk, and then we begin.

We each take a bite, concentrating on Balto, a sweet dog that I can picture chasing rabbits in the summertime, its pink tongue hanging out of its mouth, bounding into the bushes, emerging with a wagging tail. I think of the time that he defended Kallik from the group of teenagers that were drunk and high, throwing rocks at anything that could break or bruise—streetlights, car windows, houses, and other kids. The baring of his teeth was all bark and no bite, but they didn't know that—the dog panting and chasing his tail only ten minutes later. I picture the husky chasing a monarch butterfly, drinking water out of a metal bowl with reckless abandon, lying on its side in the grass, asleep in the sunshine under a momentary lapse of winter.

The cookie is dense and rich, the chocolate still soft, and gooey, melting as it touches my tongue. The sugar and flour hold a hint of vanilla, the chew so satisfying, the cold milk washing down the sweetness. There is a buttery goodness about it, a hint of brown sugar and molasses adding depth. My eyes are closed as I savor the flavors, and I know the boy is seeing and feeling similar things. There is nothing bitter here, nothing rotten—no grit, or fungus, or sour aftertaste. The dog is as close to pure love as it gets. And I'm grateful for that, honored to be allowed this window into its soul.

When we open our eyes, there is a sparkle in the daylight. We finish our cookies, down the milk, and wait.

Because we have shared this moment—because I am channeling the spirit of Balto—the boy, if he is open and attuned, might sense the spirit as well. It is the only way that I can pass this on to him, a similar moment in my childhood, when my grandfather passed on to me the curse and blessing that I may pass on to Kallik now.

I open my mouth to speak, and out drifts pink smoke, like cotton candy, winding its way out and up, strands knitting together into a winged bird with three heads, that curves and drifts in my gentle exhalation. Kallik's mouth is open as well. Orange thread undulates into the air, his eyes widening, as it wraps around the bird, stitching a cross-hatch pattern across its back, and wings, and head. The creature flaps and soars, rising up, and then floating down, before perching up in the rafters of my home, on a beam that traverses the highest point.

"Are you okay?" I ask.

The boy's eyes are still wide, and he smiles.

"Yes. I'm good. But it isn't always like this, is it?"

"No. Most of the time it is not. Can you open the door to let it out?"

"Do I have to?" Kallik asks.

"Spirits can't be bound. You may see it again, or it may merely fly from house to house, and then deep into the woods, never to be heard from again."

The boy's eyes sadden.

"But knowing Balto, I'm sure it will return. Eventually it has to move on, as we all do, maybe coming back as something else. Keep your eyes open. You may find each other in another time and space."

The boy nods and walks to the door, opening it slowly, and then heads out to the porch, to make sure that it can get out.

The creature leaps and dives into the room, circles once, and then flies through the front door and out into the shimmering whiteness.

"It seems you have the gift, Kallik," I say.

And in that moment, a great weight is lifted and transferred to the boy.

My gut churns, as a frown slides over my face.

The dead can linger, but for how long, it truly varies. If a spirit and soul is ready to move on—either eager to end pain and suffering, or seeking out ascension and rebirth—it might not stay long at all. I've seen a few instances where it was almost instantaneous. But most spirits, even when happy, having lived a long life, filled with family, and friends, and fulfillment, will still hesitate in the transubstantiation. They might suddenly worry that a spouse will be sad, or alone, giving them pause; they might realize that they weren't quite as ready as they thought they were, suddenly looking down on a life that they still cling to, their earthly delights resonating in the release; or they simply may have a moment of fear and uncertainty at what may lie on the other side of this reality.

A day, a week, a month—the dead move on when they are ready to move on—but when it comes to my work, there is little to no certainty. A soul that moves on quickly, before I can get there, will most likely be okay, as they have little holding them back. Those that linger—they have things to work out, and it's rarely something pleasant. Vengeance, anger, regret, fear—they manifest and anchor the spirit to a place and time, haunting those around it, causing havoc in their manifestations.

I have been away from my work for almost two weeks now. There are letters, and hides, and carvings in the box. I have been summoned repeatedly but have been unable to answer the call. An army of wolves, salmon, eagles, and polar bears camp out on my porch as I heal, and rest, and grow stronger.

Those that remain, they will not be happy. The kind souls have moved on. The broken, tainted spirits that are left? They fume and howl in the darkness that holds us captive. But they won't wait forever. I know this to be true.

I find something unexpected when I finally bundle up and head out to inspect the tear. A few things, actually. The wind is calm for a blessed moment, the moonlight glimmering across the birch and spruce that line the bottom of the hill. I exhale a cloud of breath into the air, knowing that I can't linger, the icy fingers of the long night already reaching through cloth and fur to scratch at my fragile flesh, sharp nails eager to pinch and cut.

Hoofprints litter the ground, starting where the rip begins, circling my yard, up and down the tree line, eventually leading up into the hills, and on to the mountain that squats in silence, ambivalent. In one spot there is a grouping of eight legs, and I try to picture what that might look like—hooves leading up to a fur-lined torso, eight legs like a spider, but as large as an oxen, or maybe a caribou. I turn to inspect the woods, finding scrapes and gouges cut out of several trees, a line of three gashes, as thick as my thumb. I imagine curling horns that twist and turn, like an antelope; I picture branched antlers tipped with sharp blades, like a reindeer; I see great curled monstrosities as if a goat stood on its hind legs, dancing in the darkness, bleating its rancor to the world. But it's the eight legs that bother me, and give me pause, a shiver running up my spine. I hope that it heads into the mountains and never returns, spinning great webs of sticky threads to catch and eat whatever hare or sleepy owl might come its way.

And then I see the figure, down on its knees, hands clasped as if in prayer, its head bowed. In the darkness I mistook it for a bush, covered in snow, frozen solid.

Death by winter.

An arctic suicide.

The first of the long night, but not the first I've encountered. I sigh and approach, tasting the air for residue. There is a faint lingering flavor—bruised apple, or moldy orange, a fruit that is based in sweetness, but now gone over, a fuzzy mold coating the perimeter. It doesn't go far, not all the way to my house. In fact, it barely registers here, where I am standing right beside it—there, and then not there; present, and then gone on the gentle wind.

Brushing off the snow to try and see her face, I realize it's a woman. Mostly it's the men that take the easy way out. I don't recognize her, but she must be local, to walk out here, to know my business. She is entirely naked, to expedite her death, her skin certainly going numb in minutes. I can't imagine the pain as she walked here, but she can't have had far to go, certainly from town. I can only hope that she lost consciousness quickly. Her pale skin has a blue tint to it, no teeth marks yet, but the wolves will come for her, the coyotes, and whatever else lingers here in the woods. I cannot lift or move her—she is frozen to the spot. It will be a gruesome undoing when they finally find her, but there is nothing that I can do now.

Aside from one fleeting gesture.

A cracking comes from the water, down by the sea. The ocean won't freeze over, but the bay might, at least here, close to the shore. Great groans and creaks rise up from the icy beach, a booming thunderclap resonating under the ice, and across the water. A thrum of bass resonates under it all, as if a giant guitar string has been plucked, reverberating into the water and up the hill.

There are boot prints that lead away from the body, and I wonder if there was someone else here with her. Did they want a better view as they expired, walking farther up the hill instead of staying here with her? Did they merely escort her to this rift and tear, to make sure the job would get done? Or did they change their mind and head back to town? The eight-legged freak that wandered this small clearing has trampled on the other footprints and indentations making it hard to decipher. And the snow has filled in everything else, obscuring boots and bare feet and hooves alike. In a few hours this will all be gone and buried, the only sign of life, this frozen sculpture in repose.

I am still recovering but there isn't much here to chew on, so I grab a handful of snow and open my mouth, instantly chilling my lips, teeth, and tongue. It melts quickly, and as I swallow, there is hardly anything to taste— bitter orange rind, sharp sassafras root, gypsy mushroom that tastes like dirt, and a hint of curdled milk that is slowly going sour.

I part my lips and a tiny, white ermine only a few inches long unfurls from my mouth, chittering in the dark, as it crawls out. Its black, beady eyes search the woods for life, or threat, turning back to me, skittering up and onto my shoulder, around my neck, and down my chest and legs, before disappearing into the snow.

"I don't know that I did much for you here, my friend, but I hope that wherever you are, you've found peace."

A great wingspan passes over me in shadow, and I pray it's my friend the snowy owl from the other day, and not something else entirely. It circles three times, passing in front of the moon, and then heads north, up the hill, and away from me.

Owl.

Definitely owl.

Almost certainly owl.

Please, be the owl.

I wonder how long this rip has been open wide, and how many days it remained tight and shut. Perhaps the skeletal bear has held off the invaders all on his own, though I doubt it, even as formidable as he was. There is evidence of something coming through, so if it could happen once, it could happen multiple times. And now I'm picturing a herd of spider deer, cricket ox, beetle elk—gathered in a black, furry pile, making a nest in the woods that might be mistaken for a bush, under the layers of snow and ice.

Like my friend here.

I have to head back inside—it's so cold out here, the wind picking up again, the snow starting to whirl. If not for the glow of my cabin, I wonder how easy it might be to get lost in the folds of white. Distance can be confusing, time elusive, elements misleading. As if recognizing my gaze, the lights in my house flicker, threatening to lose power. The streetlamps near me have all been shot out, broken now, as I anticipated. Out of anger or boredom or drunken stupidity—I don't know.

Behind me the tiny houses that line the street sit mostly in darkness, a smattering of sleds and canoes stacked against the huddled building. As their porch lights stay dark, my neighbors burrow in for the night. In the water I see the moonlight reflecting, waves hardly moving, a slow undulation barely rippling the surface. The outline of the tear shimmers a dull golden color, as if it is sleeping as well, breathing in and out, pulsing and fading, resting as it waits for whatever comes next.

I close my eyes for a moment and picture the dead, stacked like cord wood, one on top of the other. I picture glowing embers, the sound of shovels chipping and clanking against the frozen ground, seeking purchase. I see a massive feast on a long, wooden table where great beasts are carved into slices, drumsticks in piles, balls of lumpy meat under red sauce, with roasted potatoes that are crispy at the edges, bowls of sautéed spinach, and salted green peas, glasses of wine reflecting red against the crystal etchings, silver trays shining as they hold golden biscuits, steaming rolls, and pungent garlic bread. And then the lights go out, and in the dim firelight there is mold on everything, a white fuzz, a layer of fat solidifying over sour gravy, squirming white maggots crawling over slick meat, black and green spots running over bread and fruit alike. It is sour and rotten, a fermented creeping tang that threatens to coat my mouth and tongue with its disease, as bile rises from my stomach.

I open my eyes and take a sharp breath in, tiny bites at my mouth and throat, swallowing down razor blades and coppery torn flesh, my stomach rolling with disgust.

Whatever comes next, I deserve it.

# CHAPTER SIX

# THE ESCALATION

The day begins, and ends, in violence.

When I look out the back window, the praying form that I left kneeling in the ice and snow has been torn to shreds. Blood stains the snow in the dim moonlight, as limbs are scattered in the clearing, up the trail, and off into the woods, long smears and bloodstains that appear black in the darkness. They are gnawed to the bone, leaving behind only gristle and ligaments. The snow is falling down slowly right now, but in time, it will all be covered. Whatever is left here will certainly be picked apart and carried away when the wolves and coyotes return for the scraps of muscle and bone marrow that still remain. I wish I could have done more for her. It is a tragedy, these brutal acts unavoidable, once it had all been set in motion. If somebody wants to die, there isn't much you can do to stop them, I'm afraid. They'll find a way to make it happen.

I throw another log onto the fire, bundle up, and head out onto the porch to retrieve the offerings and letters, aware of the delay, and the simmering anger that must certainly linger in the hearts of those who have lost kin, or friends, or neighbors.

When I open the door, there is snow everywhere, pushed into the corners, drifting up onto the wood pile, the second, cheap flap of a door hanging askew, one of the hinges torn out of the plywood. I go to close it, holding it up, trying to click the latches shut, and back into place, but they have all been broken off in a moment of rage, the intrusion a personal violation that hurts more than I thought it would.

Somebody has been here.

I turn to the apple crate, unable to find it at first, and then I notice the splinters of wood and broken slats that lie in a pile under a dusting of snow. It has been stomped into submission. No letters, no sculptures, no hides, and no parchment.

Nothing.

This has never happened before.

But I've never been sick before, never hurt so badly that I couldn't do my job. Not for long, anyway. Not like this.

Without direction, without their calls to service, I have nowhere to be. I can't go on a leisurely stroll into town asking them to roll out their dead. It's too cold, the windchill ruthless. So I turn and head back inside, a headache beginning to form, a throbbing in the base of my neck that I rub with my hands, thick gloves discarded in haste, boots pulled off and kicked to the corner.

Hanging my coat on a hook by the door, I flop onto the couch, frustration and resentment boiling to the surface. For years now I've spent time with my neighbors, held palaver as we enjoyed a meal, their loss and suffering something that I could help to pass, a way to ease their minds, two coins placed on the eyes of their lost husbands, wives, fathers, mothers, children, pets, friends, and coworkers. It has aged me beyond recognition, torn at my flesh in any number of ways, and put my life in danger every time I set foot out the door. Mother Nature was already one landmine to avoid, manifesting her anger in every hungry animal, icy wind, or bone-rattling storm. I don't need another.

Along the way I have seen wonders as well, in the purity of an innocent baby, lost at birth, a holy reconciliation, casting light and warmth into feathery goslings, fuzzy kits, and iridescent beetles. I have seen the beauty and glory of a life well-lived, in threads of gold, whispers of tangerine, puffs of violet. I have tasted love and honor, friendship, and calming peace. It was an honor to be allowed into these private, intimate moments of grief and sorrow. I do not take this responsibility lightly.

I have been a catharsis in an otherwise heartbreaking vulnerability, providing closure, and companionship—a finality. I have been a catalyst of change for what might otherwise have remained toxic, stagnant, and diseased. I have been a guide to another realm, where hopefully something better will emerge, something glorious.

And what have I asked for in return?

Nothing.

A meal.

A kindness.

A bit of grace.

A heartfelt moment of remembrance as vegetables were chopped, meat browned, chocolate melted, sauces rendered, bread leavened, herbs shaken into a pot. One ritual of home, family, and comfort leading to another—the release of a spirit, the absolution of an imperfect soul, the blessing of a loved one as they pass on, ascend, or are reborn.

The darkness is winning.

Quicker than I could have imagined, the heartbeat of this community, the bloodline, the backbone has been shaken, broken, and tainted—the isolation and separation pushing us all to the brink of war, turning on each other, as the icy wilderness laughs in the darkness.

My stomach clenches, and I stand to go to the kitchen.

I am tired, and sore, and lost.

I close my eyes for a moment and pray.

I am standing in a field of snow and ice, the wind howling around me, as a gold compass with a luminescent pearl in the center spins in every direction, unable to show me the way. I open my arms to the spirits of the north—the land that is frozen solid, the water that slows as it darkens, the air that shatters what won't bend, the fire in my heart flickering, threatening to go out. The moon drifts out from behind a swath of rushing clouds, lighting up the sparkling field, as I slowly breathe out baby blue forget-me-not petals, white dandelion fluff, and yellow chamomile pollen.

When my eyes open, I cry crimson tears that run down my pale skin, a rivulet of sorrow in a land filled with regret.


I take a short hike, flashlight beam barely penetrating the night, through the snow that whips and twists around me, unable to sit still in my house, the anger and frustration building up, a sense of futility washing over me in a chilling wave of depression. Layer upon layer, bundled up like a swaddled baby, I step past the blanketed remnants of the woman who died praying at a tear in our reality. The opening is widening again, preparing for something else no doubt, and part of me wants to grab the edge and help it expand, maybe even break through to the other side. But the heat and sulfur drift to me on a wave of rippling gases, and I'm unable to see deeper into whatever land or world lives beyond it. The grass is always greener, they say. One circle of hell traded for another, I'm sure.

Up the trail, up the hill, to the base of the mountain, my trip today is reckless, and I know it, but I need to see something, to confirm my worst fears.

There is a pit filled with bones from a creature that stood upright, when my gut said it should have been down on all fours. An abomination that not only crossed over and came through, but thrived in the woods for a number of years.

Is there more?

Are there others?

Has this been building?

A quick glance toward the clearing tells me that it is still covered in snow, a marker on this hike up the mountain, but nothing I need to investigate further.

There is a cave filled with smears of blood, the remnants of its feasting, rudimentary drawings depicting great horned beasts, flames of flickering heat, and a horizon that never seems to come into focus, a distant sun in the shape of a hoofprint.

This is not what I need to study, not today.

Beyond that, up the trail, my cane now a walking stick proper, the incline steepens. As I hit the edge of the tree line, the last of the emaciated pines gives way to rocky outcroppings, a dotting of anemic scrub dotting the cracks and crevices.

I pause for a moment to cast my flashlight around the trees, and here, in the evergreens, I find what I am looking for.

There are several cocoons hanging from the branches of the sickly sugar pine, the bulbous droplets the size of watermelons. It's very dark out, the sun a distant memory, the moon unwilling to appear for many hours still. Holding the light in my left hand, I fumble for the hunting knife that is strapped to my belt, unclasp the snap, and pull it out. I walk closer and tap the frozen silk, grasses woven into it, a strangle of twigs wrapped around it like a shell. It is hard and sounds empty except for a rattle that bothers me, something shaking around inside the shellacked container. Against my better judgment, I slice it open from the top to the bottom, pushing hard with the sharp blade to penetrate the shell, and step back quickly as something spills out.

Falling to the ground are hundreds, maybe thousands, of frozen, hardened spiders and beetles—some strange carapace that I've never seen before. They are hollow, like a cicada husk, either molting and changing into something else, or perhaps withering and drying on the frozen ground. I think of the eight-legged beast that left hoofprints in the snow and shiver, turning the light around me in a circle.

No sign of it.

And then I turn the light up into the tree and there it is—curled up in a ball, furry legs tucked in, thick hide a dark brown. I fall backward, the light never leaving it, a string of curses filling the night air. But it doesn't move, its eyes wide and lifeless, limbs frozen and twisted at unnatural angles.

It's dead.

The elements were too much for it.

Birthed into the void, or pushing through to investigate, it seems that not much can live out here in these elements, aside from the evolutionary wonders that hibernate, or travel in packs, covered in fur.

I stand up and turn off the flashlight for a moment, gazing up to the top of the mountain. Black on black, matte on matte, something circles the peak, casting a shadow over the darkness, the color so subtle that I have to convince myself there is anything moving there at all.

That is no owl.

Its massive wingspan gives me pause, as the winds whip up and a rumble comes from the sky.

Thundersnow.

I've never seen it here before.

A crack of lightning fractures the darkness, and for a moment I can see the creature clearly, leathery wings flapping in the thick falling flakes, talons at the ends, an elongated head with its mouth open, two rows of teeth exposed for but a moment.

How long has it been here?

When did it come through?

I can only hope that it prefers the summit and the smattering of mountain goats that may still remain high up in the frigid altitude, over the lights and noises and smells of our small community. Or perhaps us humans just don't have enough meat on the bone. Elk and caribou, Dall sheep and reindeer, wolves and coyotes—it may not need to travel any farther—or at least not all the way to town.

I need to close the tear.

The darkness has stained this land for too many years. There may be no cure for a disease this far gone. But I have to try. It's my life's work.

I return home cold, tired, and afraid. I bring a few logs in with me, my day fading away, the night coming on soon, expanding the darkness, as the gloom continues. The village is quiet, buried under the muffled hush of heavy snowfall. Down the road, the houses sit in shadow, streetlights out, not a movement anywhere, everyone tucked in, bundled up, and still. The smart thing to do.

My plans are simple—a cup of tea, a bowl of soup, and an evening by the fire. Taking off my coat and snow pants, boots in the corner, gloves next to them, I collapse on the couch and fall asleep.

When I awaken, it is to the sound of a car door slamming, something heavy falling, and then silence. I stare at my front door and imagine it bursting open, but nothing comes for me, a few crackles and pops emanating from the fireplace, and nothing more. When I go to the kitchen and click on the lights, nothing happens. The lines are down. Or *still* down. Or down *again*. I don't know. I hardly know what day it is, and how long it's been since I've seen a soul—living or otherwise.

I brew the tea and heat up the soup via candlelight. The gas burners still work, even if I have to light a match to get it started, the electric ignition failing to work. I am starving, and yet sick to my stomach at the same time. The tea is filled with lavender, mint, and chamomile. I'm hoping it will make my stomach feel better. The soup is a simple potato with leeks and hints of smoky bacon. Something to fill me up.

In the flicker of the candlelight, I take a sip of the tea, letting the herbs wash over my tongue, and then something bitter emerges at the end. Did I forget the honey? I take a spoonful of soup, and let the buttery broth linger in my mouth, the smoke and black pepper merging with sweet onions, and then turning suddenly sour.

I set down my spoon in disgust.

I know what this is.

It's all too familiar.

I stand up quickly, knocking over my chair, rushing to the kitchen sink to stare out into the yard. The moon has risen, casting a pale gaze over the trees and water, but there is something else out there, hidden in shadow, ringing my property—all the way around. I can't quite make it out, something bundled up and lying on the ground, the snow shushing to a stop, as the breeze gently pushes the trees back and forth. The moon passes behind a cloud, and the shapes disappear, and then it emerges again, brighter than ever. I can see what it is.

A body.

Several bodies.

A gasp slips out of my mouth, as I realize what I'm seeing. A body has been placed in my yard, and another next to it, and then another. Bundled up in a tarp and tied tight with rope, the shape is that of a full-sized adult. Next to it is a ceremonial blanket with colorful, intricate patterns—a lumpy shape rolled up in it, secured with twine. The third body is wrapped with black garbage bags, yellow ties crisscrossing the shape, tying one bag to the next. The fourth is in a tan drop cloth, splattered with a variety of paint colors. The fifth in nothing at all—just a sweatshirt and jeans, the parka too valuable to give up, the mukluks as well. The bodies continue—all the way as far as I can see, to the left and to the right, and then completely out of my sight.

"No, no, no, no, no . . ." I say as I run out the front door, stocking feet wet from the snow, the cold rushing in like a flock of startled geese. The bodies continue out front, all the way around my house.

"What have they done?" I whisper.

A single torch sticks out of a snowdrift at the end of the stone path, the red and orange flames flickering in the dying wind. Tied to the branch are necklaces made of twine—a turtle, an eagle, a fox, a bear, a wolf, a salmon, a caribou, and a seal.

There is no sign of anyone, no feeling left in my feet, a sharp stabbing pain in my chest.

So be it.

I stumble back inside, my exposed skin needled with pain, hands aching with every movement, a fine layer of snow covering the hardwood floor from the door being left ajar.

I sit down at the table, and tuck back into my meal. I sip the tea, swallow, and grimace—spooning one mouthful of the sour, fetid soup back into my mouth after another. I lift the tea and taste fecal matter, cobwebs, ash, and dirt. I choke it down. I spoon in the soup and taste sour vomit, chunks of gamey gristle, maggot-infested cheese that curdles as I bolt it down. I hold my hand over my mouth as it fills with bile, and then force that back as well. As my eyes water, I gulp down the last of the tea—fermented fruit gone bad, the decay of a dying flower bed, the smell of cut grass composting into rotten, wet mush. With a stuttering last breath, I lift the bowl and tip it up, chewing on the potato, the broth spilling over my face and chin—rotten eggs turned green and slimy, fish left out in the sun with flies buzzing around it, pus from an open wound.

I stand up and a sheen of sweat washes over my body, my gut tied in knots. I bend over as muscles seize, my eyes squeezed shut as I'm wracked with pain. It is a mass of swirling eels nipping at the inside of my stomach, it is a rippling of my skin as if my blood is swelling to a boil, it is a tightening of my muscles as I cramp up, the contractions seizing my heart.

My eyes widen and there is a clearing filled with sunshine, birds chirping, the flutter of butterflies as they flit from flower to flower. A cool breeze pushes over the long grasses, as the warmth of the sunshine kisses my skin with a blush of color, painted onto my flesh in loving strokes. A buzz of cicadas in the distance blends with the chitter of a squirrel dashing off with a nut in its mouth, the coo of a dove, jasmine drifting to me from swaying bushes, a hint of pine underneath. The rays of light sparkle down onto my upturned face, and for a moment, I am a child again, filled with wonder, serenity, and hope.

And then I am slammed back into the darkness as if returning to the earth after a long flight, my arms heavy, my legs weak, collapsing to the floor in a ball of quivering pain. I shake uncontrollably, hands trembling, my back arched in a painful rictus. My spine cracks, and my muscles clench, my teeth bared in a feral grimace, lips pulled tight. My head is filled with a pressure that threatens to explode.

My skin tightens, a thousand cuts appearing all over my body, as if something is trying to get out—nipping at my flesh from the inside, biting and slicing, tiny teeth, and miniature talons pushing against my flesh. I roll over onto my back and claw at my clothes, trying to rip them off, buttons flying off my faded flannel, t-shirt torn in half as I rage, my fingers grasping at my herniating skin, one undulation after another. My nails dig into my pale stomach, raking across it, taking strips of skin away in red stripes. I open my mouth to scream and out spills a mass of spiders—tiny black creatures with red, beady eyes, furry backs, and tiny sharp pincers that click together like an orchestra of castanets.

"Oh, God," I moan, rolling around on the ground, seeking relief from what's coming, but knowing it will never arrive.

There is a great rending under my skin, as if a zipper has been undone from my sternum to my pelvis, followed by a sense of liquid being distributed under my flesh. There is a second tear, and I can feel fat and connective tissue being severed, a layer parting, releasing tension, like a rubber band. And then a third incision, splaying open my skin, exposing my rib cage and my internal organs.

I scream with every ounce of my being, as my rib cage splits in half, and something emerges from my body.

My vision is blurry, covered in salty sweat and spatters of blood, one long, bony leg slowly extending out from my ruptured stomach, unfolding once, and then twice, until it is planted firmly on the ground, a pool of blood widening around me. And then another leg emerges, unfolding as well, tentatively placing itself on the floor, as it trembles into life. Six more legs push out, securing a base on the ground in order to raise up a teardrop abdomen that is bony and white with spikes running up and down the middle. Out of the shimmering bulb, glossy with my blood, a thorax appears, followed by an elongated skull that ends with two sharp fangs, dripping with a yellow liquid. Pincers click open and shut. Black beady eyes sit in a clump in the center of the skull. When it opens its mouth in a high-pitched screech, two hesitant tentacles slither out, gray suction cups glistening under rubbery, black skin. And then they quickly retreat back inside its gaping maw. The creature stretches and rises up, filling the room as its body swells and expands, plates of bone separating to reveal glistening muscle that quickly snaps back into place.

In a rage it dashes around the room, looking for a way out, knocking over lamps and tables, as the last of my life seeps out of me, the room spinning, everything below my neck numb. My wrinkled skin smooths over, my hair returns to its natural shade of brown, the elderly man gone, gnarled knuckles reduced, liver spots erased. In truth, I am somewhere in my thirties, not that it matters anymore. There was so much that I still wanted to see, and do.

I cannot move; I cannot speak.

There is a clatter as I hear glass breaking, wood snapping, sparks spilling out of the fireplace, as the creature bangs into the stony chimney, burning itself. Smoke drifts to me when burning logs tumble to the floor, tiny creatures running over my hands and face, flames rising up as the rug catches fire, transferred to the papers and magazines in a rack at the end of the couch, and then rapidly onto the curtains, without hesitation.

*It will be over soon*, I think.

I've been cold for so long.

I cough as the room fills with smoke, the walls made of pine, the sap a sparking sweetness, melting plastic, the roof rolling with flames. Everything crackles around me, for I am now officially in the belly of the beast.

The creature stands over me, my face reflected in a multitude of eyes, pausing for a moment to lean in close, two ivory pincers clicking, its fangs dripping acid on my face. A drip and a sting, a drip and a sting, eating a hole through my cheek, into my mouth, before burrowing into my throat.

What horrors can still await me?

It skitters back and forth on the tips of its appendages, a dancing mad god, lifting first one side, and then the other, as the house is engulfed in flames.

With a crack and a heavy thud, the roof collapses, revealing a black sky filled with white pinpricks, my flesh burning under the fiery structure, a cold blast of air rushing in. The creature moves on, out of my sight, over the walls that still stand upright, fleeing into the darkness, its brood of hatchlings chasing after it.

I imagine it will seek out the rift, and I pray that it will work its way through and end this war forever.

And in the wonder of the universe, a blinking planet pulses in the night sky, a flicker of life from millions of miles away. And I wonder what life might be thriving there, right now, and what that might look like.

ACT TWO

# MOTHER MONSTER

—

You can make an oyster surrender its pearl . . .
All you need is persistence and a sharp enough knife.

—John Langan, *The Fisherman*

# CHAPTER ONE

# FAMILY

The earliest memories I have of becoming a mother, of growing up beyond the innocence of youth, often involved battling with creatures that lived in the desert, the plains, the crevices that split the earth, and the caves to the north. But I wasn't always alone.

As a great horned beast—my body covered in scaly armor, my cutting horn jutting up into the air, my thick hide wrinkled, scarred, and dry—I spent most of the time hunting for food, water, and shelter. Bony plates ran up and down my spine, capturing the heat of the day, to keep me warm at night. My legs were like tree trunks, ending in a flat round toe, protected by dense nails. But part of the problem with traversing the same stretch of land, searching for the handful of grassy patches and random oases, is that every other creature out here in this godforsaken hell was doing the same thing. We traveled in circles, in great loops, up and down the dunes and across cracked, emaciated soil. Out of these prolonged migrations came either violence or peace, enemies or new family, betrayal or unity. The only constant in my life was change.

My beastly children come from different fathers, and in each one of them there are strengths and weaknesses. Being a mother, I have created life in many different forms, but with that gift and responsibility comes death. Out here in the wastelands, it lingers in the air, hunches in the shadows, and waits for our most vulnerable moments to leap out and devour my progeny. Over time, this loss drained great amounts of emotion and hope from me, leaving me an empty shell. Love was lost, grief descended, my hope dashed on the rocks like a baby bird fallen from a nest.

My first brood was created by one of my kind, the natural progression and choice, one large, trundling animal mating with another. When I saw him lounging next to an oasis to the east, it was as if I had stumbled across myself, an out-of-body experience, staring at the arc of his back, the dented and scratched armor, the thick legs, and faded horn. He was my twin, a hearty echo, a calming presence.

We didn't speak much, not at first, and not at all in the end. I merely made my way down the hill, to the water, supping up the cold liquid, as nearby, brown cactus wrens chirped and fluttered, while other furry creatures observed us cautiously from a ridge to the north. I suppose this doppelgänger was used to being alone, as I had become, because he barely opened his eyes to see what rumbling monster had invaded his space. That confidence and lack of fear, I envied it. Some days I was the alpha—the largest, strongest, angriest animal for miles; and then other days I felt vulnerable—damaged, isolated, lost, and afraid.

I'd seen my kind taken down, swarmed by vast clouds of gnats and fleas, their skin turned a bubbling red, devoured alive by tiny carnivorous parasites that at first blush seemed harmless. I'd witnessed great battles with other large predators—curved horns, sharp nails, tails with spikes, teeth as long as daggers. The blood that spilled into the sand disappeared in moments, sinking beneath the surface, leaving nothing behind—temporarily slaking the thirst of this greedy, insatiable hellscape. And on one occasion, some massive winged beast that descended from the sky—taut leathery skin stretched across bony wings, its expansive pinion blocking out the sun—cast us into shade, my siblings next to me one minute, and then gone the next. Tentacled creatures living deep beneath the surface pushed up through cracks in the earth in search of prey, massive sandworms with ringed mouths of teeth roamed the hills and valleys, lurking inches beneath our feet, while roaming packs of snapping feral dogs chased any herd they encountered to exhaustion, searching for soft spots and weak links to take down, tear open, and devour. Death came in all shapes and sizes and often with no warning.

As the sun set, we huddled next to each other seeking solace in our company and reprieve from the heat near the cool water, both taking in forlorn breaths, and exhaling peace, the reassurance of our size and armor granting us a moment of quiet in a lifetime of battles. I encouraged him to help me create life.

It didn't take much, just proximity, and a few whispered words of encouragement, to tell him that there was no need for violence, that he could freely have what others might try to take. There was an aura of stability about him that gave me comfort, a sense that he might stay, might join me in my journey, the rest of my brothers and sisters taken, or lost. What might we create out here in the heat and lingering danger? I thought, if only for a short while, perhaps something special.

In the darkness, as the moon rose, he mounted me, and I received what he had to offer, merging for a moment, two lonely souls in a desolate place. It was a simple act, one that required no instruction, and when he finished, I was relieved, the pleasure of our pairing tingling my momentarily warmed skin, the moonlight reflecting off the water, bathing everything in silence and serenity. We slept by the watering hole, and for a brief moment, I was happy.

In the morning, he was gone.

Part of me feared it might happen.

His deep, large, round prints had almost disappeared in the shifting sand, but I spotted his faint tracks over a nearby hill, trailing out of sight, and I almost followed him, but decided after a long and painful consideration, to let him go. He had shown me who he was. There was no point in trying to force him into domesticity.

His disappearance was the first rivulet of worry, a screw that tightened in my chest, unlike anything I'd felt before. The deaths that would follow, they would cement my heart over time.

It could have been worse. I was alive.

The children came a fortnight later, unexpected and with considerable pain—a litter of four pink, wrinkled beasts with their twitching ears, so vulnerable and small. Writhing in the sand, gasping for breath, already screeching in unison for nourishment, I feared they would not survive. That first inkling of terror at being a new mother burst from my chest like a horde of skittering bugs. I wanted to shove them back inside me, so I could protect them a little longer. It would be months before their armor would harden, tiny nubs that would become their horns protruding from their snouts, skin slowly turning gray, as it thickened. I would need to keep a close eye on them; so vulnerable and naive.

The first child was torn apart in the night before it could even develop—strands of his pink flesh littered across the desert floor, his soft underbelly gaping wide and empty, disemboweled with his organs devoured, eyes wide and lifeless, staring off into the void with nothing but the horror of his final moments to keep him company. I never even heard the predators approach, stealing him off into the night, not a cry or bleat or muffled scream. I was heartbroken, but tried to remain grateful that the rest were not taken.

The second beast to die grew its armor well, sharpening his cutting horn on every rock he encountered with great pride and interest. Physically, the boy thickened up nicely, stout, with the potential to grow larger than myself, nearly double, I thought. The irony of his death was that the poisonous berries looked like any other edible ones, his confidence at growing and surviving a false truth, the purple and red vomit a violent cone sprayed across the dirt, reminding the rest of us to be more careful.

The third child, she learned from her brothers, balancing the physical strength and protections of one sibling with the hesitation and caution the other lacked. She was my shadow—a smaller version of myself, with her father's horn. Our conversations—as we traversed the desert, seeking grasses, hunting and defending, gnawing the meat of our kills right down to the bone—were a great comfort to me. Her death was my greatest loss. A cry from the fourth child sent her running to aid her brother, the runt of the litter in trouble again. Squeals and grunts came from over a hill, jolting me from my nap, her bleats for help intertwining with his, as I lurched to my feet and crowned the vista in time to see them both sucked helplessly down into the sand, gone in a whisper, as the sun shone on and the wind blew on with indifference. There had been no sign of this trap, this quicksand, this hole in the earth. It pulled them both in, and they were gone. Just like that. In the blink of an eye. And in that moment, my armor hardened, along with my heart, and something changed, something broke.

Barely a turn of seasons, and they were all gone. What did I have to show for it all?

Pain.

Remorse.

Doubt.

And fear.


It would be more than a year before I met the second father.

At the southern edge of the mountains, a patch of dense woods lined the base with pine trees, mesquite, and sickly scrub brush. It provided a welcome patch of cool shade, scattered grasses, and occasionally a ripe fruit or flowering bud. I didn't typically travel this far north, as the expansive desert that stretched out toward the mountainside was cruel and unforgiving, filled with one dangerous element after another—tentacled creatures, packs of rabid hyenas, and flesh-eating beetles the size of dogs. But over time, I'd grown restless and wanted to see what else lurked and lived and grew around me. Perhaps it was an unconscious desire to manufacture my own death. Or maybe it was just boredom and a broken spirit. Either way, I headed north.

I smelled him long before I saw him—the rank odor of wet fur, the sour sharp bitterness of urine, the fetid breath of something rotten, something decomposing, suffused the air around me—but by then it was too late. I scanned the horizon, searching for the source as I sat in the dense forest, resting in the shade, the chirps and titters suddenly quiet in the trees. Overhead, through an opening in the canopy, a flock of dark shapes expanded and contracted, shrieking up from the treetops into the sky, not quite birds, but something else, I thought, small, and grouped together tightly. The growl came low at first, and then surged in volume, rumbling into the space around me, filling the struggling forest with menace. And then it appeared from out of the undergrowth, slinking out onto the path.

The beast that emerged was no coyote, no hyena, not a wolf, or at least, not any wolf that I'd ever seen before. It was huge, its eyes almost level with mine, its gray fur thick, and luxurious, massive pads set down one long limb after another, its bushy tail twitching back and forth slowly, as its mouth opened to bare its seemingly endless white teeth. I was transfixed by the lustrous blue of its eyes, the panting mouth and lolling tongue expanding into a grin. It strolled closer, sniffing the air to taste my scent, before sitting gently on its haunches a few feet in front of me. A stuttering heartbeat rattled my rib cage, frozen in anticipation, as wonder held my curiosity captive.

I thought perhaps it had never seen my kind before, and I took in his regal stature with a slow inspection, impressed by his thick coat, calm demeanor, and demanding presence. This was his land, his woods, and I had invaded it. But now he sat and laughed in the shadows, holding court with no fear at all.

He was eager to talk, having been alone for some time, and saw me as an oddity, something new and different. There might be a lesson for him in this, something to help him survive out here in the dying land. So, we shared our horror stories, our histories, and our knowledge. I told him of the watering holes to the south, warned him of the cracked earth and the beasts that lived inside it, enlightening him about the grove of cactus to the west, with their edible flowers and purple fruit, if he ever got desperate enough to leave the forest. He told me of a warren of rabbits on the other side of the mountain, certainly too fast for me to catch, but meat nonetheless. He spoke of the voices in the caves above us, of a rotten tree that dropped strange decomposing buds to the earth, and then he disappeared back into the woods, and out of sight.

Before I could bring myself to follow, he returned with a dried piece of meat from a recent kill, dropping it gently to the ground in front of me, the morsel more of a snack than a meal, but the gesture appreciated nonetheless.

He asked me to stay, to wait until the moon would come out, so he could serenade the darkness with howls, yips, and great urgent cries filled with loneliness, longing, and sorrow.

And so I did.

Our pairing was not as awkward as I thought it might be, even though it surprised me in many ways. He was a gentle soul, full of poetic visions, but as the night wore on and the moon rose higher, he called out into the expanding gloom and was answered in kind, by voices both similar and foreign to his own. I told him to go, to be with his people, his pack, that the south and its desert would not be kind to him. And with a long hesitation, his blue eyes rippling in the light of the moon, he finally nodded, and then was gone, in a flash of movement, one giant leap into the woods, through the bushes and out of sight.

The litter I would birth later took more from his bloodline than it did from mine, primarily shaggy cubs, with the occasional armored helmet, or an odd spike or plate running down the spine. They were mostly canine, furry, and long-limbed, but in the desert, they were hot and mangy, seeking a relief that I could not provide. They traveled instinctively in a pack, eager to track and chase and kill, moving as one across the desert, the plains, and the deadlands. When they remembered, they would leave me an offering, much like their father had—their bounty glistening and slick with blood. These feral creatures would drift across the land, ebbing and flowing—away from me, and then back in a rush of snapping teeth and gleeful barks.

When an orange harvest moon filled the sky one night, turning redder as the darkness expanded, they filled the air with painful howls and sorrowful yips. One by one they snuffled my armored head, and licked my face, before departing into the blackness, heading north, to be with their father.

I couldn't decide if it was a betrayal or just an eventuality. In the quiet of the night, I wallowed in my emptiness, the void left by their absence too heavy to bear, struggling to understand why they had abandoned me, even though, in my heart, I knew what they truly needed, and that I couldn't possibly give it to them. It was a loss that I would contemplate for many years to come. And it never hurt any less, regardless of the truth, even as I knew they were better off without me. It was so very hard to let them go.

—

I remained alone for a long time after their departure. I spent much of my time at a tear that had materialized one day on the desert floor. Like a wound in the very fabric of reality, this giant rip in space-time gaped open with a blinding light, always facing me, from whichever direction I approached it. I would sit and stare into the winter wonderland on the other side, a stark contrast to this desolate world of mine, trying to figure out how and why the portal manifested here. I feared this strange gateway with all of my heart, and yet, it drew me to it, with the cold mournful wind and the dusting of snow and ice that swept its way through. There was life on the other side, and I thought that perhaps as this land continued to die, that they might somehow be able to help us.

I would be right.

And wrong.

In so many ways.

The third father was something much darker and more complicated.

What I thought was a dream, a nightmare, turned out to be real.

In my longing and loneliness, I'd often sleep by an oasis, as I had in the past, or in the woods to the north, looking for familiar friends, or by the rippling tear, the world on the other side so strange and curious. And in my sorrow and waning hope, I would stare at the stars, their pinholes dotting the dark sky, while the planets glowed red and yellow, fading in and out. I often wondered if there was life elsewhere, or if they too were already dead and gone. The moon was often the sole source of light in an ever-expanding darkness, filled with a creeping apathy that threatened to drown me in sorrow. I prayed to whatever gods might be listening—asking for forgiveness, seeking knowledge, eager to learn and grow, to find a way forward, to create life, and share in that companionship.

But something else was listening too.

And the response was not what I expected.

At the peak of night, clouds passed overhead, obscuring the already hazy moon, as a cold, dust-laden wind pushed across the desert, a heat rising up out of the swirling sand, the red glow of something sinister pulsing in the darkness. As it closed the distance between us, one lumbering step after another, quaking the entire landscape with each massive footfall, its true form remained hidden in shadows. Around the unseen presence, a dark aura throbbed, trembling in the void, emanating waves of darkness and dread like an inverse sun. Under the roar of the wind, the entity unleashed a stream of whispers, a cacophony of seemingly meaningless and unintelligible words, a chaotic rambling manifesto filled with recognition, desire, anger, and violence. I was unable to tell if I actually heard this strange invocation, if it was real or imagined, or if it had placed the words somehow in my mind.

When blood is spilled in the darkness, does it still glimmer red?

If nobody is there to feel it, is it still warm, and tacky?

The scent of salty flesh, something burned and smoking, a bitter, pungent incense wafted over me, and yet, my eyes could still not find the source, a gauzy veil dropped across my vision, as it neared. I cried out, but my shouts were lost in this insidious vacuum, consuming everything in its path. There were no words, no negotiations, only a void that was suddenly filled with a curious energy, a glistening velvet sustenance that hid in the expanding pitch, reverberating with hunger, malice, and glee.

And then I went under. Everything gone, blinded by a claustrophobic blanket of fear and restraint, as a singular hand was placed on my head, long nails clacking on my armor, a presence slowly enveloping my paralyzed frame, sniffing and grunting, blowing fetid air into my face. Its disease poured over me, holding me tight, enrapturing me with pain and suffering, a glorious suffering that pushed agony deep into my body, spiking a ripple across my flesh. Then came the heat, as if I were burning from the inside out, my skin crisping, flaking, and sliding off of me, a viscous liquid, sticky and heavy, coating my armor, a tar that pushed me down into the earth.

And then nothing.

In the morning, there was no evidence that anything had happened, no marks on my body, no soreness or tender flesh, not a drop of blood, or ichor, or lingering smell. I spent hours wandering in circles, trying to find some sort of confirmation of what had transpired. I even paused at the rip, pushing my head into the snowy terrain of the other side, until the bitter sting of the icy wind upon my face forced me to retreat without any answers, pine and something burned drifting to me.

In the days that came, I checked every stream of piss for blood; I inspected my body from head to toe looking for marks, bruises, and bites; I questioned every uneasy pain that emanated from my gut, wondering if it was something I ate or a new life growing and twisting within my battered body, squirming in my womb like a nest of angry snakes. But I could find no confirmation. And so, I denied it ever happened.

Which was a mistake.

One mistake in a series of mistakes that would haunt me for the rest of my life.

When I gave birth, it was to a horror that nearly split me in half. I collapsed face down in the cracked soil, overcome with convulsions and rigor, my skin on fire as if my heart was pushing pure poison through my bloodstream. I twisted and turned in agony, writhing in the dirt and sand, caught in the throes of contractions that grew closer and closer together, begging for death, begging for anything to make it stop.

It did not.

Sweat covered my flesh as I screamed into the hollow night, the horned child pushing its way out of me, one pointed tip at a time, followed by a snarling claret skull, one brawny arm, and then another, until its cloven hooves found their balance and stamped defiantly into the sand. I trembled in relief, and glowed crimson, as it strode to the rippling tear, stepping through without a moment's hesitation.

As I cried and whimpered into the silence of the surrounding desert, I knew that I had been forsaken, cast out into the darkness, punished for praying to the wrong god.

I swore that this must be the end of it all.

But it wasn't.


The fourth father was not the last, but he was the one that extinguished my last hope and caused me to lash out at the world. He helped me build the walls around my heart, to tamp down any love that still burbled within me, set my dreams afire in a rush of predatory hunger.

After my third birth sent a horror through the tear, I vowed to turn away from all mating, all family, all companionship. I would simply persevere, and when the land died, I would simply die with it.

I was done caring.

Done trying.

I'm sure that somewhere in the dark there was a great peal of laughter, the fates denying my plans with a malevolent grin, God chuckling on His throne of skulls and diamonds, as around him angels blinked with a multitude of yellowing eyes.

As I wandered the desert without a plan, I found that my anger vibrated around me like a drum. The creatures of the night gave me a wide berth, hiding on the periphery, as they barked and howled and grunted and cackled and crowed and snorted and snapped.

On a day when I was completely lost, the heat and sun pressing down on me, my vision blurred with rage and grief, there was a long swath of cool shade that passed over me. I squinted up into the brilliant sun in its wake, blinking rapidly, unable to see, as something descended quickly, covering me entirely, hot air beating around me in waves of musky chaos.

And then . . .

How can I describe it?

I was flying.

It lifted off, this massive creature, picking me up, and up, and up into the heavens. The strength, it was impossible. I felt a set of six great claws clinging to my armor, my shell, pulling my body taut, threatening to rip me in half. The pain, the rising wind in my face, the widening gap between my feet and the distant ground, filled me with an overwhelming blend of exhilaration and fear. I looked upward, away from the drop of certain death, to see flapped wings that were rippled with veins and tendons, sinuous leather held together with muscled bones, a wide and elongated head spliced with a toothy beak, its legs coated in brown feathers, sickly yellow digits ending in sharp, black talons.

Below me the majestic landscape revealed itself as we rose higher and higher—the peak of the snow-capped mountain, above the opening of a cave, where horned goats roosted precariously on sheer cliffs a mile high; vast patches of grass far to the east that imparted a lush green upon the earth that I'd never thought possible; spectacular plateaus to the west where a massive split in the earth held a looming blackness that seemingly had no bottom, gleaming with an oily residue; and a winding ribbon of deep blue to the south that must have been a river, a meandering liquid appendage ending in a crystalline lake filled with undulating masses of silver-backed fish so plentiful that they could be seen even from this great height. It was all so far away, and yet, right there before me.

Whether I was dinner or mate, I didn't know, and in the face of my demise, a strange thing happened.

I realized that I didn't want to die.

I wasn't done fighting yet.

As we crested the top of a mountain range far north of any land I'd ever seen, below me a great nest appeared through the clouds, a twisted lair made of roots and twigs and berries and branches and limbs and logs and leaves.

That is when it let go.

For a long time after that my memory is fractured, like the plates that protected my body, like the leg bones of my thick, rugged appendages. I can only piece together flashes of a diffused narrative, everything in black and white, a stuttering strip of celluloid that burns in a bubbling climax at the end.

There are open mouths and long beaks, and they snap and clack, heads lolling back and forth, pink tongues flickering in anticipation of the meal to come. There is a great pecking at my flesh, holes appearing between the gaps in my armor, chunks of meat taken, tendons pulled and snapped, blood weeping from the wounds. There is a crack of lightning, the rumble of a seething storm and a downpour covering everything in a blue chill. And then there is a sudden rush of air and I'm flying once again, then tumbling down, rolling head over tail, bouncing and twisting, until I crash in a cloud of dust, the world gone quiet.

After a while another memory rises to the surface, as I am gently lifted up, first my torso, then my hind quarters, as tufts of thick fur ripple beneath me, growls and snarls, and then a sense of movement, my body drifting weightlessly, covering a great distance as we slowly move, cool air whispering across my bent, broken, and bruised flesh. And then I am immersed in cold water, calming at first, surrounded by the pressure and then scintillating light, before a sense that I am drowning, a desperate need to breathe, finally surfacing for a frantic inhale. And then quiet, merciful quiet, as everything goes dark once again.

When I open my eyes, I am lying by an oasis near the tear, surrounded by piles of leafy greens, a pyramid of purple fruit, and the carcasses of several dead hyenas. The branches of the trees and bushes around me are filled with wrens and sparrows and doves and hawks and falcons and vultures and crows. Holding court is a great horned owl, hooting gently in the glow of the setting sun, turning its head this way and that.

I rise and stretch and they all go flying, all except the owl. He stays with me through the night until the morning, and then he quietly departs.

When the beaked creature rips its way out of me several months later, I stomp it to death without hesitation.

CHAPTER TWO

# THE BEGINNING
# OF THE END

Time here is slippery, and though I vowed to never have any more children, eventually I did—days, weeks, months later—I'm not sure. But it happened. Though, I was never the same.

The skittering bone fiend that comes through the tear is followed by a swarm of tiny spider children—beetled creatures that dance across the dirt in a wave of crawling darkness. It dances on first one set of legs, and then the other, casting its gaze around, trembling in the sunshine and heat. A shimmer of moisture follows the creatures, the last vestiges of snow and ice melting quickly. The bony spider is coated in blood, smeared with ash, and it makes my skin crawl, my stomach roll, my mouth turn dry.

My spawn were napping by the tear, a brood of armored beasts and spiky fur devils, that have grown accustomed to the cold gusts and icy offerings. They have taken on whatever deformed monstrosity has come through and never lost a soul.

This time it's different—what comes through isn't slow or ponderous or thick. It is manic and hungry and filled with venom.

So many nights my offspring have slept by the tear, watching as it slowly expanded and then contracted, like a great, heaving lung breathing frigid sleet into the suffocating desert heat.

Sometimes a harmless creature would flit though—some sort of pink, fluffy bat or perhaps a mottled moth, lost and afraid. And they'd let those creatures go, though they might chase them about at first. The other beasts that crossed over, they would attack at once, pouncing on the creature, stabbing and cutting with their horns, biting with their sharp teeth. They were an efficient bunch and worked as a team.

And when they were ready to investigate what was on the other side—the eldest going through one at a time—their siblings would gather around, stamping feet and yipping in encouragement. One by one they would pass through—angry armored beast, snarling furry hunter, eight-legged freak—never to return.

The skeletal monster immediately pounces on them, seeking soft purchase, any gap in their tough skin and plated shells, sinking its long, dripping fangs in before they realize what is happening. Those with softer coverings—matted fur and thick hides—don't stand a chance. Their spiked tails shake in anger, elongated jaws snapping at the critters that wash over them in a wave of clacking fervor. They leap up and dash around in a mad circle, uncertain as to what is happening—snapping and biting at whatever comes near them. They shake off the wave of insects, as the tiny bugs bite and pinch.

But it is too late; they are too slow.

One by one they fall, heavy into the dust, limbs stiff, mouths open, as I stand and watch in horror. There is nothing I can do to help them, their cries and bleats rising on the thermal waves to the top of a mesa where I stand surveying the land—hunting for a new mate, watching a pack of slake dogs that huddle to the east, straining to see if somehow in this dead land there might be new growth to sustain us.


I stomp my feet in anger, heavy pads and thick legs raising a cloud of dust. I bellow into the air, my cutting horn slicing at the blue sky, as flies dart around my swatting tail, as I twitch in frustration. The sun beats down on my armored shell, exposed vertebrae running from my skull all the way down my back, metal spikes glistening in the light. Though I wander the land with a sense of immortality, my defenses honed over time in order to battle creatures large and small, in this moment, I feel vulnerable and exposed, as the horror of this land expands. There is no time to descend from on high, the jittering creature too fast in its acclimation. It is not the first time something has come through, of course, but it will be the most devastating. In the past we have been able to defend ourselves, but this time, we are caught unaware.

Too fast, too precise, too deadly.

I will not be able to protect my children this time, as they are dead and gone already. There is nothing more that I can do. The next litter will have to suffice—whatever horrible beauty I birth into the dirt—filled with potential, but cursed from the beginning. There are so many ways to die here in the hellscape. And new ones being invented every day.

The only satisfaction I gain over the next few days will be from the agonizing demise of this bony freak, as it realizes there is no water nearby, the punishing heat frying its own progeny, their hard shells popping as they boil from the inside out. I watch it wrap my kin in sticky webs and fibers, turning them over and over, as if it is roasting them on a great metal spit. And when they are contained, and the shell hardens, it punctures the stiff container with its long fangs, supping out their liquified flesh and bones. It feeds on my children, slowly drawing out whatever remaining vitamins and minerals that have left, but the sustenance doesn't last long. As they start to shrivel and bake, drying up from the inside out, it realizes that these cocooned creatures will not be enough for it to survive. It eventually sets out—running up one hill and down another, but always returning to the tear, even going so far as to dip a leg in, to test the cold one more time. It leans in, considers, and then retreats. It must feel that the arctic on the other side is certain death, where this land might hold some slight promise.

It is wrong.

It dies trying to scramble into a long, narrow crack in the drying clay, too thin to provide it any shade, or relief. It is surrounded by nothing but dirt and dust and sand. Perhaps it thought there was water beneath it all, some passage to a cooler existence. And it is not wrong, there *were* caves that ran beneath the desert. At one time they were filled with trickling streams, rushing rivers, and still ponds where anemic creatures hid in the darkness. But it's gone now, most of it, dried up, and empty, like the rest of us. So, whatever it might have smelled or sensed in the fissure, it was only a mirage. An illusion.


I know where the water is, what little is left here, and where it hides. I know where there are groves of shrub brush and prickly cactus, their inner wet meat juicy and sweet. I know what plants blossom into flowers and fruits, what greenery is poisonous and deadly, what migratory patterns lead animals to my door. For I have been here a long time, and seen many things. I am a survivor, and even as damaged as I am, I have found a way.

I know that to the north, across the dry land, there eventually are mountains—rocky formations that hold little vegetation, thorny bushes with tiny bitter berries, and angry goats, with their curved horns, hidden on ledges and high up in the cooling air. I know that to the south there is an expansive desert, my legs tiring as the sands shift and pour over one rippled hill after another, giant spider nests burrowed deep into the soil, with their trap door webbing. I know of the plateaus and mesas that drift toward the west, pushing up into the sky, casting shadows over serpentine cracks, steaming fissures, and canyons littered with the bones of the dead. And to the east—the dying grasslands, where what used to be green is now dried up, broken, and scattered to the winds—pollen and dust mites filling my nostrils with bloody sneezes.

It hasn't always been like this, but my world is dying, and my bloodline threatens to go with it. Mountaintops ringed with snow, water running down its steep surface, to gather in the valleys below, has now turned to flame—coal fires burning up from the earth's core, volcanoes erupting with molten lava. To see rocks burning, fire rising up out of the ground, is a uniquely unsettling experience. What few lakes that existed here have dried up or turned saline—whatever fish once lived in them, floating in the soupy, festering wounds as the shorelines turned to salt. Some are now covered in a pungent oil that flickers with dull blue fire, ignited by lightning or gases that spontaneously combust. Beneath the desert a series of caves used to be filled with water—bubbling up and out of the surface to provide smatterings of oases, ringed with palm trees and sugarbushes with their pink and yellow flowers growing in their shade.

The world has moved on.

And there may be nothing I can do about it.

For as long as I have lived here, I have sent my children through the tear, seeking answers, looking for food and water, one after another. They have gone willingly—eager to see what lurks on the other side. They have gone hesitantly—unsure what the cold conditions might do to their hearts and minds, let alone their flesh. The have gone with anger in their hearts and fire in their eyes—tired of the hungry creatures that have emerged from beyond the tear. They have gone for so many reasons.

None have returned.

When I stand at the rip and peer through the open filament, I see the whiteness, the cold and ice, the billowing snow and let it wash over me like a blessing. I fear that I would not survive there either, unprepared for such harsh elements. Perhaps I stand on this side, gazing through, as others do the same from beyond the rip—each of us as horrified and uncertain about what lies on the other side as the other. We are mirrors, perhaps, echoes of the same voice, reverberating and dissipating in the ether.

When the creature dies in a spasm of movement, legs twitching into the pummeling heat, I finally descend from my high ground to bury what is left of my children. I impale their scrawny, cracked, bent forms, wrapped in petrified silk, one after another, and lumber toward a fissure that lies just over a hill and to the south. I hesitate the first time, realizing what is inside this cocoon—not just a sac, or a shell, but life, life that came from me. And it aches. I drop them, one by one, into the bottomless pit—the one with the black armor, who loved to sneak around in the darkness, hidden by the expanding night; the furry one with such long, gamboling strides, how she was so quick to dash up slick outcroppings, where others feared to go; the littlest one, who never quite grew his shell, still soft, and gray, where the others wore their carapaces with pride, the song he would sing under his breath when he got sad and felt alone.

When my work is done, I collapse in front of the tear, exhausted. The sun sets and the land begins to cool, a flutter of snowflakes drifting out of the rend, melting in the air. A fog creeps out in a slow stuttering exhale, filled with the scent of pine and woodsmoke. A trickle of moisture runs down the edge of the tear where the heat meets the cold, condensation appearing on an invisible layer of glass.

I have a decision to make. Stay and try again to give birth to a solution, hoping that this time, the right creature might be created to brave both lands. Or finally push through and explore the frozen tundra on the other side—whatever horrible, brutal reality might await me there.

Neither option gives me much hope.

In the distance, along the horizon, a herd of great beasts lumber across a ridge, their massive bodies shaking the earth, long necks stretched into the sky. They are outlined in silhouette—starting with the largest, and then working their way down to the newly born. Now and then, there is a low moan, or soft bray, as they traverse the hills and valleys, their thick hides holding the heat from the long day of blistering sunlight. The warmth is a light companion on their long journey, comforting as it holds back the cold of nightfall. They are seeking vegetation, not my armored flesh, so I merely watch their shadows as they migrate in the cooling night air, seeking an oasis to refuel, or perhaps a boneyard in which to shed their skin.

In the dreams that come to me, I have crossed over, and through the glimmering tear, penetrating the cold with a humble acquiescence. It is both invigorating and terrifying, as I've never felt so much dark, heavy weather on my skin. I can feel the bone-numbing chill in every crack in my armor, every pad on my feet, my desert eyes watering as they struggle to adjust to the blinding cold. I clench my jaw against the pain and survey the frozen environment around me.

In the dream, I stand alone beneath a flickering streetlight that casts the white landscape in a yellow haze. There is no sign of life—unlit windows in ice-capped houses, empty streets marred by wave-like ridges on the surface of hard snow, countless evergreens swaying silently in unison with the gusting squalls. I turn away from the light, my heart thundering in my rib cage, toward the wooded hillside nearby, and beyond it to the mountains looming in the blackness, and I start walking. Climbing higher, looking back with ever pause to catch my breath, I see the vast darkness above the sleeping village, broken only by a smattering of stars and the endless expanse of falling snow. I lumber farther upward, pushing aside sickly pines, boughs drooping with the weight of the snow, straining to keep my balance on the icy incline. The path is too narrow—struggling through snowdrifts, stumbling over deadfall, crashing headlong into bushes and shrubs—on my way to higher ground. Every desperate inhale draws shards of broken glass down into my lungs, as I climb higher and higher into the thinning arctic air, until the tree line falls away and there is nothing left but barren mountainside.

I start digging, my cutting horn cleaving the ice, snow, and dirt—a trench appearing as I scatter the clay and rocks far and wide. Under the frozen ground I churn up roots, and hibernating bugs, my head lowering and then raising until I have finally dug deep enough, and wide enough, creating a hole that I can climb into. I tuck my legs up under my body and lower myself into the trench. I bend my head down, tucking my jaw close to my chest. As the snow drifts down to me, it coats my shivering armor in a blanket of cold, my body cooling, and slowly going numb. I close my eyes and sink into the mountain, now just one more ridge, one more hill. The wind blows, and the sounds fade, as I become one with the rocks and dirt, freezing into a block of ice, my heart slowing, until it finally stops.

I wake to the sounds of thunder, as rain falls heavy on the deadlands. I can't remember the last time it rained. I tilt my head up to the heavens and am rewarded with a deluge of water. The droplets hammer the dusty, dry land, sending up steam wherever it strikes the blistering earth. As quickly as the water hits the surface, it is sucked into the sand, the dirt, the clay, and between the rocks. It runs into the cracks and disappears from sight. I drink as much as I can catch in my open mouth, laughing for a moment at the idea that I could drown here in this arid wasteland. The irony of such a death. I will store whatever water I can in the reservoirs of fatty tissue that run down my back, on either side of my spine. A crack of lightning runs across the sky as the sun shimmers and clouds pass in front of it, everything cooling a few degrees, the shadows casting out across the land. Mixed in with the rain are grasshoppers—green and lively and as startled as I am. The earth is covered in a blanket of squirming, hopping, frantic insects.

And then as fast and violently as it started, the rain stops.

In the quiet that follows there is a chorus that rises up from the bugs and insects that have been sitting still, joining the cacophony of the grasshoppers, who are waiting to see what happens next. A gentle wind blows, and for a moment, nothing moves. And then the bugs are swarmed with every hungry mouth that has been hidden in the hills, and rocks, and crevices—hawks and falcons descend from the sky, rattlesnakes and vipers strike from between rocks, skinks and bearded dragons skittering across the wet sand.

There is a spring a mile to the east, and I decide to walk to it, the idea of a bath, of cool water, and healing mud, more than I can resist. This oasis will have held on to whatever water it has just caught, the few struggling palm trees grateful for this brief, but heavy, rainfall. So, I will take advantage of this moment.

On my way east I pass the skeletal spider that lies fractured in the dirt, limbs akimbo. Its eyes are a dull white, tiny ants climbing all over its body, trying to find entry via the cracking surfaces of the bony creature, as nature slowly breaks down the husk of the strange critter. Up close I can see how large it is, the pincers and fangs sticking out of its open mouth. So very dangerous, but useless now. I notice half of a cocoon shell sitting next to it, upturned toward the rain, holding water like a cup. The shellack that coats the outside of the dried silk seems to be waterproof. It is solid, able to keep whatever liquids and moisture lurk inside the wrappings. It contains them. It holds them intact.

Which gives me an idea.

Something that might make life possible here in this fractured land.

I think of the dead creature that lies at my feet, I think of the rumors of the silkworms that line the caves to the north, and I think about the great quantities of ice that lurk on the other side of the tear. Snow and ice, glaciers and mountains—there is so much potential here.

I bend over and slurp the water from the shell—my tongue tingling, but not quite going numb, whatever toxins remain, losing their strength. I turn my cutting horn to the abdomen and thorax of the bone spider, and tear open the bony exo-skeleton, searching for the silk. Whatever glands might have functioned once, whatever mechanisms allowed it to cast and spin and weave—it's broken now, no good to me, I'm afraid.

I turn and lumber toward the water source, slowly moving over one hill and then on to the next, leaving behind the rippling tear that calls to me now, more than ever. And when I traverse the dunes and finally spy the palm trees and bushes that surround the sparkling mirage, there are cackling hyenas lapping at the water, darting in and away, as a great flying beast flaps its leathery wings above the watering hole. The rain will draw others, but for now, I am the dominant species here. I am the alpha.

I bellow as I charge the water, the mottled, rotting animals scattering in every direction, through bushes and shrubs, over the hills, and out of sight. I slide into the water and submerge myself in the cooling spring, washing away dirt and waste, sores and death. When I rise up and break the surface of the water, the cawing creature lands on my armored back, flapping its veiny wings, as its long red beak opens and closes. A forked tongue flickers at me, tasting my presence in the air. It picks at my hide, searching for whatever bugs may have scrambled out of my many crevices, plates, and folds. It must have missed out on the grasshoppers. Or maybe it's just a ritual we perform, a dance we do. I allow it to perch on my back, watching the land for signs of danger. I am the largest monstrosity here, for the moment, but there are other wandering beasts that might find me a tasty snack—cracking open my hard shell to get at the chewy, tasty bits inside.

On the ridge of the hill, I spy the pack of hyenas—a mother like me, sitting up tall, her nose sniffing the air, as she cackles and grins, her tongue hanging out of her mouth. Her kits bounce around her, eager to approach the water, thirsty and hot, but she keeps them back, one eye on me, the other scouring the land for a source of dinner.

On the other side of the bushes there is a hare and her bunnies, hiding in the shadows, licking the leaves. They chew as their noses twitch, her ears up tall, turning this way and that, watching the hyenas on the hill, watching me as I sit in the water, watching the giant bird that sits on my backside—always watching, this one. She is fast, as are the babes, but there are faster animals out here, so her response has to be immediate.

I watch a flock of wrens that line the branches of a sickly mesquite tree that is on the side of the hill. No doubt its roots go deep, the oasis and spring providing it enough water to survive. The little yellow and brown birds chirp and tweet, covering the branches in their neurotic little jig. When a last bit of thunder growls and cracks across the sky, they scatter into the wind and then immediately fly back to their same spots.

There is life everywhere here in the desert, and I'm not sure how it survives.

When I leave, the hyenas will descend. When I leave, the rabbits will scatter over the hill. When I leave, the antelope will bound over the hill and skitter to the edge of the water. But not at the same time. Not all at once.

There is a hierarchy here in these deadlands, and I know my place in it.

# CHAPTER THREE

# CROSSING THE GREAT DIVIDE

As the sun sets, the sand mercifully cools and the heat of the day dissipates, while a whole host of nocturnal creatures from deep below the surface come rising up to feed. I scan the darkness for any signs of these arrivals as I head toward the caves in the north, where the silkworms are rumored to exist. I've heard stories of their glowing chartreuse skin, several feet long, hanging from the roof of their damp, dark lodgings like stalactites—dripping and wet. Their song is supposed to hypnotize anything that tries to harvest their manifestations, their tensile strings of silk plucked like those of a harpsicord. I need very little light to find my way, few obstacles between my location and the mountain range—cactus, and tumbleweeds, and scrub brush.

As I wander in the moonlight, I pass a massive archway made of the faded bones of a long-forgotten monstrosity. The rib cage is half buried in the sand and dirt, the bleached and blistered bones curving up toward the pale moon that hangs heavy overhead. Mammoth shards of the yellowing ivory reach up into the darkness as if grasping for a distant star, or perhaps just dinner. It is a pale Venus flytrap, just waiting to snap shut. Extending in the other direction is a smattering of vertebrae, that must have, at one time, been its tail. Three huge spikes lay in a clump at the end of the diminishing bones, each one crossed over the other. But at this end, where I stand, is the skull of the ancient beast, upside down, its horns buried deep into the dirt. Snakes squirm in and out of the jaw and eye holes—red stripes, and rattles, and glistening black skin. I can hardly imagine how huge it must have been. What might have taken it down is unfathomable.

For a moment the scale overwhelms me as a sequence unfolds in my head—a beetle chased by a rabbit while being stalked by a fox who is then devoured by a wolf. And then that lupine mongrel is torn to shreds by a cornered wolverine who is feasted on by a mountain lion who gets mauled by a hungry bear. That brown furry bruin is plucked from the ground by a massive prehistoric bird who is then swatted down by a behemoth, roaring as it shakes its horned head before being gorged on by a behemoth on two legs with tentacled arms that strangle the moon out of the sky.

I shake my head and take a breath.

And then I carry on.

A fluttering silhouette passes in front of the moon, a cauldron of bats screeching into the quiet of the night. They start out as a dispersed cloud, merge into a single cluster, and then separate again. As they swoop back and forth, blocking out the moon, and then revealing it again, a larger shape floats by behind them, obliterating the moon for several seconds—so enormous that as it moves from one side of the sky to the other, the pale orb just ceases to exist. I stop moving for a moment, for out here, even I can shift from predator to prey.

As I trudge onward, a crack appears in the earth, red light glowing up from beneath the surface, gas hissing out, a sulfurous miasma of dank moss and decaying fish. In the darkness something oozes out, first one, long barbed tentacle, and then another—tentative and uncertain. They weave into existence, more dark appendages feeling their way out, testing the night air, undulating, and then retreating back into the subterranean heat. There is a rumbling beneath the dirt and sand, and then the creature emerges again—one hypnotic flailing arm after another—the end of one tentacle curling into a fist that pounds into the desert floor. I detect the movement of something slinking around the open crack, a coyote or wolf that might have thought this brute dinner. And then more of the mangy, four-legged beasts ring the rim of the crack, snapping at the swaying feelers, one of them managing to take a bite out of the rubbery arm. And then the infernal creature grabs a pup—wrapping its slithering tentacle around it, slowly squeezing as the animal barks, yelps, and then cries. It crushes the canine, drenching the arid surface of the land with blood, and waste, and viscera. The other dogs scatter, unsettled by their fallen sibling, now bent in half, and pulled into the crack.

I give the opening a wide berth, the red glow dimming as the creature descends into the fiery abyss below it.

The caves can't be that far, I consider, as a howling rises up from over a hill, several sets of red eyes peeking out of the gloom. They are either mourning their loss or still hungry. Or perhaps both. I stomp my feet loudly and bellow into the darkness, causing them to scatter into the night. We have met before, and it did not go well for them. They know to stay away. I am no leviathan of the molten core, but my cutting horn is as sharp as ever, my thick hide and armored plates tough to chew.

It is a long night, the walk cooler in the darkness, but exhausting nonetheless.

When I find a slab of rock in the middle of nowhere, I climb onto the altar and take a break. The mountain isn't going anywhere.

It starts with a biting sensation, something nipping at my hide, squirming under my plates of armor, burrowing its way into my vulnerable cracks and crevices. I cannot see in the darkness, as the moon has gone behind a cloud, the subtle pinches become agonizing stings, and I find that I am unable to move. It's difficult to breathe, my vision swimming.

Fire ants.

Demon fire ants.

I can feel them scuttling across my body, hundreds of them, then thousands of them, my eyes swelling shut, as their poison works its way through my body.

Something lumbers out of the darkness, thudding footsteps, with a decaying stench that drifts to me—a sour wave of putrid flesh, a rattling sound filling the air. I strain to move my limbs, but they won't respond. I cannot breathe, the air gone foul with the rotten carcass of the diseased creature. A swarm of flies buzz all around me, and a fear washes over me, as they waste no time laying their eggs in the tiny cuts all over my body, in the chinks between my armored plates, in the wrinkles of my hide, in my ears, and mouth, and nostrils, where they will turn into maggots and then evolve into something far more revolting.

My stomach roils in disgust, but I cannot move.

When the beast stands before me, I can hear it grunting and wheezing. This rock was a trap. And I have fallen prey to some desert spirit that now stands before me in the dark. I strain to open my eyes, feeling the pus seeping from them, and I can just make out its long, muscled, sinuous arms as they hang down past its waist. Gnarled hands end in grubby nails that are sharp and caked with dried blood.

When it lowers its head to meet my blurry gaze, I stare into its sickly eyes, jaundiced and bloodshot, filled with swirling madness. Motes and dots cloud my vision, as it takes my head between its filthy hands. It drags its long sandy tongue over my anguished face and into my mouth, licking and nibbling, tasting to see if I'm worth eating.

A crown of thorns erupts from the top of its head, its elongated snout sniffing my flesh. When it opens its wide grin to expose several rows of long, jagged teeth, its mottled tongue rolls out and down its chin. A rack of ivory antlers branch out in every direction, so long and heavy that I'm not sure how it doesn't tip over. Caught in the sharp branches are moss and sinew and vines and flesh. When it moves from shadow into the moonlight, the silhouette shifts and changes—muscles swell and then contract, its head stretching and then pulling back into shape. With every step its hooves ripple and change—wider, shorter toes emerging and then disappearing, talons extending and then retracting.

Where has it come from?

And what does it want?

It stands up, its thick, dark flesh covered in cuts and scars, and its phallus is engorged—a rigid monstrosity made of ivory, flesh, and tiny barbs that will tear me apart as it fills me with some wriggling horror.

It isn't hungry.

It wants to spread its demon seed.

I lose sight of it, and panic washes over me, as it walks heavily behind me, the earth shaking. I can feel it taunting me, as it circles my prone body, huffing and panting, snorting and rutting in the air. It is taking its time, finally trapping a worthy vessel, enjoying the ways that I squirm, and tremble, and moan. It has called forth the fire ants, it has brought with it a swarm of disease, setting all this in motion. It bites at its own flesh, tearing away chunks of meat, blood flowing out of the wounds, smearing its body from head to toe in the crimson liquid. It laughs a deep, guttural sound that makes my skin crawl and my body tense up with fear.

With the last of my energy, as I feel the world spinning away from me, the darkness creeping in, I bellow and bleat into the pitch, taking in a deep breath, and screaming into the void. And then I do it again. My throat ruptures, blood trickling down into my esophagus, my screams triggering a fluttering of bats to emerge from a rocky outcropping, filling the air with their own screeching flight.

The earth trembles underneath me, the sand rising and rippling, and a serpentine horror glides over the hills and valleys, one segment repeating after the other. It undulates up and down, diving beneath the surface and then rising up again. Its feelers and legs click and scuttle as its segments shift and turn, first one way and then the other.

How do you trap a creature that is untrappable?

By allowing it to trap something else.

And when it is occupied with the feeding, with the ritual, with the frenzied hunger and desire that has been building up over time—you pounce.

There is a sensation of everything tipping over, as the moon emerges from the clouds, and the ancient millipede rises up out of the darkness, a singular gouge and scar just under its jaw. In one fluid motion it engulfs the skinwalker, the shapeshifter, the night demon—swallowing as it chews, tearing the beast limb from limb.

It is only a matter of time before it circles back to finish me, my call an act of desperation, summoning my savior, but also my own demise.

Under the blinking stars, I shake and tremble, as the sky opens up and starts to rain. It is a cold, hard, pummeling downpour, and there is nothing I can do. Lightning fractures the sky, illuminating the hellscape for an instant, first once, and then again—a goddess' face appearing in the moon, frowning, and then disappearing.

I pass out in the cold, wet night, feeling far from anything that resembles life and home.

When the sun rises, I shake off the night—the ants and flies and maggots and sand, take a deep breath, and keep on walking north. The sand creature never returned. I was spared. The restless spirit that resides in the moon—she was disappointed but shifted the tides and gravitational forces anyway to grant me a moment of grace.

It takes me a few hours to lumber to the foothills of the mountain, carrying the heat and humidity across my back like a thick blanket, and so I stop to rest.

At the bottom of the incline, I spot something, and though I am weary, I stand up and move closer to inspect the clump that shakes and trembles in the morning light. It is hard to understand—there is fur everywhere—matted and white, dirty and stained with blood, burrs stuck to the mottled coat. I hear a bleating and spy two heads, joined together, black eyes glassy and wide, teeth bared to the sky in pain and suffering. I see hooves and legs sticking out in every direction, and four long, curved gray horns jutting out of what must be some sort of stomach or back, as flies dance all around the stinking horror.

I don't like it, not one bit.

A bony, chitinous shell has begun to form around the limbs and torsos, a carapace of sorts. Its eyes are bloodshot, bleeding red tears, and weeping a yellow pus. Its tongues loll out one side and then the other, turning into some sort of rough, white fungus.

It smells of fermented grass, and sour moss, one side of an emaciated rib cage torn open, the remnants of a recent meal spilling out onto the dirt. A dark liquid leaks out from under the pile of goat parts, staining the earth black. Motes dot the shimmering heat that radiates off of the stinking pile. And when the wind shifts toward me, it gives off a sickly heat, more than the sun that beats down on me, but also oily, and thick, and heavy. I step back away from it.

*Kill it with fire*, I think, looking around for something that may help.

I'm afraid to touch it, to go near it, whatever wasting disease or torquing poison might be working its way across this decaying amalgam. I see twitching feelers now emerging from the squirming forms, and bile rises in my throat.

When I hear the approach of padding feet, I turn to spy my wolfish friends and decide to leave it to them. I guess I'm not done walking, not yet, so I push on up the path and hill, the caves still far away, and I'm so tired, but whatever cacophony is about to descend on this tainted spot, I don't want to bear witness to it.

I've been scarred enough; I don't need to keep ripping the scabs off, as the yellowing edges of my wounds refuse to heal, picking at the gelatinous flesh beneath it.

As I leave the beasts to their meal and certain death, I hear yelping and growling, bleating and babbling, drifting up to me as I ascend. It's hard to tell if anyone is winning—it's eat or be eaten out here—or if the toxic meal will only spread its disease even farther out into the sprawling wastelands, infecting everything it touches.


On my way up the mountain, I am drawn to an unfamiliar tree growing out of its side with thick bark and twisted limbs, ending in red leaves that are ringed with spikes and thorns. All around the base of the tree are mutated acorns with an unnatural fleshy tone, blue veins worming their way through their shells. Worms weave in and out of the diseased fruit. The ground is littered with them, one close to me split open to reveal a green seed and pink interior with meaty properties—sinew, and muscle, and bone. Mixed in with the hundreds of acorns that are scattered around the base of the tree are what look like aborted attempts at life. I turn my head back toward the pile of goat horns and mangy mongrels and wonder if this is what happened to those animals.

There are mangled, diseased, and rotting carcasses—what looks to be rabbits, and coyotes, and goats, and snakes, and foxes, and lizards, and baby birds—all squirming in a mess of decay and death, one layer of flesh after another, trying to bond with what lies next to it.

Were they abandoned here or did they hatch?

Were they drawn here by something or caught in its trap?

In the leaves of the tree are hundreds of spiders, crawling around the webs and cocoons. There are flies trapped in the sticky gossamer, struggling at the ends of their lives. And there are blackbirds picking at the trapped insects. And there are snakes wrapped about the birds. There are loops of what looks like intestine strung through the branches, pumping blood from one part of the tree to another, as flowers bloom into a sickly mottled tint, their stamens glistening and wet.

I hesitate to go on. If this is what struggles to live outside the cave, what might I find inside? Or maybe this is some primal, feral warning system, an alarm system built into the mountain to scare me away.

I've come this far.

I swallow hard and take a deep breath, once more staring at the squirming pile of abominations, and then I move on.


When I open my eyes in the middle of the night, the multitude of stars that dot the black velvet sky shine down on me in a cascade of shifting galaxies. A shooting star, a comet, flies overhead, and then another—and then one more, traversing the darkness from one side of the horizon to the other. And then a rush of lights as they spill across the deep space, a shower of light filling up the silent darkness.

Perhaps they are crashing down on the other side of this planet—landing in some primordial soup, or smashing into withering grasslands, setting fire to all that lingers around it. Or maybe they never hit the earth—sizzling and sparking as they left space and entered our atmosphere, dying out before making it all the way down. Perhaps they have brought something alien here, to learn from our bestial ways.

I wonder if the entire planet is withering or just the patch of land that I can see, touch, hear, smell, and feel.

I don't know.

I remember a naked woman standing at the tear, a sickly yellow aura surrounding her body, as she prayed, and then knelt, and then froze in place—her dying words asking for forgiveness.

I remember the way the wolves tore at her frozen body, tearing her limb from limb, survival of the fittest, a circle of life come all the way around.

I remember a man, clothed in thick fur and hide, from head to toe, and the bloody aura that surrounded his flickering existence.

I curse that man, and the creatures he birthed, the broken, angry, hungry manifestations that he sent through the rip—a war I never asked for.

If only he could see that I was asking him for help.

We are all dying.

Some of us faster than the others.

# CHAPTER FOUR

# THE CAVES

Over millions of years, we evolve and change. And in an instant—BAM—something new is created, birthed into life, altered, or perhaps enlightened, as we adapt to new information, environments, and knowledge.

When I approach the cave mouth—lumbering up the wide path, gray rocks lined with streaks of white, a single cactus pushing a red blossom into the air—something shifts, and changes, and I am not what I was any more.

I stand at the opening of the cave a woman.

Here, at the mouth of this cavernous opening, it seems something else is required. Something else, that I didn't know I had in me.

I hear the thrumming of the silk threads that the silkworms spin, deep inside the mountain. It drifts out to me, a melody of chords and climbing scales, a vibration that reverberates up through the underground chamber, washing over me in a trembling sensation. I am flush with heat, and then cold, shivering, dressed in what I can only assume is some default setting, or favorite outfit—blue jeans and a tan flannel shirt, over a dirty white t-shirt, with heavy leather hiking boots on my feet. Inexplicably, for just a moment, there is a fluttering of snow inside the cave, before it quietly drifts to the ground, where it quickly melts into the dirt. A crackle of electricity runs around the perimeter of the opening, dissipating into the hillside.

I step inside the mouth of the cave and am greeted by a pale green bioluminescence that seeps out from cracks and fissures lining the walls. It originates from the silkworms, no doubt, who lie deep below.

I seem to be in the right place.

When I enter the cave, and go farther inside, I am greeted by a vaguely humanoid statue carved out of wood. Pounded into each eye are three massive nails, nearly the size of railroad spikes. A gentle fuzz of blue mold runs all across its surface. It is a tall, thin figure, with its fists clenched at waist height, a permanent frown on its face. It is wearing some sort of robe, a few lines of detail sliced here and there—pocket, belt, and cuffs. A circular emblem is carved into its chest—bisected by horizontal and vertical lines. Some sort of sun, I think, reminiscent of the Aztecs, or perhaps the Mayans. There is a noose around its neck, the end of the rope hanging down in front of it, stopping just before it hits the ground—actual hemp, linen, and cotton—as thick as my thumb. A shiver runs up my spine as shadows whirl about the room, shifting in translucency from black to gray to white and then back to gray and black again, disappearing into the gloom. The damp mossy musk of the cave rises up, a hint of sulfur on my tongue.

Overhead, a clear, viscous liquid oozes from the ceiling, a glob of the heavy goo landing on my arm, where it burns into my skin. I try to rub it off with my hands, but I only manage to spread it further onto my fingers and palms, my hands now tingling, a slight throb running under my skin. I spy a puddle of water farther inside the cave, and stepping around the statue, and away from the clear jelly, I wash my hands in the cool water, and it seems to help a bit.

The cave continues.

I walk deeper inside and am greeted by a wave of movement, the next room larger, but darker as well. I can see the veins of the glowing green streaks embedded in the walls, but it is covered by something that seems to be breathing, undulating, moving with one collective inhale and exhale. Underfoot, something crunches, and as I peer down, squinting, I see eggshells covering the ground, and a mixture of tiny bones scattered over the top, a small gasp and squeak escaping my mouth.

Which sets the walls into motion.

A flurry of sickly yellow bats pour out of the cave, over my head, dirt and dust raining down on me, dander and guano, in a storm of movement. I choke on the air, bending over, ducking my head in tight, as they flee the mouth opening, out into the dimming sky.

The tunnel goes deeper, the room I'm in now, narrowing as it descends, something carved into the walls along this long, narrow passageway. There are faces here—rising up out of the wall—some dashed in faded, scraped, red paint, others with radiant stones where their eyes should be. Rudimentary shapes and lines are gouged out of some—circles, and lines, and triangles. A few have hair—black and brown and blonde, one made out of dried hay. Some have horns—short and blunt, curved and twisting, or branching off into antlers. Their mouths are held shut in grim defiance; they are open wide in silent screams; they are defaced with long incisors and fangs. They line the wall on both sides, all the way to the next room, which opens up into a grotto.

In this room, there are cracks in the ceiling that let in light, the openings running all the way to the surface, I assume. They cast a few weak rays of sunlight into the room, moss and slick greenery lining the crevices. On the right wall, there are several skeletons sitting on the ground facing the wall, their bony wrists and ankles held in iron chains, pelvises resting on the floor. Cast onto the left wall are shadows that dance and frolic, echoing the bony remnants, though the skeletons do not move—skulls bowed down, or tipped back, hypnotized, or perhaps lost in wonder. Some seem to be straining to look over their shoulders, to try and see the shadows. The light flickers on the wall, as if we are underwater—thin lines and dappled rays running up and down the surface, outlining the shadows, painting the walls in movement.

I keep walking.

The deeper I get, the more I notice the critters that run about the edge of the tunnel, disappearing into the cracks, and then appearing later in whatever room opens up next. There are translucent scorpions the size of cats, cave spiders with furry legs as big as oranges, woodlice and centipedes in pale white and faded yellow, their segmented bodies twisting and turning as they scramble over each other, fleeing from the light.

The warm air gets thicker, puddles and trickling streams lined with a scummy spray, the stench of rotten eggs drifting to me. I walk into a much larger room, where there are bodies of water and tunnels branching out in all directions. There are all sorts of scuttling and slithering things. Crystalline snails and glassy shrimp aggressively try to avoid the spiders and water scorpions. In the multitude of tiny ponds that now appear, pale leeches swim across the water and prey on pink earthworms, a frothy foam bubbling the surface. A path runs across the middle of the room, water on both sides, movement underneath, something shimmering in the darkness, but it's nothing I want to see.

What lives down here should be left alone.

So I keep going.

As the tunnels go deeper, they narrow again, the ceiling descending, a green glow emerging from an unseen source below. The strumming of the silk threads resume as I get closer, their siren song luring me into a state of calm reverie.

Hammered into the walls of this stretch of tunnel are a series of totems, twine strung through and around each individual carving, made of soapstone and wood and ivory and jade. A turtle, an eagle, a fox, a bear, a wolf, a salmon, a caribou, and a seal.

In the cavern that appears before me, the chamber is filled with a mist—water and steam and fog mixing in the air, both hot and cold, some spring or aquifer nearby. There are plants here that I haven't seen in a very long time—rubber trees and pink bougainvillea, stunted date palms and white orchids, creeping jasmine vines and blooming lilies.

And all along the ceiling, in a web of silk, are the worms. They glow a lime green, veins of the same fluorescent color running all through the walls of the cave. The strands are woven into webs, and pockets, and thick ropes, and tense strings. The worms are constantly moving, inching up and down, across the ceiling, and over the plants.

They whisper to me as they move.

*. . . behold, we have set before you an open door, which no one is able to shut . . .*

I spy the glowing white archway on the far side of the room. But I have come here for their webs, their silk, and I will not leave without this substance.

*. . . many moons ago, there was a great earthquake . . .*

I slowly creep toward a gathering of webs as the silkworms writhe overhead.

*. . . the sun turned black like sackcloth made of goat hair, and the moon became red with blood, and the stars in the sky fell to the earth . . .*

I bend over and start rolling up the sticky webbing into a ball, my hands tingling, as the worms continue to speak.

*. . . the sky receded like a scroll being rolled up, and every mountain and island was removed from its place . . .*

I slowly accumulate the webbing from the size of an egg to an orange to a cantaloupe, rolling the sticky strands around in a circle.

*. . . you are not listening, my child; you have forgotten the face of your father . . .*

I turn my head up to the mass of glowing green worms.

*. . . time is an illusion; this is a world where nothing is solved . . .*

The walls pulse, and the worms undulate in a frenzy.

*. . . everything you've ever done, or will do, you will do over and over again . . .*

Cave crickets leap up and down, springing into the air in a frantic dance, catching in the webs.

*. . . because those who cannot remember the past are condemned to repeat it . . .*

I pause, a sheen of sweat glistening my skin, the rich scent of the jasmine and lilies making my stomach curdle.

*. . . the definition of insanity . . .*

The walls shimmer with a condensation that sweats and drips to the floor.

*. . . in the days to come you shall seek death, and be unable to find it; you will desire a rebirth, and yet death shall flee from you . . .*

The ball is now the size of a watermelon, so I stand up and take a last look around, before running for the light.

*. . . depart from me, child, for I never knew you . . .*

And as I burst through the white light of the opening, laughter spills out of me, my head tilted back, tongue lolling, eyes filled with fire.


When I awaken, I am lying in the shade of the outcropping, no longer in human form, but monstrous once again. Lying next to me is a huge ball of webbing, coated in sticky toxins, flies dotting the surface of the skein of skin. It is wrapped in elephant's ear plants and bound with what looks like vines. It rests on a tripod of sticks that have been tied together with twine to form a rudimentary sled. My friend has taken care of me here. With a grunt, and a painfully slow movement, I rise up and head back the way I came, eager to see if this can work, dragging the contents of this excursion behind me.

In this dream, I am standing in an open doorway as the rain turns to sleet and then to snow. I am watching my daughter pack up her car, leaving before the winter settles in, before she is trapped here one more year. She is headed south—to university, to a job that doesn't exist yet, to a man that may or may not love her. She hops into the silver SUV and closes the door with a dull thud. She does not look back. I light a cigarette, waiting to see if she will say anything, do anything more than drive away from me. She has a picture of me, she told me. She has a picture of us all. And so she turns over the ignition, looks over her shoulder as she backs out—always careful, this one—and then rolls into the street. She pauses for a moment, when she shifts the car into drive, her eyes to me, a single tear running down her face, and then she shakes her head and drives on. I exhale cigarette smoke, and then go back inside, out of the cold.

I spend the next several days digging a trench down in the valley where the tear is widening bit by bit. I'm not sure how much longer it will be open, time an elastic band, stretching out in all directions.

    I am a child dancing in a field of flowers—surrounded by bursts of yellow and red—bees and flies with motes of pollen all around.

I am a laborer building—tearing into the earth, so that I might create something new here—a blueprint in my head of how this might possibly happen here in the deadlands.

I am a magician casting a spell—searching for a way to cleanse my soul and bless this endeavor—as a glimmer of golden sparks cast a silhouette around me.

Enlighten what's dark in me.

Strengthen what's weak in me.

Bind what's broken in me.

Mend what's bruised in me.

Heal what's sick in me.

Revive what's lost to me.

The sun beats down on me as I grunt and labor, my cutting horn digging deeper into the desert floor. It starts with sand, and dust, and dirt. Then as I dig deeper, the soil turns to hardpan and clay, cracked and so eager to soak up whatever rain might fall. I use my horn, and the side of my head, my mouth, and my legs to push the dirt, to lift the rocks, to kick the clay up and out of the widening hole.

As darkness falls, the trench is wider than the oasis, three times as long as my battered, dusty frame, and so deep that I have trouble climbing out.

I stand at the end of the ditch I have created and glance over at the ball of toxic webwork, and then to the tear, and beyond it into the ice and snow.

Tomorrow I will push my way through and see what lies beyond. I will test myself like I've never done before.

When I lie in the darkness, the cool night drifting over me, I feel a tremble from deep inside my body, and my eyes slide open.

I am with child, again.

The moon casts shadows over the land as something flies overhead.

Perhaps this was my final pairing.

Perhaps this time my children will stay.


As light spills over the horizon, I stand up, sore, and ease over to the tear. It is as wide as I have ever seen it, snow spilling through, and then melting in the hot air.

I head for the oasis, praying that it hasn't dried up already. The walk is slow, and the dust and sand blow all around me, my mind lost in thoughts that take me to other places, and other times.

When I arrive, there is barely a puddle, a tiny trickle pushing up from a crack in the earth, the pond empty—not a single animal in sight.

It will have to do.

I kneel down in the mud and lap at the feeble wellspring that pushes up from deep within the ground. It could run out at any time, the next watering hole being several miles farther east, over so many hills that I can't even consider it. And it may be drying up as well.

When I have taken in as much water as I can hold, I head back to the trench, and the tear—my bladder full, the water deposits that line my spine full as well.

There is one more thing to do before I can cross over into the frozen tundra.

I walk to the ball of silk and webbing and cut the vines loose, peeling the leaves away from the sticky substance.

This will not be easy.

I roll the silken ball into the hole and climb down the embankment into the cool, cracked, dry soil. I stomp on the webbing, sticking it to the bottom of my feet, and slowly spread it around the bottom of the trench. It stretches and coats the dirt, my feet tingling, as it expands, and widens. I have no wet poison, like the spider spawn, to spray onto the webbing; I have no rain storm to patter the thin surface that I am slowly, painfully rubbing over the dry clay, filling in every hold, and fissure, and expanding crack.

So I have to be creative.

I squat in the middle of the hole and piss on the webbing—my stinking yellow urine spraying out, shooting up the walls before running back down to the center. I turn my ass as I slowly walk in a circle, drenching the webbing from top to bottom.

With an enormous amount of effort, exhausted from the day's work, I climb the gradual incline up and out of the hole.

The only thing I can do now is wait.


When I wake up there are dingoes running in and out of the hole, yelping and barking, drawn by the scent of my urine, no doubt. I bellow at them, and they run away, and I fear that they may have torn it, undone my work, before the shellac could harden, before the cocoon I've woven into the bottom half of this dirt cup was able to solidify.

I lean over the edge of the trench and gently tap the webbing with my foot. It's as hard as a rock. I hit it harder, and nothing happens. I bend over with my sharp cutting horn and tap it against the edge, and it clicks with a satisfying response.

The clay and hardpan underneath will support it, mostly solid, but not waterproof, I'm afraid. Unless I want to merely water a desert with a hose and bucket, this shell will have to hold.

With a glance toward the sun to try and estimate the amount of daytime left, I lumber over to the tear and finally push my way through.


It is colder than I could ever have imagined. Everything turns blue and white, the gold and rust of the wastelands left behind.

I turn to the woods and see the branches covered in snow and ice. There is a smattering of red on the ground, remnants of something violent in the powdered snow. The house in front of me has burned to the ground, the smell of woodsmoke still lingering in the air. There are no coals burning, merely ash and lumber piled on top of each other, as the frigid whiteness whips and swirls all around me.

I can't waste any time here wondering what happened to the structure or why there is blood in the snow. The wheel of time turns slowly, crushing us all, so I continue to search for my solution.

The trail and hill leading up behind the tear have potential, but it's mostly fresh powder and new drifts, which won't do. There may be blocks of ice higher up in the mountain, but I don't think I can make it there, the incline too steep, the flesh beneath my armor already tingling from the cold, feet turning numb.

So I turn to my last hope, the water below, a snowy beach encircling an inlet that opens out into the vast ocean. And it's down there I spy a solitary iceberg, a cleaved block of glacier, drifted in with the tide and landlocked into the shallow bottom of the bay.

I discover several routes that lead down to the water, including a wider, unplowed one that may have been used for boats, and cars, and man. I trudge down the snowy incline, one heavy foot after the other, until I reach the edge of the water, the dark blue and black liquid rolling about like waves of oil and molasses.

I take one cautious step into the water and it is bracing, a shock running up my thick hide. I'll have to be fast. I work my way into the freezing liquid, wading cautiously, and then I quickly lose my footing on the seaweed-covered stones, and go under, all at once.

Everything turns blue.

I hear car doors slamming, and the laughter of children. I hear the door to a house open, and the laughter turns to crying. I hear voices raised and glass breaking and the sound of something burning, something whimpering in the dark. I feel the long night wrap around me, the darkness creeping back in, a familiar passenger that I remember carrying for many years. I feel the void where life once was, the space where something once slept and cried in the dark. I feel the warmth of amber liquid and the sensation of flesh parting. I smell cigarette smoke and see the stars dancing overhead.

And then there is a great undoing—every inch of flesh slicing open, dissolving, as it sloughs off of my body. There is a burning sensation as every bit of exposed muscle is set on fire, pinpricks turning to knife cuts turning to separation. There is a wash of panic as pressure runs across my tendons, a pulling, and tugging, and then the sharp stab of something breaking apart, tearing—again, and again, and again. I am washed in a liquid that stings as it absorbs, I am ground into dust, the motes floating in the wind, I dissipate and disintegrate, as the last of my conscious mind finally slides into the darkness.

And then I come up out of the water, gasping for breath, as I lumber to find the ground, four legs churning, a massive block of ice rising up and down, pushing me under. It is three times my size, and as the waves roll and turn, it slams down onto me, knocking me under.

I cannot see, and I am choking on icy water, burning my insides despite the cold.

When I am able to finally break the surface without being pummeled, I find the shore and slowly back out of the water, bending my neck to impale the ice on my horn.

It is so heavy.

I grunt, and pull, and back out of the water, dragging the chunk of iceberg with me.

It takes every muscle I have, my back straining and popping, as I move it onto the shore. I can feel my horn sliding out of the block, the water like a lubrication, the block slipping away, but I'm able to tug it on the shore as it finally lets go, and the front half stays on the land, while the back half remains floating in the water.

I am so cold.

Colder than I have ever been.

I must find my way through the tear.

There isn't much time.

I stagger back into the water and throw myself into the block from the other side, slowly sliding it out of the water and onto the beach, where the snow-covered stones and frozen seaweed create a slick surface. There is nothing to do but push the block up the hill, and so I lower my head and heave.

I push, and groan, and cry in the darkness as the block slowly works its way up the hill, eventually stopping on level ground. I cough and wheeze and vomit up water, struggling to find my breath. But the tear is only a few feet away now, so I shiver, and tremble, and push the block through.


As the sky turns orange and the air cools around me, the block of ice sits in the trench that I have dug, slowly melting into the hole. It is a thing of beauty. I cannot take my eyes off of the brilliant white color, translucent in places as it melts into the pit, rivulets of shimmering blue running through it. The water that is slowly filling the hole is crystal clear.

It's a start. I can't count on rainwater, but this chunk of ice should get us started. It will evaporate in time, so it will have to rain at some point, or I may have to return for more ice and snow. But for now, the water is filling up the pool—the pond—my creation.

I lower my head and fall asleep as the darkness washes across the land. Over one hill and then another, yellow eyes glimmer in the expanding night. Nostrils flare and mottled beasts slowly creep closer. In the distance, larger animals pause, staring across the horizon at a glimmer of water where there previously was none. Flying creatures circle back before the sun is completely gone from the sky—marking the spot, their territory expanding toward the glimmering tear.

As a wind drifts across the land, seeds, and buds, and pollen drift toward the water.

Where there is life, there is a way.

And where there is life, there is soon to be death.

# CHAPTER FIVE

# THE HELLSCAPE

The earliest memories I have of this place are fuzzy and uncertain—so long ago, and yet, seemingly, just the other day. Things repeat, and then distort. There is a pattern emerging in the sprawling landscape, in what I see, and it makes me question everything—one hill looking like the next, one mountain repeating as if cast by a giant stamp, one bird becoming two becoming many. There are times I climb a sandy rise, or rocky outcropping or grassy knoll, expecting to be back where I started—standing at the tear, come full circle somehow. I see faces in outcroppings, hear voices in the wind, smell fragrances that don't belong here. I am haunted by the past, tortured in the present, and wary of the future.

We did not live here by the tear originally; no, we were in the grasslands to the east—where there was an abundance of shrubs and bushes, some growing flowers, and later, fruit. One had dull purple ovals with a vibrant pink interior; another, a spiky brown husk with a crimson nut inside; a third prickly green orb with a cloudy center, dotted with shiny black seeds. There were lush, long grasses and bushy trees, and low-running plants that held tiny white flowers tasting like vanilla.

I remember being so much smaller, one of many, born on all fours, with my cutting horn still a dull knob, my hide not yet hardened into armor. It was a vulnerable time for our brood—unable to defend ourselves, until we grew larger, and thicker, and sharper, and angrier. In the beginning, our survival depended on our mother.

She was not nearly as big as our tank of a father, nearly half his size, and with much less armor—mostly the plates on her skull, her thick hide closer to red than gray. When the seasons would change—blazing heat shifting to an ice storm in minutes then back to rain, and finally ending with a rippling heat again—her hide would change with it, sometimes sprouting a dense coat of hair to keep her warm, other times shedding plates and thick skin in pieces, as if she were molting. And whenever that happened, she seemed both relieved and mortified. Unsure of what she had been, who she was now, or what the future might hold. Out here in the deadlands, logic was as rare as water, so we had to adapt at a moment's notice in order to survive.

I remember following her one day, when nobody was looking, the rest of my brood sleeping in the shadow of three sickly palm trees, father nowhere to be seen. She would wander off, much like he did, only to return with a newfound energy. She never told us where she went, and we never asked. It was none of our business, and probing her, or father for that matter, would get you the sharp end of a horn.

I always kept a few dunes between us, hiding behind the curve of one swell or another, her slow progress easy to track. I didn't start to worry until the sun began to set, me with no bearings, uncertain of the way I'd come, all of the hills and crests looking the same by now. My tracks had been blown away by the wind, no way to retrace my steps. So it was stay with my mother, and keep her in sight, or die out here alone, lost to my tribe in the cold of the night, or from dehydration the following day.

When the moon broke fully through the clouds, she stopped abruptly in the middle of nowhere, collapsing into the sand from exhaustion. There was a gentle breeze pushing across the desert, and on it, a song, a humming that drifted to me. The melody flowed from my mother's lips, drawing the wildlife to her—a lilting voice, full of haunting discordant harmonies and sorrowful notes. Soon after, it was replaced by buzzing and low vibrations, something more primal.

From over the horizon a flickering of light blue luminescence in the form of animated jackdaws flittered and soared ever closer. The flock landed on my mother in a flurry of light, picking at tiny glowing seeds that rose to the surface of her skin. The birds pulled the seeds from her skin, one at a time—their long tendrils and roots either eliciting great pain from her or relieving her of some sickness—I'm not sure which, as I was too far away to read her expression in the waning yellow moonlight.

A hiss of amber scorpions erupted out of the sand beneath her, scaring the birds off in a cloud of pulsing light, as the arachnids climbed her limbs, blanketing her prone form. They clacked and clattered, their pincers snapping open and shut, searching for the tiny holes that had been made by the birds, piercing her with their stingers, causing her head to thrust backward in either agony or immense pleasure. They injected her with either a sickly poison or some flickering ambrosia, everything in the shadows out here two-faced and unreliable.

When she shook her body from head to toe, as if shedding water from a cooling dip in an oasis, the creatures dispersed, disappearing into the dark night, faint traces of their skeletal glow persisting in my vision long after they had gone. Quickly they were replaced by at least a dozen long-eared hares of a variety I'd never seen, their retinas reflecting back the moonlight, shining a bright purple. They had tan, leathery skin and elongated snouts, hackles of sharp needles running up and down their spines, their paws ending in long talons, mouths full of teeth, far too many for my comfort, even at this distance. They circled my mother and then stood before her, barking and coughing, until they hacked up furry balls that wiggled and shook, scooting together until they formed one large fuzzy orb that vibrated with an angry, orange energy. When it hopped and bounced close to her, my mother extended her neck and swallowed it whole, a ripple of dull amber energy dispersing across her flesh like glowing goosebumps.

I felt as though I was watching something that I should not see, witnessing something private, and so I slowly retreated, but not before one final transformation happened. With a shudder and a shake, she curled into a fetal position, and as the moon drifted across the night sky, a thick, white growth formed over the surface of her body, accumulating on her skin like a fresh blanket of snow, before hardening around her like a cocoon. And for a moment, I couldn't breathe, fearing that she had succumbed to the madness of the desert, her offerings not accepted, the shadow lights truly poisonous, and not the regenerative cure that I had thought. And so she stayed, for the remainder of the night, under the watchful eyes of the vigilant rabbits, while I resisted the urge to rush down to save her, as I fretted about her fate. And then, when I thought I could wait no longer, the surface of the chrysalis bulged and swelled, while the hares yelped and scurried for safety, before it burst open with a slash of her cutting horn in a shower of viscous, yellow fluid. And suddenly there were two of her—an empty exoskeleton, molted and abandoned, a shell of her former self, and outside of that clear husk, glistening and glowing like a newborn babe, my mother stood and stretched, her metamorphosis complete. She had shed her last existence, or been birthed into another—rebooted, revamped, improved, and upgraded—for the betterment of our horde, I hoped, for the survival of us all.

She let loose a great mourning call, and my heart went cold. There was so much pain and longing in her cry. And as the night shifted quickly into something much closer to frozen death than burning hot combustion, she approached her former self and let out a deep sigh, her exhale filling the hollow form, manifesting into something living. This translucent echo of my mother, animated now by her shared life-force, rolled over on its side, weeping, and trembling, and so I looked away, turning my eyes toward the shadows, as mother headed home, oblivious to my invasion upon her transformation.

It would be many years later, in a fever dream of sickness, that I realized she was aware of my presence the entire time. She was trying to show me something—to defy the labels and expectations that I had, that we all had, thrust upon her—mother, caregiver, physician, and priest. For a few brief moments she glowed in isolation and peace, alone in her thoughts and dreams. Having given everything she could to those that needed it, she shattered, and was reborn.

Our father was a quiet, massive presence, his armored plates darkened from years of wear and tear, the sun beating down on him, the tip of his cutting horn broken off. There were hairline cracks in a few plates, something he didn't like to talk about, and when we pestered him with questions and curiosity, he would stand up and walk away—toward a watering hole or just over the hills, sometimes up onto a mesa, where he knew we could not follow. The spikes that ran the course of his spine would fall out like quills, and the plates that bisected his exposed vertebrae grew dull, and tarnished, and opaque. But when he was close, we felt protected. At night when the hot land cooled, we would wait until he was fast asleep, deep into another reality, before we'd approach him for warmth and safety in the night. We would push up against each other and feel the heat radiate off of his hide. Sometimes mother would join us, but more often not.

She had felt the sting of his horn on more than one occasion and tolerated his presence with a jaded eye.

He was a violent creature—prone to outbursts and irregular emotions. One of my siblings was crushed under the weight of his massive body, when he rolled over in the night, her muffled screams lost in the darkness. When he was eating—whether it was berries and leafy greens, or the stringy meat of an impaled sloth gazelle—he would just as easily turn his cutting horn on us as the meal that lay in front of him. Until his belly was full, we stayed away from him, only coming closer to feast on the scraps of what remained. He provided, yes, but he always ate first. He had no patience, and little use for us. I never once saw him laugh.

When we crossed the red desert, seeking a rumored grove of date palms, there emerged from the sand a colossal thorny millipede, its curving body in gray segments, silver blades shining at the edge of each plate, long flickering antennae searching the air for its next meal. When it opened its jaws, ringed with pincers, we stared in horror at the gaping maw, hypnotized by the circle of teeth as they spun round and round, dripping with saliva and poison. Father did not hesitate, merely continued his steady plodding as the creature engulfed one of my kin, biting and chewing as its mouth expanded and contracted around my screaming sibling. And then it dove back under the sand, disappearing, its body taking a long time to disappear. Undulations rippled under the sand, my remaining siblings staying close to father, as it circled back. When it finally appeared again, a high-pitched screeching filling the air, father charged it quickly and impaled it under its mouth and splayed lips, digging his horn deep into its thick skin, a viscous green liquid spilling out into the sand. The creature scuttled away, up and over a hill, before burrowing back down into the desert floor. It would circle us from a distance the rest of our trip, a chattering of teeth and a low, guttural moan rising on the hot winds now and then, but it would never surface again—merely rippling under one dune after another before eventually disappearing for good.

The green poison started to eat away at his cutting horn, the tip of it turning brown over time, snapping off weeks later when father battled with a rabid hyena who was trying to steal the spoils of his kill.

I saw him one time rubbing the horn on a rock, sharpening the tip, working away the last of the dying keratin, skin, and bone. He worked that tip until it shone—so sharp that I was afraid to make a noise, fearful that he might test it out on me.

In the grasslands mother was the one who taught us how to survive. She showed us plants that leaked a thick, white liquid, and how they might be sliced open and rubbed across our hides. She would cut down the long blades and yellow fruit and transfer them to a large, flat rock, stomping on the tendrils and stems and stalks and flowers until a messy paste covered the rock. She instructed us to roll in the liquid, and then push up against each other, until we were covered in the sticky substance. It would harden our thick skin, turning our hides into plates of armor.

She showed us the rocks that father used—differentiating between the softer stones that would break under pressure and those that were up to the task. She showed us river rocks—back when there were still rivers, singular thick veins that cleaved the sand and rocky outcroppings—their surfaces worn down to a very small grain, which helped to produce a uniform edge. She showed us sandstone, composed mostly of quartz, with elements of feldspar, as well as silt and clay.

She taught us to fight, because father would not—learning to charge, and stomp, and jut out our horns with pride.

But she didn't teach us enough.

On the day our mother died, we were camped out on a rocky formation under a massive overhang, a small ridge that descended into a cave mouth. Father was asleep farther back in the cave, when the trio of big cats skulked up and out of the long grass. There were emaciated, and sickly, desperate to find meat. Their patchy coats riddled with scabs and lesions from parasitic mange, one of them limping from an open wound on its shank, long spiky tails swishing back and forth as they fanned out to attack. When they surrounded mother as she chewed on a leafy bush, it was with a speed and cunning that I'd never seen before. She didn't have a chance.

She'd never shown us how to turn in a circle, keeping your horn to the predator at all times. She'd never shown us how to take on more than one beast at a time, because she'd never had to face a pack before. She showed us how to call for help, but when she turned in circles and jutted out her cutting horn, one of the cats struck, sinking its sharp teeth and long incisors into a soft patch under her jaw. She shook her head back and forth trying to get free, but the other cats pounced as well, knocking her to the ground. Once she was on the ground, it was all but over, blood streaming from her neck, a bubbling noise rising up from her open mouth, as the animals bit and chewed.

It all happened so fast, I barely had time to stand up, and when I bleated and bellowed, my brothers and sisters stood as well. But we were no match for the cats, too slow, and too soft, and too young—we knew that—so we stayed in the shadows while she died at our feet.

We goaded father with our dull horns, begged him to do something, but he was slow to wake, and barely interested in the cats. It was only when they turned to him, seeing his dark presence as a threat, that he stood and sauntered over, shaking his head and bellowing into the sky. The cats hesitated, and when he charged, they scattered over the land.

And then he did something for which I will never forgive him. He approached mother, bowed down onto his knees, lowered his head—and ate.

In time, the others would approach and take a hesitant bite, long after father had turned and walked away.

Eat or be eaten, survival of the fittest, waste not, want not.

I hated him for what he'd done.

I hated him for being right.

I hated my mother for being soft.

And so I stomped and bellowed and pushed the others away. And then I ate as much of mother as I could. Later I would vomit into the sand, ashamed at my behavior. And then I ate the vomit, choking it back down. I would not let her death be in vain.

And then I followed in the footsteps of my father, who had survived the cats, impaled the giant millipede, warded off diving birds and the punishing sun without ever uttering a word. My father, who was as old as time, as cold as ice, and as empty as a shell. My father, the ghost. My father, the shadowy specter.

I vowed right then and there to never be soft. To make sure that I survived, no matter what. And in that moment, I devolved, and regressed.

It would be much later that I would listen to the whispers of the cave worms, but it would be a pattern that I would repeat—again, and again, and again.


I wake one day to find our father gone, a fading trail of his heavy footsteps leading off into the distance. There are six of us left, alone at the edge of a desert where the mountains loom to the north, a few palm trees providing us shade. We have a task today, I've decided. I am the oldest—my shell the hardest, my countenance grim, the others willing to listen, if only out of fear. I am a shadow of my father, but a shadow that casts long across the hot sand. A shadow that drowns out all of my light, my vision reduced to a tunnel, coated with decay.

There is a small spring between these sands and the mountains to the north where a bubbling of water rises up, providing a bit of relief. But there is also a danger in the cliffs farther away, something my siblings don't know about, but I do.

It's time to see if the lessons our mother gave us have paid off.

I will not warn them. I will not remind them of this lurking threat. I will instead simply lay the test out in front of them and see if they can pass. I have no patience for those that will not learn. And as the land dies, and the winds push over the hills, the greenery will start to fade, the waters drying up. I fear hard times may be upon us. Less to share. Simple pursuits that we take for granted now, soon to become difficult to provide.

We trudge forward toward the oasis as the sun beats down upon us. The others are distracted by an enormous dragonfly, its translucent wings buzzing in the air. Snapping at it, one of them catches it. It bites down, the crunch and green, slimy guts causing it to spit the thing out in disgust—twitching and shuddering it vibrates in the sand. They stomp it into tiny bits, laughing as they do so.

A knot of tension rolls over in my gut as we approach the shade of the palm trees and the trickle of water that has formed a small pond. A ring of small, withered bushes encircle the water, a few tiny, yellow birds taking off into the air. There are no other animals here, as they know the dangers, preferring to sneak in at night, under the cover of darkness.

I cast my eye to the mountain range, and then back to the watering hole, unnoticed. We dash into the cool water, drinking and playing, until a shadow passes over us and I freeze, my gaze cast skyward. It circles quietly and then passes over again.

The others don't notice.

I back away from the water, until I am standing by a patch of rocks, jutting up from the sand, like the spine of some great beast. I push my heavy legs and feet into the hot sand, until I start to feel the cooler grit underneath. I shake my body back and forth, pushing lower and lower, until only my head is exposed, my horn jutting up into the sky, flattening my spikes against my shell, making myself small, and inconspicuous, next to the rocks.

One of my siblings turns to me, her mouth open wide, finally glancing up as the great hawk passes over once more. She sees the bird—its magnificent wingspan nearly triple our size. The bird keeps its gaze on the watering hole and the others, its underbelly lined in thick red plates, talons sharp as razors.

When my sister turns to me once again, I finally say something.

"Blend," I whisper. "Blend in."

And I shift the color of my armor, the tint of my thick hide, until it matches the rocks around me—a mix of gray and brown, with white marbling running through it.

She turns to her brothers and sisters, and then back to me.

And then she is gone.

A stream of blood follows her ascension as the great bird rises higher and higher, taking off for the mountain range to the north. She never makes a sound. It will eventually dash her on the rocks, cracking open her newly formed armor, to feed on her organs, pulling tendons and muscle from her split corpse like taffy. It will burrow out her eyeballs and fracture her skull, until her gray brains leak out into the dirt.

The others only stand there and gawk, so I bury my head in the sand and dirt and close my eyes. In quick succession there is a great cawing and shrieking, several more shadows passing over the water hole, until there is finally silence, an earthy creosote filling the air.

I have not brought my siblings to their certain death.

I have tried to teach them that life is brutal, and then you die.

Unless you are prepared.

Unless you have steeled yourself for such inevitabilities, and already imagined the worst. If you do not wall yourself off from others, if you do not cast a protective shell around your soft bits and leaking sacs, if you do not turn away from those that ignore the warning signs, then how will you ever survive?

I tell myself this when the nights are dark and long.

I play back the scene in excruciating detail.

And I reiterate the importance of this lesson.

Sometimes I even believe it.

When I open my eyes to the silence, one of my sisters is tucked up close to me, shaking uncontrollably. She is the same color as the mottled rocks, hidden in plain sight.

She does not understand now.

She may not understand later.

But she has survived.

When the sun begins to set, we stand up, shake off the sand, and make our way home. Along the way, we see a rattle-snake eating a desert rat, forcing the stiff, gray shape down its gullet; a fennec fox slurping up a clutch of eggs, the yellow yolk running down its chin as its large ears turn like radar; a hyena with its head in the rib cage of a fallen antelope, the creature's long, twisted horns tipped in blood.

I don't say "circle of life" out loud, but it's what I'm thinking.


I am standing outside the cave, staring deeply into the gloom.

I am standing outside the cave, staring deeply into the gloom.

I am standing outside the cave, staring deeply into the gloom.

Nothing changes.

And so, I repeat the cycle once again.

In this dream I am covering up the bruises with makeup. I am wearing a long-sleeved shirt in the middle of summer. I am wiggling a loose tooth, the root giving way, tossed in the trash can, as the cold winds whip around outside. I am lifting a bottle of mouthwash that is not mouthwash. And I am cooking him his favorite dinner, as the winter storm crackles and snaps the timber bones of our aging house. I am cast under the gaze of those who have no understanding. And I pass it on. Unwilling, or unable, to do anything else.

And then there were the two of us, mother long gone, father only a memory, and so when we stumble across the rotting carcass of a female coyote, we pause for a moment to stare at the flies that dance around her, the wriggling maggots that fester and squirm in what's left of the poor creature. She's been picked over—face chewed off, gutted from the inside out, organs wolfed down—nothing we haven't seen a hundred times. There is a pungent stench and I don't want to linger.

It's when we start to move on, headed back toward a glimmer that I've spied in the distance, away from the watering hole, and toward the west, that I hear the yipping from under some scraggly undergrowth just over a small hill, not far away.

It's her litter. The puppies are small, and furry, and can hardly stand. Perhaps she was defending them from some predator. How they survived I don't know. As we move toward the mesa, and the outcropping by the glittering filament, they follow us, the pups.

I can tell already that they aren't going to make it. Without their mother, with no pack around to protect them, they will starve and die out here in the heat.

My sibling turns to me, eyes heavy, head bowed.

She knows they will not make it, either, but she is not entirely dead inside, she still has a glimmer of hope.

Yes . . . she would take on this task, slow us down, endanger us with these niblits that will certainly draw something to us as we move across the dirt and sand.

"There is nothing we can do for them," I say.

"We can take them with us," she says. "We can protect them."

"We can hardly protect ourselves. It's dangerous. I won't do it."

"Why won't you try?" she asks.

"If you'd prefer, I could stomp them to death right here and end this stupid game we're playing. They will not make it. There is nothing we can do."

I keep walking, but she stays behind. I am filled with a boiling rage that I cannot let go. So I fume and I stomp toward my destination for the night—a glimmering golden filament with puffs of snow leaking from it.

When the moon comes out and the night grows long, I consider walking back to the bushes where she has hunkered down, the yipping mutts bouncing and bounding all around her. I haven't seen her smile like that in a very long time. Maybe ever. But then I thought that perhaps this would teach her a lesson, one night alone with the annoying critters, and then in the morning, maybe we can find a way.

I fall asleep thinking about what might be possible, that maybe I should listen to her more often. It may not cost much to bring them into the fold. Maybe she is right.

When I trod back over the hill in the morning there is nothing but carnage.

She is gutted from her throat to her anus, tough hide split open, rib cage torn wide, hollow inside. Around her are balls of fluff, missing their heads. Whatever came in the night, it was fast, and quiet, and efficient.

I take a deep breath, and then turn away.

Never again, I tell myself.

And I let that shell wrap around me, tighter and tighter, until I don't care about anything or anyone ever again.

# CHAPTER SIX

# TRANSUBSTANTIATION

I spend the day hunting and gathering, visiting old haunts, wandering familiar grounds. I travel as far as the eye can see to acquire seeds, and pods, and flowers, and stems. I swallow black seeds and red seeds, most of them tiny, some of them almost too big to choke down. I find slender tan pods with white down poking out of them, and square orange ones that have barbs at the end, and white circular ones that are mostly filled with spores. I stop at the oasis, which has dried up now, not even a trickle leaking out of a series of cracks and fissures, the dirt and mud as dry as a bone. I chew and swallow any burst of color I can find, and then move on to the drying grasses and other reeds, and then anything that is nearly dead, but still retaining elements of life—petals and stamen and leaves. It is a rainbow of faded colors in orange and pink and yellow—taken in one bite at a time, where around us, most everything else had faded to gray and brown.

Every time I stop at a location—withered oasis, rocky outcropping, dying grassland, or dusty mesa—I lumber back to the new watering hole I've created and vomit what I've eaten into the water. I can only hope and pray that something sticks.

As dusk settles over the tiny pond, I collapse by the water, sipping at it, the solid hunk of iceberg liquified into warm water, melted all the way down. It didn't take long, only a few hours, and now the water glistens in the fading sunlight.

As dusk settles over the tiny pond I've created, creatures start to migrate toward me, and I'm too tired to do anything else but lie here, my great head resting on the ground, jaw in the dirt, horn sticking up into the air. I am suddenly exhausted, empty inside, a spark of something changing and growing, not entirely void of emotion. The darkness inside me has a flickering flame, and I'm afraid to breathe for fear of blowing it out.

What emerges over the hill, and from the earth, and out of the sky are beasts I've never seen before. If they have united today to plan my demise, so be it. I have nothing left to give this hellish world. I am spent.

An avalanche of rocks pours over a hill to the north, gray and brown, with veins of white all through them, rolling up to the water and stopping suddenly. They shift and jumble into a pile, turning into stone foxes, their tails made entirely out of moss and blades of grass. A ripple of electricity runs over and through their bodies, the mother sitting up taller, as the kits rumble and shake at her feet. She takes a sip of water, and light shimmers across the surface, rippling as static fills the air. From the bottom of the trench something tiny scuttles about, glowing in the looming depths, like tiny plankton set on fire with icy blue filaments. The fox and her kits lie close to each other creating a rock formation that blends into the earth, a whiff of musk drifting to me.

Over the mesas and plateaus to the west, a massive blue stingray floats and swims in the air, long tentacles and barbs twitching from up by its mouth, which is ringed in red. Two dorsal fins on the top of its long, scaly body undulate in a soft breeze as it floats overhead. It circles the hole as if in a dream, slowly moving through the sky, getting closer and closer, until it slides into the water, nearly twice as big as the trench. Bending its back and arching upward, it leaves its tail in the water below. It births a cavalcade of shiny white eggs into the water, where the tiny fish sit curled up like fetuses inside the rubbery shells, drifting to the bottom of the pod. They settle in next to each other, a dull glow emanating from the clutch. A dozen little black eyes peer up at me from the water, as the last of the light leaves the sky. Done with the delivery, the stingray slides effortlessly into the sky, and out of sight to the west, back to wherever it came from, a deep bellow resonating in the air like a whale searching for a mate, deep within the ocean.

From the east, out of a massive fissure that lies just beyond the sterile oasis, a smattering of red crabs scuttle over to me, nearly as big as I am. Their glowing shells are like embers in the darkness, and they climb over each other in a hurry, running around the edge of the pond to get to the far side. From between the cracks in their claws and abdomen and legs, there is a molten lava that spills out, ringed with light. When they open their mouths—which were closed tight, two eyes on the ends of long stalks—flames erupt into the night sky, an explosion of color, fireworks sparking the dark. They pile on top of each other and then mushroom into orange and red leaves, a fiery bush that now holds court on the other side of the water. The air smells of sulfur and smoke, the leaves pronged like a maple.

And from the south, a lumbering four-legged beast in silver approaches, with a jagged hood that is lined with vivid colors—turquoise and fuchsia—an enormous horn that doubles as stigma and ovary, in a dull yellow that glows like gold. A bunching of stamen spill out of the center of the flowery head, sensing the air. It is blind, without eyes, but seems to know where it is going. It sits down next to me, roots sprouting into the earth, going down deeper and deeper, and then slides up close to the shell, where they merge with the outside of the cup. A web runs beneath it all, white tendrils piercing it, but no water seeps out. They have become one with the structure, and with a great sigh, the creature blooms into a squat palm, amber trunk leading up to a shock of blue leaves that shake into life. Tiny round fruit manifests within the branches, hardening into a brown, hairy husk to protect what sweet meat lies within it.

The moon rises and a sparkle runs across the surface of the pond, as greenery emerges from the water—algae appearing on the surface, grasses piercing the perimeter, scraggly shrubs pushing up through the earth, wherever a crack resides.

The filament glitters in gold dust, as beyond it the snow comes down heavy, large flakes sprinkling out of the tear in a huff.

I have nothing left to give.

And so I sleep.


In this dream, I am standing naked in the snow, the cold wind biting, tears streaming down my face. My feet are red, and my hands are tingling, but I walk forward anyway, nothing left for me here—the children gone—a glimmering fissure calling to me from across the quiet town.

Everything hurts. And nothing matters.

By the time I make my way up the street, and around the house, I am numb from head to toe, a whimpering sound drifting to me from the woods. And then I realize the noise is coming from me—a slow keening building up, the wind confusing me, the snow falling heavier and heavier, and so I fall to my knees and pray.

I ask for guidance, make promises that I probably won't keep, and then shut my eyes. I am dead inside, gutted and empty. So why not finish the job?

It is getting harder and harder to breathe, the ice crystals in the air cutting my mouth and throat as I take in a thin, aching breath, and then release it slowly, a stutter in the air. Every frozen cloud of breath puffs out in front of me, condensing into a thin sheet of ice on my pale cheeks and freezing on my eyelashes. All around me, the snow swirls, blurring out my surroundings in a tempest of white.

The golden filament has parted, widening, to show me something else. It is the great beyond, some other world. Perhaps I could have just gone on through, but I am so tired now, my blood cooling, my limbs numb and useless, my heartbeat fading. And it seems so very far away—a lifetime, perhaps. Or more.

I have not asked for mercy because I don't think I deserve it. I will never learn, if I am forgiven again and again.

And so I ready myself for whatever comes next. It will not be pleasant; I am sure of that. I will not be rewarded for drawing to me one angry, violent spirit after another. I know that's not what love is. I have moved through the world like a toxic oil spill, coating and drowning everything in my path. I have sought to trap those seeking flight, unwilling to let them be free; instead, preferring to drag them down into the poisoned waters with me, rather than suffering alone, or seeking help. I have oozed over one habitat after another, slowly and surely, one horrible, inevitable inch at a time.

To the one who fled south, unable to look overhead, so focused on the moment at hand, I forgive you.

To the one who stayed behind, to protect those more unfortunate or vulnerable than herself, suffering in the process, I am sorry.

To the one who was unable to defend herself, never having been taught how to fight, forgive me for not doing better.

To the one who remained—a dark, sulking presence, cold and distant, as those withered and died around you—I place a pox on your soul. May the buzzards of the sprawling desert pick at your organs for all of eternity. May the cold specter of this fractured land haunt you for as long as you take breath. May you never find peace, never find fulfillment, never know love again—in other words, may you become just like me, and all that I have brought down upon myself.

And may you burn in hell, never finding absolution.

# ACT THREE

# THE BOY WONDER

—

We must accept finite disappointment,
but never lose infinite hope.

—Martin Luther King, Jr.

# CHAPTER ONE

# A TRANSFER OF POWER

I witnessed what they did to Sebastian. The endless night, the expanding darkness—I've seen what it can do to people—kind, generous souls turning angry and vindictive—but this was beyond my worst fear. It was a betrayal of the highest kind. I stood at the window of our small home, watching as one neighbor after another brought out their dead, wrapped in makeshift shrouds—blankets and trash bags, tarps and drop cloths, some in nothing at all. It broke my heart to see them surround his house, to abandon their loved ones there, knowing what it might do to the old man on the hill.

And now he is dead. His body desiccated, torn to pieces, giving birth to something horrific, that then vanished through the tear.

His house had been gutted by the blaze, leaving nothing but a skeletal framework of charred pine and birch logs, interred in a wide circle of ash and soot on the pristine white snow. Inside the burned-out structure, only vague remnants of his homestead could be identified—warped appliances, twisted pipes, and scorched furniture. The wreckage smoldered for days after the fire, flaring up each time the wind gusted, carrying the acrid stench of melted plastic and woodsmoke to the townspeople below.

It is an abomination, and every time I look at the remains, it breaks my heart all over again.

I understand the traditions, the reasons why they were impatient, why they acted—fear of their loved ones being stuck in some sort of purgatory, or hell, unable to ascend to heaven, to be reborn, or cleansed of their sins. They didn't want their bigoted brother, or alcoholic father, or vengeful sister to be birthed into some wasteland as a rabid hyena, blood-thirsty vulture, or deviant goat. I get it.

My training was incomplete, and now Sebastian is gone. All I'm left with are a handful of rules—finish what you eat, or run the risk of partial absolution, and permanent damage to myself; the worse the human being, the more horrible the creature and birth; and if it isn't released close to an open tear, it will stay here in this community, poisoning and tainting everything it touches. It's obvious to me that this has been going on a long time—the forgiveness and the acts that demanded a cleansing. And how not every manifestation made it through the rip.

I'd heard whispers for years about something hovering in the mountains, folktales and rumors, a presence floating and drifting in the cloudscape, an ominous shadow soaring on the winds of winter madness. I've seen my classmates behind the school trading bits and pieces of strange things they found in the surrounding wilderness. I'm talking about weird bones and oddly shaped skulls with abnormal horns. Animals that cannot be identified. I've found my own evidence when out hiking with my sister—gouged-out scratches on trees from three sharp claws; shards of rust-colored eggshells much larger than any bird that lives here; long snakeskins with patterns and gold threads that don't align with any serpent I know. This land is both sacred and haunted, blessed and tainted, honored and betrayed. So, this is what we get. With more coming soon, I fear.

I turn away from the window and head to the kitchen—rice always in abundance, whatever fish is in season, and sweet rolls on the table, the cinnamon dusting the air.

Mother has gone to work; her job at the research center pays our bills. I don't know *exactly* what they do there, but it concerns climate change. She helps them study the atmosphere chemistry, ecosystem dynamics, plant and animal life cycles, and sea ice patterns as well. It's all over my head, but she seems to enjoy it. As much as she enjoys anything these days. She comes home tired, face flushed, as she peels off one layer of winter clothing after another. It's not that she doesn't love us; there just isn't much left in the tank after a day of tests, manual labor, and extensive note taking.

I get my blue eyes from her, and when they are not dull and glossy from fatigue, they sparkle like the ocean. She has seen such wonders and often tells me stories about rare albino seals, streams rising out of massive cracks in the earth, and mutated fish from the depths of the ocean. She wears her hair in a long, dark braid that runs down her back—a different pop of color every day in the ribbon that she ties at the end. It's a little ritual that we have shared going back to when I was just a child.

"What color should I wear today, Kallik?" she'd ask.

"I don't know," I'd muse, running my hand over my chin, as if I had a long, gray beard to stroke.

Maybe I'd lick a finger and hold it in the air to test the direction of a nonexistent wind. Sometimes I'd get down on my hands and knees and pretend to listen to the earth. Other times I'd sniff, like some twitching rabbit searching for a scent.

"Feels like a cold one today—I say indigo."

And then she'd laugh, tittering like a stuttering songbird, and hunt down a ribbon that matched. She has a large music box, carved out of local wood, a pastoral landscape with mountains and wildflowers painted on it. It plays "Dance of the

Sugar Plum Fairy," which I always found to be sickly sweet, but every now and then when I was little, I'd sneak into her room and lift the lid to hear the sound of the tinny notes. There was something magical in the song, and when she was working late, my sister off with friends, Balto and I would sit and listen to it, conjuring up ballet dancers, and fairies, and colorful sweets.

My sister, Allia, has headed south over the winter break to see friends in another city. All it took was a menial week at the fishery—baiting hooks, setting lines or traps, hauling in nets, and sorting the catch—for her to realize that she didn't want to be up here any longer. Taking a year off had been a good idea, so whether college loomed or just a warmer climate, I don't know. She tried to work at one of the grocery stores, stocking shelves, with overpriced goods that were hard to come by up here. But when a case of soda exploded during the first week, having frozen in transit, covering her in sugar water, she quit on the spot. She didn't last more than a few days in her next job either, at the local diner as a waitress—tired of locals sitting there nursing a bottomless cup of coffee all day, earning only a few coins in tips for a day of pouring; sick of the occasional pinch to her ass as a drunken ape guffawed into his eggs and bacon; fuming from burning her long, slender fingers on hot plates and spilled cups of coffee. She even worked at the tiny local airport for a while but grew bored of passengers complaining about the constant delays and cancellations, the repetitive flight schedule in and out of town, and the monotonous forecast always cloudy and cold, with a chance of snow.

Allia would hike the trails with me, and she could split timber with the best of them, tall and athletic, always eager to find a reason to get out of the house, no matter the weather. We'd take Balto for walks in the summer, down to the waterfront where the giant whalebones created an arch by the edge of the shoreline. Skeletal whaling boats sat upside down, some carved from the great creatures themselves, their bones bleached and white during the endless light of summer, others made of metal, their aluminum framework secured with screws and bolts. Quite a few were hand-carved from pine and birch, nailed and glued together, shellacked and waterproofed, labors of love. Some of the schooners were covered in hides and skins, patterns and shapes painted on them. Others had modern, fiberglass hulls in bright colors so you didn't get lost at sea. No one wants a white boat in a white storm surrounded by white ice. In one moment up here, you could be stuck in the 1800s—a trapper, fishing and hunting to survive—and then you'd find a few modern conveniences and were back in the present with cell phones, and sonar, and radar to guide your way.

Allia loved fishing, whaling, hunting, and foraging—it was always an adventure to her. She didn't mind getting dirty. I'd seen her covered in blood and guts, urine and crap, cobwebs and slime. But somewhere along the way, I think the isolation got to her. On any given day, I expect her to be gone for good—a ghost, a wisp of smoke, an absence where she used to linger. Even right now, going south to visit friends, a part of me aches with the knowledge that she just might not come back. It's always a possibility.

So I sit at the folding card table and eat my white rice, boiled whale meat and muktuk, which is frozen blubber, sliced thin, salted, and then layered on top. Sweet rolls with icing are in the center of the table, soy sauce and sriracha to add flavor to the main dish. A glass of water sits there, ice cubes clanking and cracking, a miniature sea, with tiny icebergs floating in it.

I am surrounded by repetition and simplicity. The same wooden cabinets, the same coolers, the same worn-out ulu knives, snowmobiles running up and down the street—quieter now as the temperatures drop, the polar night expanding. I walk a circuit from the kitchen to the living room with its couch and recliners, a fire always blazing in the woodstove, to my tiny bedroom, overflowing with books and clothes and games.

There is a fluttering at the window, a flash of pink, something feathery and bright, but when I run to the door and stick my head out into the falling snow, the wind gusting, there is nothing there.

"Balto?" I yell into the darkness.

He's gone.

But maybe he'll come back.

It was good to see him, even if just for a moment.

It gives me hope.

I've always loved food—cooking, eating, foraging, hunting. It has been a part of my life for as long as I can remember. It is so many things to me—survival in a tough environment; connecting with nature, as we live off the land; comfort in the dishes that have warmed me all my life, prepared by family, traditions to pass down; independence in how I can take care of myself, as well as others. So it's no surprise that I earn a little extra cash working at the nearest restaurant to me, a local diner titled—appropriately enough—Local Diner #1, the same diner Allia quit. I don't know if they were planning to expand at some point and never did, or if they just felt it was important to state the fact that they were the *first*, the *best*, the *only* diner. With so few options within walking distance, I'm just glad that they hired me in the first place. Jobs can be scarce, if you don't want to work for the government, or the research facility, or the fishery. As much as I enjoy listening to the short-wave radio and cheering on my neighbors when a bowhead whale is harpooned and pulled onto the land—cut up and divided among whoever turns up with a cooler—there are some days that I just want a cheeseburger and fries.

Today is one of those days.

As I trudge through the drifting snow toward the establishment, bundled up from head to toe against the weather, the thought of a sizzling patty, spiced with salt and pepper, sauteed onions in a tidy pile, and then topped with lettuce, tomato, ketchup, and mustard, makes my mouth water. Today it will be pepper jack cheese, not cheddar, as I want something with a little kick. And if you get the French fries hot out of the frier, salted and crispy, there is nothing better. I'm old school in that I dip them in ketchup, not mayonnaise like my sister, the freak. Some days it's a chocolate shake or malt, but today, all I can think about is an ice-cold Coke, the cubes cracking and popping in a tall glass.

The diner is small—basically one large room, the outside clapboard painted a faded red, with dull yellow lining the windows and door frames. I don't know if it was an ode to the aforementioned ketchup and mustard, or some subliminal attempt to recreate the vibe of McDonald's, but it sure stands out in the snow and ice, lights encircling the roofline, metal poles and covers protecting the bulbs. Streetlights are one thing—I've shot out a few in my time, but the state pays to replace those. A private business is another thing entirely. We're in this together, after all. Everything is more expensive up here, even lightbulbs. And we wouldn't want to lose a great burger, bowl of chili, or plate of onion rings over some prolonged cabin fever.

I enter to the sound of bells ringing over the door. The food here is standard diner fare, with some classic elements, but less 1950s and more edge of the wilderness outdoor vibe. There are booths on each end of the space, with tables filling up the middle. The tile floor is a scuffed white, with flecks of black in it, and the booths are wrapped in a dark red fake leather to match the outside of the diner. The tables are simple squares, with more ornate curved legs made by a local craftsman. Not the standard

Formica tops—we have those running over the counter. There are windows running down the front of the building, thick glass that can handle the ice and snow. On the walls is a mixture of retro diner classics—oversized forks and spoons, photos of local football teams, and Coca-Cola platters—mixed with more festive, outdoorsman totems like a moose head, with full antlers, and a large circular clock ringed with pine trees in silhouette. On the tables sit the usual condiments, plus a variety of hot sauces, and a silver napkin holder in the middle.

Margie, the owner, looks up from the counter. She is wearing her usual uniform—cornflower blue with tiny white flowers, a white collar, and a dingy apron cinched tight around her well-rounded frame. She has cat-eye glasses on a bejeweled chain around her neck, resting on her considerable bosom. I mean, she's hard to miss, but she's more of a mother or kooky aunt than anything else to me here. She's never done me wrong, but I know enough not to cross her. There is not only a rifle in the office, leaned behind the door, but also a wooden baseball bat beneath the counter. If you fuck with her, or her place, or her customers, you're leaving whether you like it or not. And maybe with a lump on your forehead to remind you of what an asshole you were. One long, dark winter many years ago, she supposedly killed a man, but she won't talk about it, or give me any details. And when it's brought up, her eyes gloss over and she turns away. Must have been rough. I mean, we all know each other here—only a couple hundred people living in town, within walking distance. So I can't imagine gunning down a friend who has lost control. But it happens from time to time.

It's quiet now—that calm period between the breakfast rush and the lunch crowd, which is why I'm here. I get a free meal before every shift, and the place smells like heaven—a mixture of sweet onion, savory meat, and a hint of vanilla from something baked. I'll try to save room for a piece of pie, as Margie is known for her desserts. Not the savory salmon pie that so many like, but more traditional offerings like apple, strawberry, cherry, and rhubarb.

"The usual, Kal?" she asks.

"Yes, ma'am," I say as I head to the back to hang up my gear and store it for my shift. "Just a Coke today, though; not a chocolate malt, and pepper jack cheese, please."

She nods her head and writes on her note pad, and then posts the ticket on a turning metal holder that sits in the pass-through window. Oliver is working the grill right now, and I don't see a waitress, so Margie must be holding down the fort. He leans out of the kitchen and gives me a quick wave, cigarette hanging out of the corner of his mouth, quickly burning down to ash. Wouldn't be the first time a bit of it landed on my plate—or someone else's. We've been relieving each other's shifts for months now, but we hardly have any time to talk—two ships passing in the night. Rumors are that he's an ex-convict, ex-military, ex-cop. I don't know if any of it is true, but he wouldn't be the first guy to head this far north to get away from a sordid past and dark acts committed after the sun has gone down. He loves it here; never seen a guy who liked the long night more than Oliver. Something about the darkness and shadows appeals to him. He seems to bask in the pitch black, shrinking in the light. He is perpetually skinny, always with stubble on his face, a small scar by his left eye, his hands like gnarled tree branches. But he knows how to work the grill. The art of frying an egg is more complicated than it looks, and I prefer the lunch shift due to the smaller menu.

Margie will rustle up something at home every now and then—meatloaf and lasagna and stew—which ends up becoming the daily special. Some days hardly anyone comes in, other days we sell out of everything fresh. We have a variety of soups that the people like—just don't tell them they come shipped in huge metal cans, premade—chicken noodle, and tomato, and vegetable the most popular. Though the chili recipe is all her own. She has been competing with Yara for years now, and it drives her crazy. She's always sticking a pencil in her rat's nest of a hairdo, gray and white swirls with strands of black, and begging me to try her new variation. She adds all kinds of strange extra ingredients, trying to find the right combination—sweet potatoes, beer, whiskey, soy sauce, brown sugar—you name it. And it's always good. But never as good as Yara's. We have yet to crack that secret code.

"Cop a squat," she says and slaps the counter, sliding a bottle of Coke my direction.

I sit and we chat about the long night and local gossip. Rumors of what lies beyond Sebastian's destroyed home, though we never use his name, just allude to the trail and hills behind his property. We talk about the bar fight last night, and how one guy was so drunk that he didn't even notice the dart sticking out of his back—an errant toss by one of the patrons. She shares the latest drama about a phone number scrawled on the bathroom wall, the offers of a good time classic trolling, as we try to figure out what sweet local girl broke some townie jerk's heart, without actually dialing the number to find out. We'll leave that to Oliver, who has no shame. She inquires as to my love life, which always embarrasses me, but it's an easy thing to deflect—I just ask her the same question. She's very private, and so that usually ends with a smirk, a squint, our conversation done.

"You good?" she asks. Margie rubs her hands on her grease-stained apron.

She knows I was close to Sebastian, and is well aware of what he does. What he did, I mean. I nod my head, eyes in my lap, trying not to think too hard about it.

"Order up!" Oliver belts out, smacking the metal bell that sits on the pass-through window, tearing the order paper from the holder as he completes it, that one gold tooth always bugging me, in the middle of his crooked grin.

She hands the cheeseburger and fries to me, and then grabs the ketchup and mustard, scootching the holder closer. I add condiments to the bun, a smile working its way across my face. I'm not worried about eating here, as nobody is aware of my brief apprenticeship with the old man. And it's not like she has a dead body in the freezer. I know because I check every time I come in. All it took was one deer carcass hanging there and startling me to keep me on my toes. The dead out here pop up in the strangest places.

You never know.

Especially these days.

The burger is everything I wanted it to be—soft with crispy edges, salty with a pop of pepper and smoke, the cheese adding depth and sweetness, the crisp lettuce and savory tomato blending nicely with the mustard and ketchup. Perfection. In fact, I'd say it's better than any burger I've ever had here before, which I chalk up to the lonely house, the cold walk, and the death of Sebastian.

I swallow, and it is delicious, sad that the meal is over so quickly, work looming, as I dread the more serious tasks that are certainly moving closer.

When I hiccup and a fuzzy, white aphid springs out of my mouth, I am surprised.


Luckily Margie is too busy making another pot of coffee to notice, so I watch the tiny creature flutter and fly away from me, toward the back room, and then out of sight.

What in the hell was that?

Where did it come from?

I look around the room and we're the only three people here—Margie, Oliver, and myself. I get up and walk out the front door, the bells jingling. The wind picks up, and the lights on the front of the diner push out a dull yellow arc into the snow. I hear a snowmobile or two in the distance, down to the left out of sight, revving and running hot. Kids, I think, when the laughter drifts to me; probably people I know, some jerks from school, most likely—reckless as usual. And then I see it—a patch of blood, so fresh it hasn't frozen yet—a black squirrel, flattened and crushed into the snow and a faint red line of treads running off into the night.

Poor little guy, must have gotten confused, or infatuated with a French fry he found, as he sat in the middle of the street.

And it seems I've taken on Sebastian's powers.

I'll have to be more careful now.

This sweet little guy must have been an exemplary squirrel—chittering and leaping around up in the branches, not a care in the world. There wasn't an ounce of anger or regret in that burger. So I can only take a deep breath and sigh, knowing he lived a good life, the best little squirrel life he could.

We could all do so well.


It's hard to concentrate on work, unsettled by what I've just seen, but I throw myself into the mundane aspects anyway, sticking my head in the sand for a moment.

I turn on the radio, and the prep work goes quickly—*mise en place* in order, vegetables sliced and diced and julienned. I have filled up bins and bowls with onions, celery, peppers, garlic, tomatoes, potatoes, and much more. Sautéed onions are pushed to the cooler corner of the grill. The oil and butter tins are filled up. Hamburger and hot dog buns are close at hand. The special of the day—Margie's famous meatloaf—is warming in the oven, ready to be sliced up and dispensed, a huge pot of mashed potatoes sitting on the stove—salt and pepper, butter, freshly minced garlic, and my secret spice, smoked paprika.

And then it's one cheeseburger after another, hot dogs piled with condiments, and an endless supply of fries. Cold weather means comfort food—a hearty caribou soup with a torn off piece of bannock and a slathering of butter. Meatloaf and mashed potatoes go flying out the window—we're sold out in no time. The secret ingredient in *her* recipe is just a tablespoon of barbeque sauce, to add depth and sweetness to the ketchup.

With my long hair tied up in a man bun on top of my head and a hairnet over the top, I am a ninja chef—brandishing my stainless-steel spatula as my weapon of choice. I flip the burgers that line the flattop with the precision of a professional athlete. I drop a lid on them when they are ready to go out, steam rising up, melting the cheese quickly. When they are crispy on the edges, it's time to plate them.

I can hardly see out the pass-through into the dining room, relying instead on Margie to guide me through the orders. I can only hear a chatter of conversations from the other side, and the occasional glimpse of a cute girl with blonde hair, or a burly fisherman in faded flannel.

"Did you hear about the . . ."

"I'll never go there again; what an asshole . . ."

". . . and then I threw it back in, that weird third eye freaking me out . . ."

"Did you ask him yet? It's his responsibility too."

". . . so I put it out of its misery . . ."

"You think that six is enough?"

"Good riddance to bad rubbish."

"It's not a good sign, my friend."

There is grilled cheese on wheat, buttery and melted, this one with tomatoes, adding a savory depth to each bite; a charred hot dog with tangy sauerkraut, and a plate of onion rings, crispy and sweet; a BLT, the smoky fat of the meat dripping down over the crisp lettuce and tangy tomato, with a side of cheese fries, the gooey layer covering it all; a fruit plate with a bowl of cottage cheese in the center, each cold bite an explosion of orange cantaloupe and red watermelon; salty patty melts and seared double cheeseburgers and open-faced turkey sandwiches with hearty gravy.

It's a blur, as always, but I like it that way. Even the variations are fun, breaking the monotony of the same old orders—a PBJ with potato chips mashed into the middle; an order of beanie weenie with extra onions and diced venison; a cheeseburger with blue cheese and an egg on top. Whatever they want, I'm happy to give it to them. Life is short, order whatever makes you happy. That's what I say.

In the middle of the rush, Margie hands me a chocolate malt, a sheen of sweat on her forehead from working the counter and room alone.

"You look like you needed this," she says, smiling.

It's cold and delicious and I suck it down without thinking.

When she walks away, my eyes widen, and I pause and wait a second, afraid of whoever might have run over a rabbit on their way into the parking lot, or stashed a dead uncle in the trunk of their car, or collapsed from a heart attack outside shoveling the sidewalk.

Nothing happens—I'm okay.

But I think of what may be coming. Others who needed Sebastian's help. And how it is my job now to help close the tear, to cleanse this small village of human beings doing the best they can to just survive. What was sent through, that abomination, it should have sealed it shut.

And yet it didn't.

Why?

This town is filled with good people, for the most part. But there are rotten apples in the tub. And the tub is freezing over. And the tub has nowhere to go.

For today, I flip the burgers. I turn up the radio and let the rock and roll flow over me. I work up a good sweat, and feel grateful to be alive.

Tomorrow is another day—a day turned to night. And when the light is gone, and the darkness expands, all kinds of bad things happen. What thrives in the darkness would normally be extinguished by the light.

I have to prepare myself.

There is nobody else I can rely on.

And some days, that's how I prefer it.

# CHAPTER TWO

# ORIENTATION

I find myself standing naked in the cold, the glow of the tear a shimmering wrinkle that speaks to me in bursts of electricity, humming and crackling, as the very night contracts around me. The woods are filled with the sound of air rushing through the pines, as overhead, the northern lights shift and morph from mere lines and ribbons into full curtains of color that spread out across the heavens. I am horrified to be out here like this, so vulnerable, and yet blessed to be in the presence of something that feels so holy.

How I got here, I don't know.

But this is extremely dangerous; I could freeze to death in minutes.

On the hard-packed snow next to me is a kneeling corpse, hands clasped as if in prayer. Her skin is bone white with a tint of blue, covered in a thin gloss of ice, formed as her warm body cooled in death. The dark hair pulled back tight against her scalp sparkles with hoar frost in the moonlight. Squatting down for a closer look, I recognize her as a woman from down the road. I can't remember her name, but I know her face. A perpetual frown was her default state, always a cigarette in her long, stained fingers. I never heard her speak, just saw her standing on her porch all the time, always looking out into the woods, down toward the water, up at the sky. What she was looking for, I don't know. Answers, probably. The same questions we all ask ourselves.

Why am I here?

What should I do next?

How do I get through this?

I heard stories. Everyone saw evidence of fights out here—clothes flung out into the street, sometimes freezing, like a row of miniature tents; broken bottles and windows or slashed tires and graffiti sprayed onto the hood of cars—violence that bubbled over and took residence wherever it could; an eternity of slammed doors, rattling her small house or insulating a car or truck before somebody sped away, never coming back.

And then a moment of guilt washes over me, as I remember her coming into the diner one day, hands trembling, bruises on her face, a split lip, and a swollen eye. I saw her and Margie chatting, voices raising, and then falling back again. There was a spilled glass of water, and then laughter, later the sound of a hefty thud on the counter, as I peeked out to witness a pistol lying between the two women. When Margie caught me looking, she squinted and shook her head at me, and I ducked back behind the wall, eyes wide, and kept on cooking. The following week, I'd spy that same gun on her desk, tucked under a pile of papers, so the woman didn't take it. Maybe she had another weapon of choice, or maybe she wasn't ready to do the deed. Either way, I wish I'd done something for her that day, even if it was just giving her some extra French fries on a frigid afternoon.

When you get into somebody's business out here, quite often they don't like it—preferring to suffer alone, in silence, or deal with the matter in their own way. Nobody wants to admit a weakness or addiction. Then again, people disappear all the time up here—lost in a whiteout, falling overboard while fishing, or simply ghosting in the middle of the night.

It happens.

But what did I know; I was just a kid at the time. Still one now, really. I didn't have much to offer her, self-preservation a skill we all learn.

I stare at her naked form through the falling snow, wondering why she came here, how she got out here, what drove her to make this final, desperate choice. Hitting a dead end in my mind, I notice bite marks on her arms and back, chunks bitten out of her, but the meal she could have been was left unfinished?

Why?

A smell of something rotten drifts toward me in the glow of the tear—and I'm not sure if it's coming from the other side, or from her. It's a sharp, bitter tang, with a layer of sour decay underneath, and then I notice her wounds glistening, starting to leak streams of blood down her arms and back. She seems to be warming up, melting, thawing—her flesh taking on an almost living hue, no longer so translucent and pale.

And that is when she turns her head toward me with a low creaking sound as if her spine were about to snap under the strain, her eyes growing wide with a dull, yellow glow, veins of blue spidering across her frost-covered face. When she opens her mouth, I expect her to scream, but instead she vomits a thick green moss that spews down over her chin and onto her bare chest, a cavalcade of mutating, shifting growth that spreads out over her pale thighs onto the snow beneath her. In this creeping vegetation there are tiny red dots that at first I think are somehow berries. But when they sprout legs, and chitter about with tiny feelers sensing the air, I fear they are something unnatural, birthed out of anger and regret, an expanding manifestation of dark emotions. Also squirming in the undulating mass that sprawls toward me are tiny white maggots with miniature pincers, and little yellow heads, a faint squeal emanating from their collective wriggling. As the seething mass grows and expands, threatening to engulf us both, her eyes never leave mine, boring into me with the heat of a thousand suns.

She is angry.

I take a step backward—the needling of my skin numb now, from head to toe, a scream rising in my own throat—back into something solid, and meaty, a wave of musk and urine rising to me, as if a cloud of bloody dust has been puffed into the night. A snort of hot breath warms my neck and naked back, and I'm afraid to turn around and look, waiting for the inevitable bite or goring that must be coming.

The woman hisses something that I can't make out, a cone of icy vapor expanding from her open mouth into tiny clouds that sparkle and dissipate into the darkness.

"Get out, run away," she repeats into the night air. "It's not too late for you."

And then I'm impaled from behind by the unseen beast, blood-soaked horns running through me, exploding out of my chest, lifting my feet from the snowy ground in one rapid, brutal motion.

I wake up in my room, covered in a sheen of sweat, my hands and fingers frantically probing my body for the protruding horns, the open wounds, a sensation like blood trickling in rivulets down my back and thighs. But there is nothing there. In the pale light of the bathroom mirror, I find only two tiny puckers—as if there is an old injury here, wounds long since knitted shut, healed, but not without leaving scars.

What has Sebastian gotten me into?

I can't stop thinking about the woman. And so I take a walk, down the street to her old house to see what I can find out.

We don't get much mail this far north—no way in, and no way out by land—so all letters, postcards, and packages have to be delivered by air. And then they are driven around to our tiny community, when the passes aren't closed, and shoved into mailboxes. Packages can't be left on doorstops up here, so if you don't answer the door, they leave a note, and a slip to retrieve it later, forcing you to trudge down to the post office to pick it up. Why? Because everything freezes up here. Any sort of liquid will freeze, the water in a six-pack of soda expanding inside the can, as the volume becomes greater than what the container was designed to hold. This pressure causes the can to become strained and to eventually explode. It happened to my sister at work. I heard of somebody leaving eggs in their car, and they did the same thing—froze solid, and then ruptured later. Cleaning supplies, aerosols, perfumes and colognes, liquid medicines, canned goods—all susceptible to freezing and expanding, nasty explosions. I'd seen many a graphic splatter on a doorstep, or in a car, or on the sidewalk—only to realize later it was vegetable soup, or Coca-Cola, or a bottle of Goo Gone.

When I arrive at the house, the property is enveloped in shadows, nearby streetlamps providing a paltry source of light. It's the middle of the day, but the darkness makes me feel like I'm sneaking around at three in the morning. The street is deserted, as the temperatures are dropping, and I make a mental note to make this fast. I'm bundled up and prepared, but you never know when things might go sideways in a gust of wind, a smattering of sleet, or a heavy downpouring of thick snow. I find the windows of the residence unlit, but a thin column of smoke rising up from the chimney.

My first stop? The mailbox.

There are three pieces of mail in the dented black metal box, the pole slightly askew, either from a snowplow hitting it, or perhaps a baseball bat swung by teens in a passing car. The first piece of mail is a gas bill, the second is a phone bill, the third a postcard from one of her daughters.

The card is from Seattle, and the details percolate up from somewhere in my memory, rumors of her eldest heading south, as so many do, to escape the solitude and the cold. On the front, there's a picture of the city, the Space Needle in the background, a line of mountains behind that. A large ocean liner sits docked in a bay, buildings lining the shore. The sky is awash with bright colors—lines of orange, and yellow, and rust—a sun setting over a skyline. Though when I think of Seattle, I think of rain, and Nirvana, and depression. But it looks like a bright, chipper city, and compared to this place, it probably is. What might a postcard look like from here? Probably nothing but black ink, with maybe a single streetlamp struggling to push away the darkness. My limbs stiffen, and I stamp my legs as the cold penetrates my clothing.

The card is addressed only to her mother, and it's very short, the words echoing into the expanding gloom around me. I chew on them for a few moments, trying to rationalize their presence on the card.

It says, "Get out, run away. It's not too late for you."

And though I'm already cold, a shiver ripples through me— these words so familiar, visions haunting my waking life, echoes reverberating across the empty landscape. And for a moment I consider it—the idea of running. Pack my stuff and go. Maybe my sister was right. I don't like holding the card; it feels unholy, and my witnessing it some complicit act that is part of a larger story that I can't quite see. Too many tentacles, too many frozen roots. It's all connected and I don't like it.

I place it back in the mailbox, though I know she is no longer here, no longer alive. I don't need to talk to the husband and father to know that this is true. I know what I saw in my dreams, and I know what Sebastian has told me about the woman freezing to death behind his house, torn to pieces by the wolves. I don't need a police or coroner's report to know that she is gone, and gone violently, from this cursed place.

I creep up to the house on the snowy walkway, leaving unavoidable footprints, and trudge around the side through a knee-deep drift, trying to stay out of sight. There are three garbage cans lined up one after another, the lid of one blown open, filled all the way to the top with beer cans and empty bottles of liquor, all blanketed in a light dusting of snow.

When I peer in the frosted window, there is only the flickering glow of the television set in the living room, a large man sucked into an aging, brown leather recliner, his head shaved, wearing faded blue jeans and a dark sweatshirt with *The Punisher* logo on it. The room is every room up here—dirty, damaged furniture arranged around a source of heat, in this case a pot belly stove, and a large television set, over sixty inches for sure. It is the same dark, depressing space that so many inhabit up here. A nearly empty bottle of cheap bourbon lingers on the table next to him, what looks to be a local favorite—Very Old Barton. A plastic tumbler rests in his hand, several beer cans on the ground by the chair, spilling out of a small, metal trashcan that looks exhausted from overuse. On the coffee table in front of him, there are only two things—an ashtray overflowing with cigarette butts and a handful of hunting knives, some sheathed and some not.

The man laughs, having the time of his life, fat and happy, his drunken eyes sparkling liquid as he chortles in the darkness. His daughter is gone, the son as well, if the rumors are true. His wife has walked into the wilderness, dying alone, frozen to death, as her heart broke, and her mind followed it into a pit of despair.

To him, these are thorns that have been removed from his side, these are distractions that no longer push into his orbit, weights that have been lifted, so that he might be free again.

On the kitchen table are bags of potato chips, pretzels, and cheese popcorn. In the living room, a new rifle—a Winchester magnum—still in the box, leans into the corner, with several boxes of ammunition on the ground next to it.

I wonder what this man might taste like—something rotten, sour, and putrid, no doubt. My mouth goes dry, stomach churning at the thought. And I have a moment where I think about what Sebastian has done, and where it got him. I think about this history of the sin-eater, and the absolution of those who needed it the most. I ask myself if they deserved it. Or if maybe in death they should face the consequences they may have avoided in life. I think about a lot of things, and then I walk home, unsure of what to do next.

On the way home, I am lost in these thoughts when a chorus of frantic shouts from a side street breaks me from my reverie. At this hour, in this weather, it could be anything from a drunken brawl to mischievous kids. With my curiosity piqued, I pop around the corner, unsure of quite what to expect.

Three shadowy figures are standing beneath a lone streetlight in a tight circle, each of them swinging and kicking wildly at an object on the ground. Each blow elicits a strange yelp from the prone victim that clearly isn't human, bringing more shouts of encouragement from the boys with sticks.

"Hey, what the fuck are you guys doing?" I yell, as I walk toward them, realizing as I close the distance—seeing more clearly the bats and ax handles in their possession—that approaching unarmed may not have been the best of plans.

They stop in unison at the sound of my voice and collectively turn toward me. It's then I notice the fourth kid sitting off to one side in a snow bank, outside the circle of light. With their bundled-up faces, I don't recognize any of them, but even in the shadows from the overhead lamp, I can see that the overweight one's white pant legs are smeared with blood.

I stand my ground with caution, keeping enough footsteps between us to make my getaway should things go sour.

"It attacked us," the tall one said, out of breath, an aluminum bat in his right hand, tip dragging on the icy pavement. "We were coming back from the shop and it just jumped out and bit Randy," he says, pointing to the fourth one, the smallest in the bunch. Moving closer, I see all four are boys, about my age—a few years older, a few years younger. The one sitting in the drift is a kid with short blonde hair, his hat in the snow, feathers erupting from fresh tears in his down jacket, blood smudged across his cheek. He looks about two breaths away from bursting into tears.

"I didn't do nuthin," he says. "We were just walkin'. That fuckin' mutt came out of nowhere."

I look toward the target of their rage and see that the dark lump on the ground is actually a German Shepherd. It lies nearly still, panting and wheezing, limbs broken, head turned to one side, one eye swollen shut, blood pooling beneath it, appearing almost black against the white snow. As I step closer, I see it is laboring to breathe, but it's still alive. I reach out to help somehow, but a snarl on its lips, teeth bared to the night, tells me to keep my distance.

"Jesus Christ, guys," I say, scrutinizing each of them for a long moment, each one avoiding eye contact. "Do you always walk around with baseball bats and sticks? You just looking for trouble or what?"

"Man, this time of year, you never fucking know," the fat kid says, sweat running down his nose, seeping through his ski mask, choosing to keep it on and stay covered up.

I try to take it all in, looking up and down the road, but there is nobody around. Just these idiots, the bats probably for the mailboxes, or anything else they can bend or break. Which doesn't surprise me. People do stupid things then they get bored, and up here the restless kids are often resentful, isolated, and sick of being cold.

"That's Rascal, anyway," the youngest says, nodding toward the dog.

I look over and see a collar around its neck, and a thick chain running off a few feet, the anchor pulled out of the ground. The poor animal was chained up outside somewhere. I realize that I know this dog, and it's the meanest, loudest, nastiest creature I've ever had the misfortune to run across. To be fair, the owner is a piece of shit too, leaving the dog chained up every time he goes anywhere—to the bar, the grocery store, the post office. He's never home, and when he is, he's usually drunk or passed out. I'm surprised the old mutt hasn't frozen to death, to be honest. I feel bad for him, but I also remember him breaking loose a few weeks ago, and how everyone that was outside at the time ran indoors as it snapped and barked and charged around town. If his owner hadn't come out sooner, I think somebody would have shot him down in the street. The dog, I mean, not the man. Though that may have been the better choice, in the end. Many a night I've been walking home from work and had the dog scare the crap out of me, leaping out from between the houses, nearly throttling itself on the chain, as it flipped over backward, trying to take a piece out of me. So I get where they're coming from.

Damn dog.

But this is pretty cruel.

"Shit," I say, turning toward them. "Well, you, big guy, finish him off then; just make it quick. I don't know if he's rabid or crazy or just hungry, but there's no turning back now. Put him out of his misery."

He hesitates, then steels himself before walking closer to the poor animal with his bat overhead, prepared to hit him again.

"That's not going to work," I say. "We could be here for twenty minutes, that dog's got a thick skull, and that bat is dented already," I say, and he turns to look at the weapon for damage. "Use that," I say, and point to a large stone sitting at the edge of the road.

"I can't pick that up," he says.

"Fuck you can," I say. "You all started this, you all finish it. All four of you shitheads, pick it up and do it together."

"I don't wanna," the youngest one says, and now he *is* crying, sobbing, as snot bubbles out of his nose.

"I don't either," I say, "but he's suffering, and whatever he did to deserve this shitty life, his cruel owner, and this messed-up town, let's end it."

And we walk over to the boulder, staying wide of the immobilized dog as it struggles to snap at us despite being in the throes of death. I feel the agony and sorrow in its suffering, still angry despite its pain, whimpering as we move away, breaking my heart, no matter how terrible a dog it could have been. We pry the rock off of the frozen ground, and then the three of us lift it up to waist height, the youngest kid helping to guide us over, until we are standing above the creature, all sweating, some crying, the fat one out of breath, asking ourselves what we did to deserve this horrible moment.

"One . . ." I start.

"Two . . ."

"Three . . ."

And we drop the rock on its head with a dull thud and a muffled crack. The street goes as quiet as a graveyard.

The biggest kid turns toward the forest, stumbles a few steps and vomits into the bushes. I can't bear to look at any of them, so I look at the body of the dog, my stomach turning over. I've seen worse. Unfortunately, I've seen much worse.

"Get out of here," I say. "I'll clean this up and bury the body."

They scramble to grab their sticks and bats and stagger away from me, unsettled, and still weeping a bit, blood splattering their pants and boots. And now, mine too.

"I hate this place," I say to the dead canine and sit down next to it, an idea forming in my head.

I manage to roll the rock off of the dog and to the edge of the road, out of the way of tomorrow's traffic. It takes every bit of energy I've got left, and I thought I was already emotionally drained. After a bit of searching, slowly catching my breath, I find a faded, torn tarp around the side of the nearest house, which I can use to drag the dog up the road and over behind Sebastian's old house. The burnt husk of what was his house is now covered in a dusting of snow, purifying and sanctifying what I know underneath is death and betrayal. I try not to think too much about whether or not his remains lie at the center of this funeral pyre, and instead focus on dragging the mutilated animal toward the tear, where I collapse, sitting on the cold ground again, the golden filament flickering in the dark. This is the least I can do for the mutt.

I know the other kids were just defending themselves, but still, it's not something I ever wanted to see happen, even if it does present me with an opportunity. When we hunt, or fish, we respect the kill—always trying for a clean shot and instant death. If we don't get it right, it's up to us to track it down and finish it off as soon as we can, whether it's a deer, a rabbit, a pheasant, or a trout. You do it quick, and you don't fuck around. It's that mercy that separates us from the animals, aware of what we do, being grateful for the sustenance. And then next time, we do better. Or we don't get the shot.

Sebastian had just barely started to teach me, so there is quite a bit I don't understand about this process. My only experience was with Balto, and he was the sweetest dog I ever had. This guy, he was quite the opposite—abused, angry, hungry, and scared—he was a scourge of the town, and I'm not sad to see him gone. But I never want to see an animal suffer. Or a person for that matter.

But maybe he can teach me something here.

I know he was once a good dog, and that over the years he got meaner, and more violent, turning rabid in his desire to bite anyone and anything. And I don't blame him. You learn to hate the boot that kicks you, and then eventually you grow to hate all boots, everything that is black and leather. It's all the same—pain, and suffering. So why not lash out at it first? Get it, before it gets you.

So can I handle this?

It's more than Balto.

But less than a human being.

Kneeling in the snow, I take a Snickers bar out of my pocket, and then slowly inhale, before biting into the candy, a favorite of mine for as long as I can remember. It starts out with the rich milk chocolate, which melts in my mouth, before quickly turning into the thick sweetness of the caramel and thick chew of the nougat. The crunch of the peanuts gives the candy bar a satisfying depth, chomping and crunching before swallowing my first bite.

This is nothing like Balto.

The chocolate becomes rank and bitter, like coffee left out in the rain, watered down with dirt and grime, a layer of oily slime on the top. The caramel turns to sinew, something meaty and foul, the sensation in my mouth causing bile to rise up in my throat, strands caught in my teeth. The nougat transforms into flesh, a thick pelt that I cannot penetrate with my teeth, instead forced to swallow it whole, choking it down. The peanuts become fermented soybeans, turning ripe and sour, a thin coat of white foam appearing on the edges of my mouth as it continues to rot while I try to force it down my gullet.

I swallow it all down with a low moan, my stomach churning in response. It does not sit well, threatening to rebel.

I look at the dead dog lying next to me and shiver.

"You were a very bad dog. Bad dog," I say, laughing, as I try to choke down the rest of the bar, tears emerging at the edge of my eyes. In times of stress, I tend to joke around, but the laughter is short-lived as I am in a great amount of pain—muscles clenching, stomach rolling, my back aching as if under a great strain. But I understand the creature better, everything it has been through, the slow journey from innocent pup, to faithless dog, to senile mongrel. It's tragic and bruises my soul. It didn't happen overnight; this was something the man did over time, on purpose, shit rolling downhill. I make a mental note of this, hoping I can do something about it later.

And I may have ruined candy bars forever. Which upsets me a great deal.

With the last bite, I gulp it down, grabbing a handful of snow off the ground to try and cleanse my palette, just a hint of cherry and vanilla at the end. Which seems to come out of nowhere, flavors that don't make sense to me. A tear runs down my cheek as I realize once upon a time there was a poor little puppy dog that needed a new home, and what he got was one long, dark, abusive night after another. I feel bad for the guy.

And then I start to retch.

There is a great rippling beneath my skin, and I bend over, clutching my gut, my back arching as I open my mouth. My hands stiffen and curl back, tightening up. From deep inside me there is a rumbling, a snarling and snapping of teeth, as if a pack of wolves is attacking my insides, fighting to get out. There is a war going on inside me, and I'm not sure what collateral damage might befall me. Up and down my spine a hot wire of pain electrifies my back, heat rushing over my skin, like a fever, pushing me into a space where the world floats, and everything trembles, the taste of acid in my mouth.

I can feel the squirming, up through my chest, pushing my lungs apart, squeezing my heart against my sternum. It's in my throat, choking me, forcing its way out of my body, my jaw threatening to dislocate. When I bend over, ready to vomit out what feels like a seething mass of rabid beasts, a strange thing happens.

Out pops a fluffy white rabbit, with cherry-red eyes, a whiff of vanilla in the air. It takes one look at me, twitches its nose, wiggles its ears, and then hops off into the woods, avoiding the tear, never looking back.

What the hell?

# CHAPTER THREE

# SOMETHING ISN'T RIGHT

I sit in the cold for a few minutes, knowing that I can't stay out here too long, but also aware that something has gone wrong. This isn't how it's supposed to happen. The dog was a violent cur. It had bitten many locals, torn apart people's fences and homes, and should have been put down a long time ago.

And yet . . .

There was a moment, when I first tasted its spirit, its essence, that stood out from the bitter flavors that ringed my mouth with disgust. It was that slight pop of cherry and vanilla, and with it, some imagery from many years ago—a litter of puppies, all fuzzy and sweet, their breath like little furry angels, their tiny sharp teeth nipping at each other, but a danger to no one, innocence embodied. We are all born blank slates, I think, and what comes next, how we are treated—that's part of how we become who we are. It's nature versus nurture, the genetics and breeding of each species lending us certain tendencies, but also the domesticity and evolution coming in the ways that we are raised and treated.

The wind rushes through the trees, and overhead the lights drift and sway, colors merging and overlapping, the northern lights brushing blue and green across the expanding night, a swath of pink lining the horizon, just over the mountains.

I close my eyes and commune with the benevolent giants as they dance across the sky, offering up warnings and wisdom in equal amounts. I ask for guidance as I try to explain the history of what has happened here, certain that Sebastian has communicated this before, in this exact spot most likely, speaking to these drifting colors as they took on the rough outline of whales and seals, morphing into one fin and tail after another, and then back into abstract shapes and colors. And I am rewarded with a vision, something to help guide me on my way.

I see a field of yellow flowers in the summertime, the high grasses still, as overhead something soars on the thermals, eagle or hawk most likely, the sunlight a blessing across the land.

There is a colony of rabbits near the edge of the woods, a mother hare in brown, with several little kits nearby, twitching their pink noses as they chew on clover. She is on full alert, her ears up, every now and then leaning over to take a bite, and then her head is back up, ears turning this way and that like a radar shield. She is watching out for trouble.

On the other side of the field there is a band of coyotes, the mother chewing on berries, as her three pups finish off the remains of a deer that was taken down by the pack earlier that day. There isn't much left on the creature, but they harvest what they can, gnawing on the bones in a lazy manner, as flies dart about.

At some point, the respective groupings lie down in the shade and take a nap.

All except for one rabbit and one coyote. They are curious, and awake, looking for adventure, and so they sneak away through the grasses and end up meeting in the middle of the clearing.

At first they are shocked and startled, back on their hind legs, the bunny ready to flee, the coyote pup wondering if he is indeed full, or perhaps still hungry. They tremble next to each other, uncertain what to do next. This is new to them. And then a strange thing happens. They both nudge forward, sniffing each other, and then suddenly take off, running around the field as if possessed by demons. The pup chases the kit, and then when cornered next to an outcropping of three large boulders, the bunny turns around and chases the coyote, startling the little guy, who dashes away, surprised by her sudden playful aggression. When they have disturbed enough dragonflies and gnats, they curl up in a ball in the middle of the field and fall asleep. They are comforted by the similarity in their small bodies, their fluffy fur, their sparkling eyes, not yet bitter and suspicious. They see more in common than they do their differences.

Later, when they are called by their respective mothers—a howl and bark from one side, a growl and hiss from the other—they dash off, never to see each other again. The pack will move east, as the rabbits stay put, a bit west.

This is not the first time such a thing has happened.

And then the aurora borealis shows me another sight, something much darker.

There is a single brown bear rumbling through the forest at the base of the mountains, as fall turns to winter, snow starting to drift down. She is angry. She has seen great violence in her long life—her cubs shot by humans when they were merely rummaging for food in the middle of the long night, deer eviscerated and left in the woods, limbs hacked off, antlers shorn, blood pooling into icy puddles. She has seen salmon torn apart by her own claws and teeth, the orange meat savory and sweet—eyeballs swallowed whole, spines left in the dirt. She has eaten grubs and worms and maggots out of the carcasses of dead animals, out of the rotten husks of downed trees. Everywhere around her, the bear sees death, so she responds in kind.

Eventually, she has no family left, shot or sick with disease. Whenever she encounters life of any kind she roars and attacks, animal or human, leading to a flurry of arrows, or a stray bullet wound here and there.

When she is old, and sick, and dying herself, she collapses in the same field that once held court to a tiny rabbit and her friend, the coyote pup. She is exhausted and ready to move on. The last thing she feels is a nipping at her fur, a tentative inquiry, followed by a rush of growling and snapping teeth. She is not surprised. Everything out here is death, she thinks, there is nothing good in the world.

*May my diseased flesh make them vomit and collapse; may I take as many of them with me as I can carry to the great beyond,* she thinks.

She does not remember being a bear cub, or the hunters that spared her mother and her kin. She has forgotten the calls of, "Hey, bear," that echoed through the forest, the children coming home from school, exploring, but aware of the dangers, trying to scare them off, looking to avoid trouble. She does not recall the way she and her family piled together in the cold winter—brothers and sisters next to her massive mother and father in an effort to stay warm through their hibernation. No, none of this comes back to her. Her heart is black as coal, solid as a rock, dead for a very long time now.

But once, she was innocent and full of life.

Once, she held wonder like cupped water in the palm of her meaty paws.

It was snuffed out by greedy men and the cruelty of nature.

When the tiny rabbit passed, it was an old brown hare, and if I had been present at its demise, it would have tasted like cotton candy. When the coyote pup died, having fathered three litters, mangy and skinny but content to let it all go, he would have tasted like caramel and brown sugar. The bear? She was black and oily, bitter and sour, a tangy decay bubbling over my tongue like a rotting, erupting fungus.

But at the end of the swallow, there would be a hint of sweetness—mint and juniper, a crisp, refreshing note.

I open my eyes and think of the possibilities—who we are, where we came from, and the ways the world comforts and crushes alike. I think of the opportunities we are given and the choices we make. Which beast do we choose to feed—love or hate? And what then do we become?

For a moment, I look at the trees, skeletal in the winter, their branches like bony fingers. They are nails, sticking up from the ground, spiky and sharp. And I can be a hammer if I want to.

Or, I can be something else entirely.


In a snap of panic, I realize that there have been eyes on me for some time now—neighbors in the shadows, coworkers on the periphery, friends right in front of me—my actions starting to draw attention. I have not been nearly as sneaky and devious as I thought.

Walking home from the visions I have just seen, the tear widening, when it should have been closed, I realize that it is only a matter of time. What went through the tear—whatever Sebastian birthed—should have closed it, bought us time, perhaps enough to last us until the *next* long night, nearly a year away. But no, it didn't. The tear was closed. I see it in my mind's eye, the pulsing, drifting lights showing me so many things, and then it immediately ripped back open again. What was sent though certainly went on to do its job, to battle what lay on the other side, whatever was waiting there a challenging adversary. But the actions of this community—the way that the creature was conceived and torn out of Sebastian like some urgent c-section gone horribly wrong—has placed a stain on this town, which continues to spill outward, seeping into the cracked, frozen ground, as it infects one person after another. It is a plague, an infestation.

This cannot continue.

What Sebastian has been doing isn't working.

There must be another way.

As I walk home, the snow drifting down to me, wind whipping around the houses like ghostly race horses in mad pursuit of some distant prize, I can see now what I missed before. And I realize how things are going to change.

I can picture Margie with her eyes opening wide as she sorts silverware and fills napkin containers, the image of the white aphid I coughed up reflecting in their metal surface. She mutters blessings and protections under her breath, in three different languages, reaching out to a variety of old gods. I can see Oliver just behind her, peering into the pass-through, squinting behind a puff of smoke, as he chops onions with a chef's knife, head tilted to one side, a frown working its way over his face. They understand the role that Sebastian played, but they don't like these ancient rituals and how they might come home to roost. No, keep it at a distance, they think. Up on the hill, down the road, out of reach, away from the rest of us, closer to the woods and the mountains. Don't invite it in, don't palaver with it, don't commiserate with such unknown forces, for they might corrupt one's soul, a blight upon what meager crops we aim to raise within each one of us—something tender, in need of our mercy.

I understand their fear, for I once had it as well.

Hands thrust deep into my coat pockets, the freezing wind makes my eyes water, and I remember more now, see it as it truly happened.

I picture Yara standing outside of Sebastian's cabin, a Tupperware bowl of chili in a sturdy bag, the container still resonating heat and spice as she raises her hand to knock on the door. But she never lowers it, never knocks. Instead, she walks away with flushed skin and tears forming in her eyes. She is afraid of Sebastian, and always has been, though she went to great lengths to hide that terror, to spare his feelings, to try and befriend this hermit, this sin-eater. And now that I have taken on his qualities, watching as we commune over the spirit of my beloved Balto, the pink fluff rising in the air, taking flight, she steps away. She understands, but she is still afraid. She is afraid for her soul, and for mine as well, even as she crosses herself and prays over the memories of her newly departed mother. Yes, she will place the coins on her deceased family's eyes, but that doesn't mean she likes the rituals. She will startle awake at night, visions of glimmering gold eyes and flickering flames, hoping and praying for pillars and clouds and pearly gates to wash away the uncertainty.

I take a deep breath as I approach my house, the world silent, my thoughts ricocheting like pinballs around my aching skull.

I see the boys, on their way home, horrified by the dog we have put out of its misery, but also curious about what I will do with the carcass. They have seen death out here as well—in the gutted deer and its vultured remains, as well as in the skeletal fish spines and tails down by the water's edge. They have lost relatives and pets, spending many a sleepless night staring off into the long, icy darkness, one hour after another unfolding into something quite unknown. They've spent hours spinning the tip of a hunting knife on their index finger, drawing a drop of blood, every gun in their tiny houses accounted for as they lay awake staring at the ceiling. The location of each weapon was like a blueprint unfurled upon a tabletop. I see them creep back toward the edge of the forest and beyond the burnt frame of Sebastian's destroyed cabin, watching as I cough up a fluffy white rabbit, with cherry-red eyes.

The rumors will spread, if they haven't already. I imagine Margie and Oliver chatting, as Oliver lights up another smoke, and Margie places one hand on her hip, shaking her head from side to side, filled with worry. I imagine Yara down at the grocery store, bursting into tears when she drops a bottle of orange juice, the glass shattering all over the dirty floor, coating her with shards and sticky fluid. The shopkeeper will come over and help her, asking her if she is okay, and she will confess to her knowledge, and her fear of the great unknown. I imagine the youngest of the boys waking up in the middle of the night, screaming, as his parents try to calm him down, amidst rants and pleas filled with feral dogs, alabaster rabbits, and glimmering golden tears that smell of sulfur and creosote.

Much like Sebastian, I don't really have a choice. When they approach me to ask for my help, and they will, I won't turn them away. That is part of the job, the responsibility. But this time it may be different. I am not Sebastian, and my blessings?

They will be doled out in a way that amplifies the righteous, and condemns the wicked.

*For thine is the kingdom, and the power, and the glory, for ever.*

A smile crosses my face, and I reach out to open the front door to my home.

A reckoning is coming.


It is only three days later when I am finally approached by somebody. Her name is Victoria Johnson, and she lives on the north side of town in a quaint little cottage painted salmon with crisp, white trim. It looks like it might be made of spun sugar or confectionery wafers, windows framed with cutouts of hearts and suns and moons. She lives a little closer to town, across the street from what used to be Sebastian's house, the frame a pile of burnt timber and ashes now.

I've seen her come into the diner a few times, a bright pink knit hat on top of her head, a fuzzy ball topping it off. Won't lose *her* in a storm, that's for sure. She moves slowly, her puffy light blue coat running all the way down to her knees. Her cheeks are ruddy, with a tan cardigan sweater over a white turtleneck, a silver charm necklace in the shape of a heart. No doubt pictures of her husband, or children, are nestled inside. Her face is weathered, but full of life. She has looked like this for as long as I can remember. I've heard some kids calling her Grandma V, and she often carries a paperback with her—Agatha Christie or maybe John Grisham. I worry about her walking around, sometimes with a cane, but most days not. The ice and dogs and snowmobiles—she's just one day-drunk-jerk afternoon away from some idiot running her over, or a spill that could break her into a thousand tiny pieces. But she perseveres, and I'm always happy to see her in here.

Most of the time she gets a chicken salad sandwich on whole wheat toast. She drinks a Diet Coke (no ice) with a fruit plate alongside it, avoiding the French fries and onion rings. Watching her girlish figure, she tells Margie, every time the fruit is questioned. And she'll take a cup of whatever soup we have, most days, to shake off the chill—no preference over tomato or chicken noodle or beef barley. Quite often I've also seen her ask for a slice of pie—sometimes begging Margie to split it with her, which she usually does. Who doesn't want a bit of warm cherry pie with a scoop of vanilla ice cream on top?

We've never really spoken, just the occasional, "Howdy!" or "How are you?" or "Cold enough for you?" between two neighbors. Sometimes just a nod of the head and a wave if we're too bundled up to stop, our voices muffled behind scarves and ski masks.

So when she comes in for the lunch shift looking especially frazzled—her hair poking out from under her hat, taken off in a rush, makeup a little crooked, eyes darting this way and that, cheeks flushed—I know something is wrong. She's looking for something or somebody, and she's in a bit of a panic, from what I can see. She doesn't even sit down, just walks up to the counter, the lunch rush gone, leaning over to whisper something to Margie, whose face runs the gamut of emotions—shock to sadness to curiosity to understanding. Margie nods her head, and then says something back to her, telling her to sit down. She gets the visibly shaken woman a cup of coffee and sets it before her, and the poor old woman raises it up, her hands shaking furiously, spilling liquid everywhere. Mrs. Johnson mutters a little gasp and sets it down quickly, holding back tears. Margie wipes up the spill as she hands the woman her note pad, pointing to it with her index finger, stabbing it a few times with the tip, glancing my way quickly, and then back to the shaking woman.

We get a few orders in as some high school kids I know stroll in loud and covered in snow—burgers all around, fries too—so I'm busy flipping and buttering buns and salting fries for the next fifteen minutes. When I look up again, the woman is gone.

It's not until the end of my shift—as Oliver loudly comes in the back door shouting, "I'm not a bear," (an old joke of his) that causes me to reply, "Hey, bear,"—that Margie takes me aside, asking me into her office. For a moment I think I'm fired—running situations over and over again in my head—burnt fries tossed in the garbage, wasting valuable, costly food; burgers that were still frozen in the middle, unhappy customers sending them back; butter left out overnight, turning sour, dotted with dead flies in the morning, dumped into the garbage with disgust.

"Kallik, have a seat," she says as she lumbers behind the desk, its surface covered in wrinkled papers, yellow legal pads, and stapled invoices—but no gun to be seen.

"Everything okay?" I ask, still covered in grease, my arms dotted with tiny burns, my brow a sheen of sweat, as I sit down in one of the two padded folding chairs.

"It's fine, it's fine . . . no worries," she says. "But I need to ask you some questions. Close that door behind you, would you, please?"

I lean over and do that, and then return to the chairs that sit there mocking me, as if I don't know what I've done, what I've become—and why I'm here.

"You saw Victoria, Mrs. Johnson, this morning, right? She comes in all the time, sweet woman, always tips well?"

"Chicken salad sandwich on whole wheat toast," I say, nodding, and Margie smiles.

"Yep, that's the one. Pink hat and all."

I smile and nod back.

"I . . . I'm not sure how to put this so I'm just going to blurt it out. Sebastian is gone. I know that, you know that, and how it happened . . . well, come the thaw, there will probably be questions, as well as consequences. I didn't like it one bit. He was a good man, as far as I knew."

I keep nodding my head, my lips tight now, as I remember what happened.

"You spent time with him, right? You knew him pretty well? Did things out there—chopping wood and whatnot?" she asks.

"I did. A nice guy. I know Yara was close to him as well."

"That's right," she says, and I know she's thinking about chili, but I let it go with a tight smile.

"What's your question, Margie?"

She takes a deep breath, and asks, "You know what he did then, right? The services he provided to this community?"

I think about everything I've seen Sebastian do, the rumors beyond that, and all that I both desired and feared in these noble, cursed acts. Part of me wanted to shake off the shackles of responsibility. Part of me longed for anything meaningful and exciting, to break up the monotony of the long winter. In the end, did I really have a choice?

"He'd been here a long time, hard not to know."

"You ever see him do it?" she asks, her eyes widening a bit, a curious sparkle in them, somewhere between starlight and glistening motor oil.

"Once. Aside from whatever happened that night in the storm. I'm not sure what I saw exactly, as his cabin burned to the ground," I say, starting to get angry, picturing it all on fire, as he burned to a crisp inside.

Margie closes her eyes and leans forward, rubbing them in circles with the tips of her fingers.

"That's going to leave a mark on this place," she mutters. "Fucking assholes," she whispers, forgetting I'm in the room for a moment, and then looking back up. "It didn't have to be like that," she says.

"I know."

"But Victoria, Mrs. Johnson, she . . . just lost her husband, Anthony. Nice guy, didn't come in much—had a bum leg, and arthritis, mostly worked with the research facility, something online. I'm not sure—crunching numbers, tracking the whales. I never quite understood it all. He just passed last night, and she's rather upset, as you might imagine. He was no spring chicken, but still. She knew Sebastian, and now is at a loss."

"I understand," I say. "And you want to know if I can help, is that it?"

"Yes, Kallik. It is. I don't know how it works, how close you all were, if he taught you anything, or if I'm just wasting our time here, but I had to ask. She's a sweet woman, and she's worried her husband is going to burn in hell. She wants absolution, and I'm not sure if you can provide it."

"I'm not sure either," I say. "I did it once, with him, when Balto passed, but there is so much I don't understand. We didn't have time . . ." I say, and trail off as I'm overcome by a wave of emotions.

When you lose somebody, you never know when it'll pop up, when that grief will show, at the oddest times, triggered by so many random elements. Could be something a person says, could be a cologne or perfume, could be a song on the radio, or some stupid catch phrase your old man used to say.

*Shit fire and save matches.*

*You're as useless as tits on a boar hog.*

*You look rode hard and put up wet.*

Outside, I can hear Oliver banging pots and pans around, which means we must have customers, and this is his subtle way of getting our attention.

"Shoot, I'm sorry," she says, standing up. "No rest for the wicked. Can you go talk to her, please? See what you can do?"

She hands me a piece of paper from her waitress pad, with the woman's name, address, and phone number on it.

"Sure, Margie. I'll go see her right away. Maybe I can help."

And at that, I can see the relief wash over her, as she opens the door and yells at Oliver, out into the restaurant in a flash, the smell of onions and grease wafting in.

I mean, I can't make things any worse, right?

CHAPTER FOUR

# MAKING THINGS WORSE

M y shift over, I wander outside, bundled up to withstand the elements, always worried about freezing to death— the arctic cocoon we're in filled with sharp edges and numbing distractions. How the human body works at all is a mystery to me—the ways we create life, and give birth, so fragile at every step along the way. The miraculous feats we are capable of—whether it's superhuman athletes, the perseverance of the strong-willed, or the ingenuity of the human spirit—never cease to amaze me.

And then I think about how often we throw it all away, turn on each other, or hunt the land with greed in our hearts, and I want to burn it all to the ground.

As I plod along against the wind, head down, watching my steps on the icy road, I'm thinking about my mother, and how I hardly see her these days. I miss her, and at the same time, can feel her presence wrapped around me like a heavy, faded blanket—comforting and smothering at the same time. I want to ask her for advice, but know that this is way beyond her. And the advice she might offer? It's the kind of advice you offer somebody at a regular job, dealing with normal issues, in a standard way. But for me, it's like telling me to put a Band-Aid on a severed arm; to just *buck up bucky* as a demon pushes through the tear; to *sleep on it* as specters circle my bed, chanting ancient incantations that entrap me forever. So no. I don't think there is much she can do here, but that doesn't mean that I don't think of her, or wish that she *could* help me.

I think about my sister for a moment, the ways that we are so similar, and yet, entirely different. We're blood after all, and in my actions I can see her reactions—a smirk, a frown, a laugh, a growl. She's so far away right now that her presence is more of an echo. But I still wish she were here, as she knows me better than anyone. She's seen the horrors of the woods, the way the cold kills, the dangers all around us—and she takes it all very seriously. She would not be surprised by my abilities, though she'd probably just hit me over the head and pack me up like a suitcase, and then head south, far away from all this, before she'd let me spend the rest of my life absolving the sins of this community. Then again, I don't think she's ever seen that rip, that tear. She might understand if she did.

But she's more concrete than my father—so little known of him, rumors of abuse, so few yearbook pictures of him, the same elongated face as me, his ears sticking out, but his eyes with that same long gaze, as if looking off into the future and horrified by what has been seen. In the group photos of the ROTC, I can hardly make out his features—the uniform oddly formal—and so he remains a mystery to me, another shadow in a long line of shadows that ring the periphery of my vision, always at a distance. I wonder which of my attributes come from him—my big heart or my quick temper, my love of animals or my fear of nature, my independence or my need for validation? I don't know, and probably never will. It haunts me, though.

I decide to walk to the woman's house right away, Mrs. Johnson, to see if this is something we can set in motion, uncertain of the rules and rituals, trying to remember what Sebastian told me, fearful that her dead husband might move on quickly, if he has little to worry over. He may be ready to go, little holding him back, and she'll want to make sure he's protected, blessed before he makes the long voyage to wherever he's going. I'm hoping he's a good man, but you never know. Nobody's perfect, so there will certainly be some lingering darkness in him, some tainted beliefs, and unsavory deeds done under the cover of darkness. We all have our skeletons.

Headlights drift past me, up and down the street, fishtailing on the icy patches, wind gusting, and then fading, while I contemplate what comes after.

Is there really a God, the imagery of pearly gates and white clouds, a man more like Santa than Zeus, harps and sunlight, and everyone you've ever known or loved gathered in a group to greet you? Doesn't seem likely to me, too much of a pipe dream, too much fiction written into the Bible for my taste. Something there, certainly, but not that caricature.

Is it more like Valhalla, the old Norse mythology, with a hall of slain warriors who live there in peace under the watchful gaze of Odin—a glorious palace roofed with shields, where the soldiers feast on the gamey meat of a boar that is slaughtered daily, made whole again each evening? Drinking and fighting and camaraderie, as they wait for the Ragnarok to descend? Seems unlikely.

Or is it closer to home, the Inuit beliefs in a cold upper world filled with famine and a hot underworld, where there is plenty of warmth and abundance? A life lived in squalor and lacking purpose might delay the transcendence, whereas a violent death leads to a quicker transference? I contemplate myths and rumors of the elderly walked out into the cold and left to die. I don't know what's true, but it sounds questionable as well.

Is it more like reincarnation—the sin-eating of Sebastian cleansing any soul, no matter how corrupt and rotten—rewarding those who sought enlightenment with a more glorious rebirth, punishing those who didn't learn, forcing them to repeat lessons over and over again until the individual evolves and can finally ascend to a higher state of being? Buddhists, Hindus, and Sikhs—maybe they have it right.

I shudder in the cold, as I let these images wash over me—gold and foliage and ice and rebirth. Allah is Jesus is Buddha is Love. Maybe they're all right, and maybe they're all wrong. Maybe it's all the same.

Maybe there's nothing.

But the idea that there is no purpose, nothing after we die, no rhyme or reason, nothing supernatural or spectacular or karmic in the afterlife? Well that's just too bleak for me. And so I let the confusion and uncertainty float around me like heavy clouds, confident that I can navigate these rough waters and find a way to help those who are in need of such services.

When the white van pulls up alongside me, I hardly notice it, the drifts of snow clouding my vision, wind roaring in my ears as the storm picks up, and I try to walk north to Mrs. Johnson's house, my head down, braving the elements. I don't hear the door slide open, and there are no shouts from inside either, merely a handful of men in dark snowsuits, goggles reflecting what little light descends from the streetlamps, their hands on me before I even know what's happening. Muffled words are shouted, and although I can't understand them, their intentions are pretty clear.

I'm to go with them, somebody has beckoned. And as I'm shoved inside and we work our way up the mountain, I have an idea who it is. The rumors rush back to me, and I think about the troll on the hill, the goat at the pinnacle of the range, the dark shadow that floats high above our town. I've never seen this man, only the aftermath of his violence, rumors of his barbaric sense of justice. And then one more detail floats to me, something I heard in the diner, whispered across the counter and between the booths, a story that perhaps he was sick—maybe cancer or heart disease—dying on the icy ridge, as he gazed down upon us mortals, filled with hatred and vengeance, driven by greed.

In us he sees waste, he sees futility, he sees mediocrity. And that's nothing he wants anywhere near him, no infection he wants to catch, no disability to slow him down. No, he wants only the best, and if his time is coming, it's no surprise that he's escorting me up to grant him clemency. He certainly relishes his strength, the ways he has pushed back, taken what he wanted, and driven others out. But now, as he gets ready to pass, perhaps other fears are bubbling up to the surface, worried about retribution, or what might come after. Whatever his idea of hell, does it wait for him somewhere, in some form?

I don't know.

And neither does he.

Mrs. Johnson will have to wait, it seems.

I'm needed elsewhere.


I've never been this high up the mountain, not on this road anyway. We've already passed through several gates, all of them heavy wrought iron, opened by a remote, or a code keyed into a panel on the side of the road, cameras popping up on the periphery, the woods thickening, the incline increasing. The van struggles and slips, even in low gear with studded snow tires on, but I keep my mouth shut, the men around me giving off a primal heat, something feral and barely contained. They're either hungry to tear me apart, or fearful of what might happen if I'm not what I am rumored to be.

I open my mouth once, to ask what is going on, and am greeted with a backhand across my face, splitting my lip, blood running across my teeth. The only reason I'm not hurt worse is the padding from layers of winter headgear soften the blow. And as I gaze into my attacker's eyes, they glitter a diseased brown, and I can tell he wants to hit me again, not satisfied with the results, my pain not enough, my reaction not satisfying, but his companion turns to him, placing a hand on his shoulder.

"Easy, we have to deliver him in one piece. He has work to do."

And the man leans back, fists still clenched, barely restrained. Four black shadows rippling with tension and uncertainty, eager to break something, to take something beautiful and make it ugly again. Like them. Something nasty and broken. Something that might tremble and flinch at their mere presence.

It's not that I'm fearless, I just know what the man wants, now that Sebastian is gone, and so my life has value for now, while they are merely pawns. He needs me for absolution, I'm guessing. There is nobody else. How long I remain valuable, I don't know.

The woods outside grow impenetrable, thicker and thicker the higher we go, snow smothering everything in a heavy blanket, the switchbacks winding up the mountainside. I can't believe how high this goes, how far it is, a few small yellow lights up ahead, what must be a dwelling, still quite a distance away.

"You know Sebastian is dead," I say, risking more abuse. "And you hope that I'm his replacement, right?"

The man in the passenger seat turns to face me, but doesn't speak.

"Then let me do my job," I say, full of bravado. "I need to eat his sins, but I can't do that with a broken jaw. I'm happy to provide my services and to then head back down the mountain."

The man stares at me, his grimace tightening and then releasing.

"Is he dead already? Or is he just lining up his ducks?"

Nobody answers me, the man squinting behind his ski mask and goggles, contemplating some answer, obviously not liking my line of questions.

"Alive then," I say. "If he was dead, you probably wouldn't have come for me, unless you're a superstitious bunch. Somebody has to ascend to the throne, though, right?"

The man speaks, a low, guttural growl, "Just shut up and maybe you'll make it out of here alive."

"Trust me," I say. "You don't want him haunting you," I embellish. "Whatever powers he has now, they are limited by being a man, being human. Whatever restless, angry wraith he might become? You don't want that," I say, almost believing my lies and exaggerations.

And then we're at the compound, a high wall built around the lodge, stones and bricks eight feet high, with wrought-iron spikes on top. The gate is open, two men standing guard outside, automatic weapons in hand, straps running around their torsos. Brutal conditions to put his men in, I think, but that's not surprising. If you can't stand in the cold and guard the king, then what use are you to him? I imagine losing a digit to frostbite is a badge of honor up here.

We pull up to the mansion, and the building is more than I thought possible. Massive, easily the largest home I've ever seen, built out of entire trees, and then fortified with concrete, steel, and stone. The courtyard is ablaze with light, kerosene torches burning in their stands, flames flickering into the night, numerous expensive cars lining the driveway. Hidden pot lights illuminate the massive stone stairs that lead to the front of the building, a yellow glow spilling out of every window into the snow. Through the frosted glass, I see people moving about, mostly men, some in similar outfits to the guys in the van, others in more functional clothing, a mix of para-military garb—blue jeans, black cloth, and flannel shirts. Even from here I can see all the way into the living room, the man who lives here unwilling to obscure his view of this domain for the sake of safety, the glass most certainly bulletproof.

As we exit the van, a henchman grabs my arm and pulls it nearly out of its socket. I am escorted up the steps, the house filled with light, a tableau unfolding in front of me as I gaze through the window into the main room. There is a stone fireplace with an inner firebox large enough to hold a man, and I fear this may have been done before, someone pushed into the gaping maw as flames licked and stabbed at a screaming, burning enemy. Around the hearth are fine leather couches and regal armchairs, tables crafted out of hearty wood, secured with ornate legs and metal framework. A long oak table runs the length of one wall, comfortable chairs with leather seats, a vase in the center of the table overflowing with flowers in shades of red, orange, purple, and green. Where they got fresh flowers at this time of the year, all the way up here, I have no idea.

On a medical bed near the fireplace lies a large man, covered in white sheets, all except for his massive, hairy chest, a full beard covering his face, long brown hair forming a crown beneath his head. Spotting the lions posed in marble outside the front door, life-size, their curls cascading, mouths open in a certain roar, I see the resemblance to the man inside. I am still outside, easily fifty to one hundred feet away, and yet he casts a shadow out into the night that is large, and thick, and intimidating.

I'll have to be careful around him. This will certainly be dangerous.

I assume the people surrounding the bed are family members—a wife most likely, tall and thin, beautiful in her curves, glistening skin, and lustrous hair. She sits next to the bed, crying, with several young men near her, most likely their sons—smaller versions of the swarthy man, as if a gathering of bear cubs had accumulated around the great beast. A few elderly specters haunt the edge of the room, statesmen and grand dames, I'm guessing older brothers and sisters, or perhaps even mothers and fathers, or business acquaintances. There is a range of emotions—grief, love, relief, fear, loathing—and all of this saturates the air, a palpable sensation, so thick you could cut it with a hunting knife.

The room is sparkling with life, but also echoing great gouts of death.

I glimpse all of this from the outside, my vision telescoping, like gazing into an enormous fish tank, while I'm shoved roughly up the steps and toward the double oak doors that split and open as if granting me entry to some medieval castle. Right before we enter, a flash of light draws my attention to the nearby woods. There is a smattering of tiny eyes filled with a glowing wonder emerging from the undergrowth, a beating of wings overhead as something black erupts into a flock of movement, and then I'm through the front doors and into the keep.

I hear voices, and doors slamming, the sounds of footsteps moving away from me, all echoing through the hall as I cross a marble floor, the walls covered in medieval weapons and armor, paintings of family, antique guns and bows, an opening to the left, the main room beckoning. I am shoved into the makeshift hospital room, the man at my side disappearing suddenly, the doors closed behind me with authority. We are suddenly alone, this man and I, the room cleared, the only sounds filling the space a cracking and spitting from the fireplace and the hissing and beeping of the machines around his bed. The blend of caustic antiseptics, lingering woodsmoke, and a sweet, heavy cologne causes my eyes to water and my stomach to roll.

Though his eyes are still closed, and he remains reclined, he raises his right arm and beckons me closer.

Pilip Silla—god of the sky—is dying.

And he wants me to grant him safe passage.


"Cancer?" I ask as I approach the bed, taking off my gloves, mask, and hat.

He nods, sitting up, his eyes clear and dark.

"You are Kallik? Son of Ahnah, brother of Allia?"

He says all of this to let me know that we've been seen—to stretch out his long reach to my mother and sister—a friendly reminder of what he is capable of, while merely asking a simple question about who I am.

"Yes, I am, sir."

He labors to breathe, heavy features carved into his face, thick wrinkled skin, like tanned leather. There are dark circles under his eyes, and though he wheezes, there is a fire in his gaze that fights off the sickness.

"Please, call me Pilip. Sit, my son, we need to talk. I am dying, as you have noted, before my time, but the doctors say that it is beyond help, stage four, having spread through my organs, and into my brain."

I unzip my coat and slip it off, the room suddenly very hot. I take a seat in a high-backed cloth chair that moments ago held his weeping wife, my boots puddling water and snow on the floor.

"I'm sorry," I say.

"Karma or chaos, the last laugh of some long dead gypsy, or perhaps just a lifetime of drinking and smoking leading to my certain demise." He shrugs. "I've lived a good life, my family is taken care of, and now in this darkest hour, I have found myself growing superstitious," he says with a deep chortle that turns into a cough, a handkerchief raised to his mouth, coming away with a bloody kiss from his parched lips.

"How long do you have?" I ask.

"I don't know," he says. "Days, weeks, months."

He reaches over to the bedside table and grabs a snifter of what looks like cognac, and takes a hearty drink.

"I'm dying," he says, as he laughs through teeth slicked with blood and clenched with pain, "but I'm not dead yet. Might as well enjoy what's around me."

I nod my head, understanding the futile actions, the last bits of pleasure before it's all gone. I take in the tubes and machines, understanding how he clings to life here, his grip on this all still strong.

"Sebastian and I go way back," he says. "I was distressed to hear of his passing in such a brutal, selfish way. If I had more energy, and focus, I might send retribution down the hill, but then again," he says, shrugging, "I also might have done the same thing. You have taken over for him, I hear?"

"I don't know, sir . . . Pilip. I have only seen him do it once, and even then, it was only for my dog. Sebastian died before my training was complete, so my knowledge is rudimentary at best."

The man frowns, and the room seems to dip in temperature, his mask slipping, revealing his baser side—the man who gutted a betrayer, a mole in his family, stringing him up by the whale bones down at the water's edge, like some skinned seal. The man who would launch arrows of fire down the mountainside for sport, occasionally setting a small shack or home on fire, laughing as some drunken bastard burned to death in his sleep. The man who demanded every ounce of ambergris be found within a hundred miles of this port, the rare whale vomit quite valuable.

"But, I think I have time to learn," I say, and a light returns to his eyes. "A woman in the village has just lost her husband, and she has asked me to help him cross over. He sounds like a gentle soul, so what I might have to go through—the pain and suffering of my experience, whatever I might conjure and birth into this village—should be relatively painless," I say.

He takes a sip of his drink and grimaces.

"You've seen the tear? If you knew Sebastian, I assume you've been to his home, seen the ripple, know what he does when his work is done?" I ask.

"We've spoken," the man says. "I'm aware of his work here, and what he sends through. We've been battling this war for a very long time. He has even come to me, now and then, seeking ammunition, my men known to be hard, violent, angry individuals. Bad things happen when you're at war, and I've lost many good soldiers as I sought to acquire rights, oil, gas, and land. I'm a businessman first, Kallik, but quite often people don't want to do business—with me, or anyone else. I do my best to convince them to sell, to part with family plots, to let go of these distractions at a greatly increased price. They don't always acquiesce."

I think back to the sale of waterfront properties, to the mysterious deaths of professional whalers lost at sea, to the caravans of families fleeing in broad daylight, or under the cover of darkness, and it all makes sense now. I'd turned my eyes away from such things, still a kid after all, and not concerning myself with the wages and pursuits of others. But today I feel ancient, so much older, maybe a touch wiser, but less innocent for knowing, for seeing the truth of this land.

"If you'll allow me to hone my craft, and I know you don't have much time, I think that I can help you. I need to prepare myself for your passing, Pilip. I have a feeling that it will be a much more painful and difficult birth than what I've known."

The man smiles, taking this in as a compliment. For a moment his aura flashes a dark shadow around his body, flickering golden light for a moment, before dissipating and disappearing entirely. When I blink my eyes, I see his skeleton, his muscles, the sinew underneath his skin, a green mottled sickness coating his organs.

"You know where I live," I joke, "so if it's okay with you, I'd like to return to my village, to my home, to try and absolve the sins of Mr. Johnson. I can learn a lot from this death, and can then apply what I learn to your eventual passing. Whether it's days from now, or looking at how strong you are, weeks, or even months, I will be ready to battle your demons, to cleanse your sins, and to absolve you of your past transgressions."

I say all of this as a sheen of sweat starts to form on my forehead, knowing that none of this may be true. I bury my true intentions as deeply as I can, hoping he can't see through my half-truths and exaggerations.

"Good," he says, taking a remote out from the layers of bedding and pushing a button. Immediately, one of his men returns, entering the room with a smile on his face and a large hunting knife in his right hand.

"Now," Pilip says, "we seal this deal—blood brothers, your word sworn on the lives of your mother and sister, even your deadbeat father down south. You will swear on the lives of your coworkers and your neighbors, and you will do so with your blood."

Pilip takes the knife from his goon and slices across his left hand, separating the flesh, as blood wells up and runs down his palm, his eyes on me the whole time, a smile pushing across his face, buried in his beard like some glistening spider. His eyes flicker, reflecting the flames of the fireplace.

*Reflecting*, I tell myself, *reflecting*.

I take the knife from him, and pause for a moment, knowing there can be no turning back from this pact. Not that I really have a choice. With a heavy sigh I run it across my left palm, and it stings, eliciting a yelp from me, and then a dull moan. He extends his left hand, and I greet it with mine, this backward handshake—the faces of my mother and sister wafting up to me, my stomach turning in knots at the events I have set in motion, thinking about the last time I spoke to Margie, the smokey glare of Oliver, and the distant specter of my father.

"Thank you, Kallik. We'll be in touch," he says, closing his eyes, and leaning back, resting again, as a nurse appears from out of nowhere, bandaging his hand. Another nurse shoves a bandage into my bleeding hand, leaving me to wrap it up. The room starts to fill back up with family, the noise level growing, a smile on his face, as underneath it all his skin turns translucent, his heart pulsing in a staccato beat, the sickness in him rising up to the surface, his forearms suddenly mottled, spider veins rippling across his face. He sneers in pain, his eyes still closed, a rotten moan seeping from his barely parted lips. A low faint growl reverberates from within him, as somewhere in the distance something screeches, consumed with pain.

I might not have as much time as I originally thought.

Grabbing my coat, I put on my hat and gloves, ski mask tucked into a pocket, as one of his men grabs me and escorts me out the way we came in. I am surrounded by his family, as they crowd him again, so many faces filled with light and love, and I wonder how they sleep at night, knowing what he does, what this monster in their midst does for a living.

And then I wonder how I might send him straight to hell.

# CHAPTER FIVE

# NOT QUITE ABSOLUTION

In the darkness of my deep sleep there is a rustling next to my bed—boot steps and a zipper coming undone, a heavy sigh, and a dry cough—but I'm so tired, so far under that I can't quite make it up to the surface. I get a faint whiff of lavender, and something that might be red currant, a hint of cigarette smoke, and a kiss of faded bourbon on my forehead, as my mother blesses me in the deep night, pulling the patchwork quilted blanket made from old t-shirts, torn jeans, and baby onesies up to my chin. She brushes some hair out of my face and whispers an ancient blessing over me, the worry manifesting in the trembling of her words, and the ghost that is my mother stands over me, praying for my protection.

"May the sun bring you renewed energy by day, may the moon restore you by night; may your aim be strong and always true, may the breeze blow strength into your might; may you walk gently through this frozen world and know its beauty and bounty, as is your right."

I stir and turn over, wanting to hold her hand for a moment—those long, swollen fingers—to climb up into her welcoming lap, a small child again, to huddle by the fire as it crackles and flickers, to feel safe in her embrace, away from the elements, innocent to the horrors of the world, and this brutal, unforgiving land around us. But when I open my eyes, she is gone, no sign of her anywhere, and for a moment, as my eyes cast a longing gaze out of my room and into the kitchen, a single bulb pushing soft light into the living room, I wonder if she was here at all. Not just today, but like . . . ever.

I take a deep breath, still exhausted, and start to go back under. Maybe in the distance a key turns, and a car starts up, belching exhaust into the night, as a door slams shut, the frame creaking as a large bulk slips into the driver's seat. Maybe a woman shuffles across an icy parking lot, watching her footfalls with caution, slick black patches so dangerous in the darkness, one snowflake in a storm of millions, lost and yet part of something boundless, trying to find her way. Maybe she senses the danger that I've brought closer to us all, putting distance between her and our house, and my spirit, out of preservation and fear—not wanting to anger the gods any more than she already has. Or maybe she's oblivious to it all—ignorant of the burnt husk of Sebastian's house, looking past the blood splattered on the side of the road, or the bones in strange sizes and quantities that circle our whaling village like a diseased doily. Maybe she thinks of my sister, and counts her blessings, believing that *one* of us got out. Who was *she* to be greedy, asking for the safety and fulfillment of us both? Let alone her own dreams. Maybe she tries to lasso it all and send it south to my father, certain that this is *his* doing, or *his* karma, and as such, should be owned by the lost, angry, fractured man.

The snow falls heavy overhead, as the moon emerges from behind thick, dark clouds, my eyes closed, but this natural majesty a scene I've witnessed so many times that I often feel like my gaze is casting paint and brush across the landscape with blue and white strokes, filling in this tapestry, dipped back into a heavy black tincture to smear all of the rest with an impenetrable darkness that pushes all the way to the edge of the canvas.

It is both real, and thin as paper, this reality.

The last thought as I lose consciousness is of my sister, standing outside, smoking a cigarette, in a red flannel top that is unbuttoned, a white waffle thermal shirt underneath, blue jeans ending in gray sealskin boots topped with white fur, silver rings sparkling under the street lamp, her left hand cocked on her hip. She is looking up at the same moon that now hangs over my head, the same silent orb that watches over my mother on her trek to work, the same sphere that bathes the sky god in both life and death alike. For a second I want to cry out to her, to summon her back, or maybe push her farther away, but I don't want to taint her with this blessed curse that has descended upon me. And yet, what I wouldn't give to hear her laughter, to have her punch me in the shoulder, to watch her run a brush through her long, brown hair over and over again in a hypnotic rhythm as she hums a tune—something sweet and full of hope. Or to sit silently at the kitchen table, no need for words, as we eat a simple meal—rice and fish and tea—her cheeks flushed, nails painted some garish color. No, I wait until she finishes her cigarette, and then I inhale with her, a long, slow, spicy breath, and then exhale expanding clouds of weariness and surrender.

What will be will be, I tell her, letting her stay where she is, trying to tell her that I'm okay, when I know no such truth. What comes next—the rituals for the dead man in the gingerbread house, the coming extinction of the dinosaur lumbering on the mountaintop, and whatever else might linger in the shadows, just out of sight, or perhaps over the horizon—there is nothing she can do. To ask her for help would only put her at risk, and she's rolled the dice enough times on this frozen earth, in the darkness, and alleys, and trails, and bars. No need to call up snake eyes just for our amusement. There is an ache building in me, a void that is expanding, and it gives me great discomfort. It is a sign of things to come, and what it means, what images and sensations wash over me—fluttering wings and gnashing teeth and moaning death rattles—cause my skin to heat and chill in equal quantities. This state of flux is unnerving, and I fear it's only the beginning.

Day or night, I'm not sure, the haze and snow overhead blocking out what might be a sun or a moon. Not that it matters. There was a text message on my phone when I woke up, the diner closing for a few days, Margie headed out of town. I can't remember the last time the restaurant shut down, and it makes my skin crawl, picturing Margie packing up a suitcase, looking over her shoulder, as Valkyries circle the mountaintop, death feasting on this village like it is some dark, festering, gelatinous buffet.

I don't like it. Not one bit.

Even though it's been less than twenty-four hours since I left the diner and tried to make my way to Mrs. Johnson's house, it feels like a great amount of time has passed, and that I've been delinquent in my duties. But when I was dropped off by Pilip's goons in the white van, her house was dark, and I didn't have the strength or courage to knock and wake her up. I imagined that she must have grown tired, waiting for me to appear, exhausted from the emotions and loss.

What I wasn't expecting when I returned was the huge funeral pyre out behind her house, wood stacked up ten feet high, built like an altar, logs layered one on top of the other, with a pyramid over the top, the now deceased Mr. Johnson tucked into the middle of it all, frozen solid, dead and gone, but his spirit still lingering, waiting for me to arrive. The smell of gasoline drifts to me, the noxious odor keeping the wolves at bay, that might otherwise make a meal of the man. And to help us with the blaze that is certainly coming.

I have so many questions, but perhaps the answers don't matter.

Did she do this alone—this thin, frail woman in the pink hat with the fuzzy ball on top—working herself up into a sweat, as her body creaked and moaned? Or did her husband help her to build this over the past couple of weeks, knowing that the end was coming, chopping wood, talking to her about the design, laboring over the larger logs that most certainly had to take more than one person to lift. Maybe more than two. Did he climb on top of this structure once it was built and give out his last gasping breath, exhausted across his body, mind, and soul?

Were they building this as Sebastian's home burned to the ground?

Were they making trips deep into the woods as the neighbors gathered in a ring, laying down their dead, waiting for Sebastian to eat?

I don't know.

But as I stand in the backyard and take in the sheer spectacle and size of the pyre, I can't help but feel anything other than peace. Worked into the logs, branches, and kindling are bows tied in a multitude of colors, tiny animal skulls attached to places here and there, hawthorn and holly branches still holding red berries, the scent of pine suffusing the air, the boughs and needles green against the white snow, ripe with sap and scent.

They only had each other, from what Margie had told me, and as their world froze around them, and things got ugly, they did what mattered to them, honoring his last wishes, leaning into their faith and religion, with the patience and perseverance of Viking priests.

What death does to us all, I think. Such strange, wondrous, haunting rituals we perform. And in the cold I cross myself anyway, taking on change, whispering my own prayers in the darkness, as overhead and on the distant horizon the lights dance, the wind howls, and the trees bend and creak in the expanding night.

I have a job to do, and that's what is important.

Before I can knock, she appears at the back door in the same clothes she wore the other day, a bit dirtier, dark smudges on her face, and a few tears in the fabric of her blue puffy coat, her eyes bloodshot, sunken into her skull. Her pink hat with the fluffy ball on top is a bright presence that nearly brings me to tears, her coat hanging off of her, the tan cardigan over a white turtleneck, as she wrings her hands, a whiff of sour body odor drifting to me.

"I'm sorry that I took so long to get here," I say.

She opens her mouth to speak, then hesitates, before starting to cry in a series of shaking sobs. I look away toward the darkness of the trees, holding my breath, giving her time to compose herself. When she recovers, she gestures toward the pyre, drying her eyes with the back of her hand.

"This was his idea, something tied to his Icelandic roots, Norse blood or something. We were in such a hurry, trying to outrun death, that I never pushed him for an explanation. He just said it was important to him, and that was enough for me," she says, breaking into a dry cough to avoid weeping again. Her voice sounds frail, empty, rambling, and exhausted, as if she hasn't spoken to anyone in days. "After what happened to Sebastian, I begged him to take it down, but then he got sick. Sicker, I mean, and it was too late to do anything else. I'm so tired, but I need to try and help him cross over, to leave this world behind and find whatever is next."

"I'm sorry for your loss," I say, unsure of what else I could possibly say to comfort her. I take a deep inhale as I choose my next words, tasting a thin layer of his lemony presence in the night air. "His spirit is still here, so it's not too late. I want you to know that, to be assured of that at least. But I also think that he was probably a good man, based on what Margie has told me. So he won't linger too long, from what I know about all this."

She offers me a weak, warm smile and wraps her arms around herself, shivering slightly in the darkness.

"Come inside and eat," she says. "I'm a bundle of sticks and exposed nerves, and I need to help him move on. I watched him go from a virile, young man to an aging, distinguished scholar to a wheezing, skeletal ghost. We were connected, and now I feel incomplete. I've been gutted, hollowed out. Everywhere in this house, it's like there's something missing. I watched him grow old and get sick and die, but then I think he's in the other room. It's like being haunted by a ghost I can never confront."

I offer her a sympathetic look in return, visions and emotions of last night's restless sleep coming back to me in pieces.

"It will get better," I say. "Not forgetting, not filling that emptiness with something else, but more of a letting go, a lessening of the pain, a way to both honor his life and to let his death expand into a memory, a recognition, a presence that can stay and grant you peace. It's different," I say, "and it will hurt for a while, but one day you will conjure up his spirit in a whiff of cologne, or a favorite meal, or a song, and it will be comforting instead of painful, and that's when you'll know that you're okay. That the wounds have healed."

"How old *are* you?" she asks me, squinting in my direction, her face a mix of curiosity and exhaustion.

"Old enough," I say.

"Thank you," she says, beckoning me to follow her inside. As I enter her house and sit down in the middle of her gingerbread house, lined with frosting, shingles made of toffee bark, the scent of vanilla, and bread, and coffee burbling in a pot. It is warm and comforting, a grandmother who has lined every surface and shelf with something pleasing to the senses. There are fuzzy blankets laid over inviting gingham couches, and cookie jars in various sizes, prairie style lamps with soft yellow light draped over it all, as if casting a spell, a glitter of sparkling dust twinkling in the dusk and gloom.

"I'll make you his favorite dish; it won't take long. I think you'll enjoy it."

My stomach rolls, and I think of my dog, of Sebastian, of the man on the hill and what this might all turn into. And I hope my plan will work.

It turns out that his favorite meal is something called muesli. I'm familiar with oatmeal, but this is a little different. And as Mrs. Johnson puts the bowl together, she tells me about the ingredients, lovingly layering one item over the other.

It starts out with a bright, shiny Red Delicious apple—which she slices and cuts into small pieces, leaving all of it intact—the skin, core, and seeds kept in the bowl.

"Isn't there cyanide in the seeds?" I ask.

"Not enough to do anything," she says. "You'd have to eat a bushel or two. It's the symbolism of the whole, not wasting anything, keeping it all together. Be glad I don't make you eat the stem too," she says, smiling.

"The dish has Viking roots, a Nordic history, something Swiss," she says.

To that she adds cold, rolled oats, which have been soaking in water overnight, more than twelve hours.

And then there are nuts—almonds, hazelnuts, and walnuts—again, cut up and sprinkled over it all.

To this she adds some golden raisins, a variation she says that her husband liked, a bit of sweetness and chew to break up all of the crunch.

She tosses in three red raspberries—one for herself, one for him, and one for their son, who passed away a long time ago.

She cuts a lemon into quarters and then squeezes that over the mixture, running a spoon through it all, mixing it up.

And then a spoonful of honey, drizzled on the top, to add a bit more sweetness.

Finally, her secret ingredients, a mixture of seeds that were supposed to be good for his health—chia, sunflower, pumpkin, and flax.

"I like to add milk to this all," she says, "otherwise it's a bit dry for me," she says.

"Sounds good," I say.

Outside, shadows pass over the pyre, as the sun, or the moon, or whatever hangs overhead, seeps out from behind the clouds for a moment and then disappears again.

"He was a good man, your husband?" I ask.

She pours the milk over the mixture and comes to the table, placing it in front of me, and then sits down.

"The best," she says. "He was generous to a fault, eager to listen and learn, talented in a multitude of ways, a lover of all things artistic, and a supportive member of this community. When Margie opened the diner, he was a silent investor and the first person to eat a burger and fries at the counter. He was part of the governing board that proposed a rule change to all whales caught in these waters, making sure that every citizen that wanted whale meat or blubber would be allowed the opportunity to take some. He helped extend the hiking trails up into the mountains, and erect the whale bone arch that greets whalers and tourists alike, when you come into the bay. He helped six different local children go to college, as an anonymous donor, all of them graduating from universities down south—engineers, scientists, teachers, and even a doctor."

She takes a moment to collect herself with a deep breath.

"Will this hurt you?" she asks, gesturing to the food.

"No, I don't think so. Not much, based on who I think your husband was. But my services here may be a bit different from Sebastian's," I say, and a frown passes over her face.

"What do you mean?"

"I won't be absolving your husband of his sins."

She stares at me, and the room grows colder.

"I am not a sin-eater," I say. "Not anymore. Maybe never, and certainly not like Sebastian. I have spoken to the northern lights, I have communed with nature, I have studied what Sebastian did, and have seen what he sent through the void, and out into the world. And his way, the old way of doing things, it didn't work."

"So what does that mean? I don't understand. Then why are you here? Will he be okay?"

"If he is indeed the man you say he was, then yes, he will be fine. His minor transgressions, his mistakes, his mortal sins, and other smaller flaws were never going to be something that held him back from whatever waits on the other side—whatever his definition of Valhalla or heaven might be. No, those absolutions are for those that need it, people that are tainted, bad seeds, evil-doers that are looking for a pass, a forgiveness at the end of a long life of crime, violence, and greed. I won't be granting that. Instead of absolution, I am granting recognition. I am not a sin-eater, but a gift-giver, an amplifier of good, instead of an erasure of bad."

She doesn't say anything.

"You are my first client," I tell her. "This is all new to me, building on what Sebastian did, understanding how it works, but I think, in the end, that the process, and result will be the same. For you, there is nothing to fear. For others? This will be something else entirely."

With a slow, heavy breath, after licking her lips, and running her hands over her face, she smiles, and speaks.

"Eat. I have nothing to fear. If what you're saying is true, then there may be hope for this town after all."

I pick up my spoon and dig in.

The muesli is delicious. It starts out with the thick, hearty taste of the oats, what tastes to me like the oatmeal of my youth, minus the brown sugar and butter. The crisp, sharp bite of the apple adds a layer of crunch to the softer grains, with just a touch of sweetness. But truly, it is the honey that really makes the dish, and the raspberries that blend in with it, to coat my tongue in a glossy, sweet nectar of the gods. And then the crunch of the nuts, the earthiness of the walnuts, and the tiny snaps of the seeds as one by one they pop in my mouth. There is nothing bitter in this bowl, I think, as I take another spoonful. She watches me eat, smiling, as my eyes glisten with emotion. The layers of flavor coat my tongue and slide down my throat like a velvet rainbow of hearty, sweet goodness. It is unlike anything I've ever tasted, so satisfying, and fulfilling. He *was* a good man. One of the best.

I finish the bowl in only a few minutes and lick the spoon, turning it over and over again.

"My God," I say, and she beams, tears leaking out of her eyes now. "I'm only sorry that I didn't get to know him better," I say, as my face flushes and my head spins.

She holds her hands together, as if in prayer, resting her face on them, hugging herself, so happy to hear what I've said, to see what kind of man he truly was, even though she certainly felt that he was something special. To have this confirmed, in such a holy, biblical, ancient way—causes her to radiate, to glow with love and peace.

And then my stomach buckles, and I bend over.

"Oh no," I say, as I scramble to my feet, quickly dressing, putting back on my coat and boots, as I feel some great rebellion working its way into a frenzy in my gut, pushing up my stomach into my esophagus, eager to find its way out.

Maybe he wasn't as good a man as she thought.

I'm out into the cold, and I know I won't make it across the street, to the ripple that glints in the darkness, and what lurks inside calls out to me. I fall to my knees at the base of their makeshift wooden altar, staring up into the unlit funeral pyre as the icy winds whip around me, and the sparkling constellations emerge out of the darkness.

Night. It turns out this is the night.

In a great rush of golden light and buzzing electricity I open my mouth and vomit out a brutal lashing of orange fire that cuts through the darkness of the backyard, illuminating the whole backyard. I struggle to find a breath, my body heaving and spasming, desperate for oxygen. I manage to inhale again, pulling scorched air into my lungs, roasting me from the inside out. The pain staggers me, but before I can even think to scream, fire erupts from my gullet again, branching out into feathers, and wings, connecting with the other segments of color—burning red, and yellow, and orange—to whirl into the shape of a great bird, its wings spread wide, beak open in a shrieking caw. It soars out over the pyre, setting it all aflame, as glittering white-hot cinders spill out in its wake like the tail of a comet, extending and growing behind it. Golden sparks shimmer out of the creature itself, as it twirls, ascending high into the sky, briefly setting the surrounding trees and rooftops ablaze. The flaming pyre crackles below it, a bed of fire beneath the beast, circling the altar, spilling embers behind it, showering us in the sparks.

The night is lit up by the inferno, bathing us in a blinding light, melting the snow, threatening to ignite the entire forest, crisping and singing their leafless branches. The phoenix circles again, and then soars toward the ripple, across the street,

lighting up the remnants of Sebastian's house, belching a flickering gouge into the wood, and snow, and melted remains,
reigniting it with an epic heat that immediately consumes
whatever is left, burning it down to the bare earth. In seconds
it is reduced to ash, flattened into nothing.

And in one fell swoop it glosses over the tear, sealing it shut.
Just like that, without so much as a hesitation, or struggle, or
warning.

I blink, and it circles the town, not touching anything else,
merely inspecting the grounds, once and then twice, trailing
light and sparks behind it, and then it dives back toward us,
crashing straight into the pyre, shooting flames high up into the
sky, a towering hellfire.

There are no words for what I've seen.

There are no spiders running across the lawn, no wolves
hiding in the shadows of the forest, no lumbering beasts with
horns on their heads, gnashing their teeth and snorting out
great gusts of fury.

There is only the crackle and spit of the flames, a wall of heat
pushing off of the pyre in waves, as if standing at the door of a
blast oven. I remain on my knees, a whisper of smoke drifting
from my parted lips and singed nostrils. The old woman stands
in the doorway of her house, one hand covering her mouth,
eyes wide in wonder, her tears glinting in the moonlight like
fractured diamonds.

High on the hill, up on the mountain, many eyes turn our
way, and dancing shadows circle tighter around a dying serpent,
eager to see how this might absolve their tainted leader.

# CHAPTER SIX

# A RECKONING

I kneel in the heat of the burning, pulsing, roaring fire for as long as it takes to consume the pyre. And that isn't all that long. Like the flames that the firebird breathed onto the wreckage of Sebastian's house, the heat is so intense that even the thickest of logs are reduced to ash in minutes. I have to back away from it all, smoke drifting out of my mouth, my skin flushed, as Mrs. Johnson stands so very still inside her house, lingering like an apparition in the dying fire reflecting off of the glass of her back door window. We are silent in our wonder, and any concern I may have had that she would have to bury her husband's bones later and deal with the aftermath of shoveling away the coals and embers, some herculean task—is now gone. There is only the powdery residue of ash, and as new snow falls down over the scorched ground, melting as it lands, a glow covering the space where this righteous man and his pyre once stood, it will soon cover it all like an uneven blanket, as everything cools, and grows cold, and eventually freezes solid.

Before I head home, in a moment of contemplation, I consider what might have happened to this community if their sins had not been absolved and sent through the tear to battle some distant creatures. What if, instead, those who were decent, those who had asked for forgiveness, those who had made mistakes, but learned from them and grew, were honored and recognized here, had their spirits released into the wild? Would the tear have gone away, no longer drawn by the violence, and hatred, and greed? Or might this community have healed itself from the inside out?

Across the village, the tiny embers and motes of light dot the dark sky, floating and drifting, refusing to die out, perhaps tied to the last of his spirit, as Mr. Johnson slowly evolves as he dissipates—smoke to lemon to a whiff of pine. Like luminescent fireflies, they dance over the village, glowing and then fading, blinking out, then coming back with stubborn bursts of light, the entire village showered with sparkling stardust, swirling above the rooftops in the night wind. Eventually, the tiny lights grow faint and burn out. Which is my sign to go home.

I turn to Mrs. Johnson, and she has her hands over her mouth, still crying, but less now, tired, and yet touched by the ritual, converted into a believer in a matter of minutes. What's the saying? There are no atheists in foxholes? I tend to agree. In the face of such evidence, how can you not believe in something greater?

I simply wave to her, a final whisp of smoke escaping from my mouth, and out of my nostrils, and she waves back, eyes glistening with tears, her cheeks puffy and flushed. I feel as though I have been gently baked, my face singed as well, but nothing serious, a tightening of my skin as if getting a slight sunburn. Turning away from the glowing rectangle of coals and embers, I stumble home, exhausted but confident that this new way of crossing over may actually work. The big test still to come, of course, with the man on the hill, surrounded by his family and his thugs. I have to bury this knowledge I have so very deep, out of a fear that he might pick up on it, his flickering eyes piercing me the last time we spoke, making my skin crawl. He's perceptive, and quite possibly something more than human.

As I saunter home, the few illuminated streetlights guiding me through the flurry of snowflakes that continue to descend on this town, I see the effects of the dusting in the houses up and down the street—individual scenes come to me like movie reels flickering in an abandoned theater.

One man, in his snoring slumber, rolls over and then back again, wrestling with a decision from his past that still haunts him to this day. And in a moment of reflection and forgiveness, he decides on mercy and understanding, putting aside thoughts of the sledgehammer and can of gasoline, his favorite hunting knife that sits on the kitchen counter glistening. No, he will reach out to his betrayer and accept the apology, ridding himself of the toxin that has been coursing through his body for years now— growing like a cancer, pushing out tremors, causing a violent rash to erupt across his blotchy skin—poisoning the angry man from the inside out. And in the letting go, he will heal.

A woman a bit farther down the road decides to hire the most qualified candidate, though she sat at the interview in a seething rage, hating every exposed patch of dark skin, every scent that reminded her of something exotic, something foreign, snarling at certain colors that were exposed in a bracelet, some country other than this one. She lets it all go, choosing instead to see the talent, the bright white smile, the generous manner—everything she was looking for in an assistant. She pushes back against generations of hatred, and lies, and conspiracy, and instead takes an emotional leap forward. And it brings her peace, her heart resting for a moment, a calm she hasn't felt in years, washing over her body in a wave of euphoria. She is awake now, and grateful for the vision.

A father texts his child a message in the dark, telling them to come home, that they can figure this out together, so much of this new to him. Teach me so I can understand, he texts, because I can't stand the thought of losing you, like I lost your mother, like I lost so many friends. The only horror left now are the three blinking dots on his phone as he waits for the response, as he waits to be forgiven—a sick feeling in his gut, not wanting to be pushed away, to be ostracized. He is just beginning to understand what it might be like to live in the minority, to feel like an outsider—he has seen the tip of the iceberg, and in that knowing can feel the weight of what lies submerged below it. And that's a good thing—that empathy and sympathy. That compassion.

I take a deep breath, cold in, and hot out, a cloud of mist drifting up into the glow of the streetlight. One step at a time, I think. One step at a time.

When I get home, I peel off my clothes and throw them into the aging washing machine, smelling of smoke, dark smudges on my hands and cheeks. I stand naked in the utility room, shivering and vibrating, as emotions bubble to the surface, a wave of sickness and uncertainty washing over me. What I've done, and what's to come, there is a connection here, a relationship, and I must get it right.

I move to the bathroom, where I slump in the steaming water until there is nothing left, letting the water run over my exhausted flesh, not trying to rid myself of the spectacle I've just witnessed—the images still running through my mind like some animated movie—but to merely wash away the grit, ash, and dirt that has accumulated over the last few days, to erase the pinnacle of these exertions from the ritual tonight. For a moment I can disappear into the warm mist of the shower and let the world fall away. I need to silence the voices, to sheathe myself in peace, so that I can move forward with confidence, leaving behind the failures of the past.

I collapse into my bed, pull the sheets and blankets tight around me, and fall into a deep sleep.

It starts with a gradual warming up of my room, the smell of creosote, and a shimmering haze in the air, as if I am standing over a patch of gasoline, translucent waves rippling in the growing heat. A russet light pushes into the room, as an oily smoke creeps up from the baseboards. I feel pulled in several directions, pushed under, as if submerged into a bloody water, a red light like veiny marbling creeping over the walls. The sheer drapes covering the windows flutter, as though a profound presence is permeating the room. My eyes begin to sting, and out the window, the hellscape unfolds.

Skeletal beasts lumber forward, their spines distorted, spindly limbs traversing the hot sand as they cross a great crimson desert with a lake of boiling oil at the center, shooting random geysers of ignited gas into the black sky. Flickering bushes composed of scarlet and orange flames ring the bubbling, viscous liquid as sinewy, glistening black serpents undulate up and down, rising out of the simmering, fetid waves, screeching into the air, elongated snouts over gaping jaws, lined with endless rows of needle-like teeth. Packs of dehydrated feral creatures swarm down over the hillsides, and into the shadowed valleys below, barking and yipping in a frenzy, their decayed yellow teeth clacking in the gloom.

Up a wide, spiral staircase made of stone, dark shapes struggle with cumbersome sacks and barrels, up and up until they reach the peak, dumping bones and sinew and great quantities of red liquid into a vast, simmering cauldron. Watching over it all, winged beasts linger, perched on the edge of the rim, snapping at each other, their long, forked tongues flicking in and out of their ruined mouths.

Across the land there are pillars of dirt that have pushed up through the earth, woven through with veiny roots. Metal spikes poke out of the columns, and on these sharp, rusty spears are swaths of tanned flesh stretched wide, drying in the heat.

Hairs poke out of the skins, which range in color from a pale white to a bronze tan to a glossy black.

Running through and over and into the crimson soil are a horde of insects—black beetles clicking and scuttling, climbing over each other, a rolling wave of shiny carapaces, mixed in with brown, buzzing cockroaches, antennae flickering in the hazy heat, wings vibrating, surrounded by nearly translucent centipedes with their multitude of legs, twisting and turning as they writhe over and around each other.

What might have once been a man raises a long, heavy hammer over his head, bringing it down onto a pile of obsidian, shattering the dark stones into tiny shards. All around him are jagged fragments of the black rock, his muscles glistening in the haze, as overhead flying creatures expand their wings to fill the sky with musty air, beating their dark, leathery appendages in supplication. His legs are coated in a coarse hair, his upper body sweaty and wrinkled, covered in scars from a lifetime of cuts and tears, legs ending in bisected hooves. On his head are two massive curling horns, and as he turns to look at me, there is a great telescoping, and my gut clenches, as either I rush toward him or he is pushed toward me, zooming in on his wide nose, a golden ring hooked through it, eyes as black as coal, two quivering, hairy ears twitching atop his head. In a widening sneer, he places the hammer down, exhales a rotten breath, and takes a single step toward me. In that moment I recognize him, a memory that was transferred to me by Sebastian, some greasy stain that had been cleaved during an absolution, and cast out, driven into the desert, down into the depths of some distant land, where he suffered in isolation. I have seen him before. He has haunted my dreams, as well as the land around us, and a series of different settings—dense woods, frozen tundra, dry plains, and barren desert—all hold his visage, worse for his presence.

Perhaps things have changed now, and the past cleansings that had previously been sent through the rip—only the darker parts of our tainted humanity here in the frozen wasteland—will now stand intact. He beckons to me, asking me to send him my progeny, seeking the runoff and tainted flesh that might come from past rituals.

But this time it will be different.

I will not send him half, but whole. I will not cleave one aspect of humanity away and offer it up as a weapon in a war that doesn't need to be fought. No, I will leave these stained, rotten husks intact. No forgiveness, and absolutely no absolution.

And as he reaches out to me, I tell him, "Not now, but soon," and with a wave of my hand, a great smear across my vision, the room turning pitch black, he is gone.


I sleep for hours, possibly days, empty from the rituals and excursions, unable to wake and do anything even remotely demanding. And in the darkness, there is a loud bang and corresponding thud, as if a great shockwave has pushed across the land, sending something massive tipping over and crashing hard into the snow and ice.

I sit up with a start.

Pilip is dead.

They will be here soon.

And so I ready myself—a quick shower, an anointing of oils, a burning of sage, and a laying of runes, written onto my flesh in ash. Around my neck a cross, and an ankh, and prayer beads, and a tiny amulet of Buddha. I am taking no chances. And then it's into the kitchen where I grab a pot of cold coffee and drink it straight out of the container. I force myself to wolf something down—shoving a bagel into my mouth, something that will stick to my ribs, cold chicken unwrapped from aluminum foil, gnawed off the bone, scraps of skin falling to the floor. I am already sweating, waiting for the knock on the door, and it doesn't take long for them to appear.

The black uniform stands outside my house, the man saying nothing, the van behind him, engine running, exhaust pushing out of the tailpipe as the streetlights glimmer and buzz in the darkness. The sickly lights sputter and then snuff out entirely, and I am pushed deeper into the darkness, fearful of the man in front of me lunging or lashing out, and then they pop back on with a crackle and a hum, slowly brightening in the gloom. He has not moved. Under that mask I wonder if he smiles or snarls, or is mostly just dead inside.

I grab my coat, and hat, and gloves, and close the door behind me, following him to the van that rumbles in the street, vibrating with energy. As the door slides shut, I take in my house with a glance that feels fleeting, a moment that I worry may be the last of something. It may be the beginning, but my gut tells me this is not as simple as light and dark, as success and failure. I swallow down the worry and bile, as we ride up the mountain in silence.

I don't ask if he went peacefully, or even if he is actually gone, because I already know he is no longer with us. Not really. Though his spirit lingers. Even from this distance, there is a radiance emanating from the mountain top, a bitter taste filling my mouth, as the house comes into focus again, Pilip's essence still present in the air.

Are they relieved at his passing?

Are they already making mental notes of what to do next?

Are they thinking about succession, position, and power?

Or are they, as I fear, nervous as a long-tailed cat in a room full of rocking chairs? Eyes turn to me, glancing quickly, stealing a look out of the corner of their eyes, wondering what I'm going to do when I get there.

Am I a blessing or a curse?

They are honoring his wish, but they are jittery, and that's dangerous. They will respect the family, but for how long? Which man among them is next to sit on the throne? Who among them is the hungriest, the greediest, the angriest?

I don't know.

What I do know is that I may not survive this, and so I close my eyes for a second to get my bearings—to pray and summon strength.

I think of my mother and her tired face, leaning back in a chair, pushing a strand of hair out of her face, cigarette in her right hand, smoke rising off of it, as a slight grin works its way across her mouth. I think of my sister, lying in her bed, covered in blankets, a body next to her, snoring, as she sits up in a panic, eyes to the north, to me. I think of Sebastian and his guidance, the soft, sweet fuzzy creature he birthed into the air, the tiny bit of communion we shared, and the beliefs he held for so long. I think of Margie, and her kindness, but also her awareness of what might go down here, her self-preservation stinging, but also a smart, calculated move. I think of a great armored creature that I saw through the tear, some massive beast that lay by a pool of water, taking in a deep breath, exhaling a lifetime of worry and now, perhaps, finding some peace.

I open my eyes when the van rolls to a stop outside the massive house, exterior lights flooding the woods with a bright yellow glare, the mansion overflowing with brightness, as the forest around us surges with the motion of shady creatures.

The man in charge doesn't get out. None of them do; he only motions with his hand as the door slides open, toward the house and the opening that leads into the dark god's castle. Stepping out, I look to the trees and hear more movement, bushes rustled by bodies hunting, stepping, hunching over. I hear a snapping of teeth, and low growls, as overhead something spreads its wings and soars closer, blocking out the moon for a moment, and then moving on.

I am alone, and yet, surrounded.

I bend over and vomit into the snow.


Standing beside his bed, I take in the family members that line the edge of the room, the light dimmed now, the warmth from the fireplace filling the space with crackles and snaps. They are here to bear witness, but they are also a respectful distance away. They feared him in life and they fear him still in death.

I taste him; he's still here for sure, something sharp and pungent like burnt broccoli, a verdant aura emanating from his still form, with a thin corona of gold around it all.

Gentle whimpers emanate from the shadows at the edge of the room, muffled sobbing, and the occasional cough, or deep sigh.

I approach him with care, as his body still holds a great weight, and in some ways I fear that he may not even be mortal, able to die. Memories of him ghosting the village, his entourage around him as if he were royalty, the stories of his violence like mythology handed down from the mountains to us peasants, laboring at the water's edge. His presence has poisoned this land for some time now.

But when I get close to him, I see his pale skin, the tinge of something sick rising to the surface, a tinted mix of jaundiced yellow and festering green, spidery blue veins running across his pale flesh. A chill runs through me as I place a hand on his bare skin—cold as marble, his arm solid with rigor mortis, his eyes closed, his lips pulled back in a slight snarl.

There is a simple wooden table next to him, pushed up close, with fine linen and silverware laid out, the only thing missing the china and food for me to eat.

"Well, we'll see what happens now, my friend," I whisper to him as I sit down.

His body vibrates slightly, moving under the blankets and sheets, washing my skin in panic, everything soft and pliable, uncertain; and I am eager to get on with it, a jittery heartbeat hammering my chest. He's still here. More here than he should be. And so I try to keep my mind empty, my heart pure, pushing away vengeance, and a panicked glee, uncertain how this will all play out.

When I close my eyes for a second, trying to compose myself, I see his head turn toward me, the jaundiced whites of his eyes flooding with blood, as his mouth gapes open to reveal an engorged black tongue and jagged rows of abscessed teeth. A putrid smell of spoiled fish and lush compost washes over me and my stomach churns at the thought of the meal to come. The clatter of a plate set before me on the wooden table snaps me out of this terrible vision. I swallow hard, gripping the edge of my jacket tightly in my fists, reassuring myself that his grotesque transformation was only an illusion, and that his calm features remain pointed toward the dark spaces of the ceiling, his prostrate body lying still.

Still dead.

But still here.

In front of me is the most succulent grilled porterhouse I have ever seen, flawless and exquisite. No doubt dry-aged Wagyu beef, the delectable scent of the seared-to-perfection flesh and melt-in-your-mouth marbled fat causing my half-empty stomach to gurgle in anticipation. It starts with a smokey aroma that curls up from the fine cut of beef, reaching deep into an ancient, atavistic part of my brain that holds memories of the first man to hold hunted game over a fire, followed by sweeter, more tender notes of the broken-down sugars and amino acids from the seared brown crust on the outside of the steak glistening with luscious juices and melted butter, pooling in the grill marks that cross each other. Lastly, the spices drift up to me—a garnish of flaky salt, red peppercorn, roasted garlic, sprigs of fresh thyme and rosemary—an herbal ribbon tied into a bow on this culinary gift. I salivate uncontrollably, almost drooling in anticipation, knowing that this could quite possibly be the single best bite of food that I will ever taste.

It is perfect.

I never see the hand that drops off the plate, and can barely feel its absence as it retreats into a hidden door toward the kitchen. I steel myself and pick up the cutlery, knowing I have a singular focus, and it is this meal, and what lingers on the other side of this new ritual.

I cut into the steak and it is perfectly rare, browned on the sides with a bright-red glistening center, marbled with glorious fat. I take the first bite and it is ambrosia, melting into my taste buds, the smoke and fat blending, a hint of the salt, and spices, the butter and garlic, a satisfying depth of meat, a touch of something nutty, and then I swallow it down.

Everything changes.

I choke, as the flesh turns rancid, something gone horribly wrong, the fat congealing as I try to swallow, a metallic, blood-like tang catches in my throat, choking me as a rotten flavor of sour milk and cigarette ashes fills my mouth.

On the bed, his body convulses again, more violently, the sheets starting to slip off of him, as the pallid skin of his face and torso suddenly flushes with color.

I force a swallow and the hunk of meat goes down, lodging midway in my esophagus. I pound my chest with my fist, gasping for breath, eyes watering, retching, barely holding back the overwhelming urge to vomit, until the bite slips down like a hefty stone into my stomach.

An intense heat radiates from his body, like an engine revved until it's glowing red, with steam rising off of his trembling corpse, but I tear my eyes away from him and force my attention back to the steak. There is so much left to devour, and I hesitate, momentarily overcome by the task at hand.

I frantically cut it up into smaller pieces, knowing each bite is going to be harder to ingest than the last, but I decide in the moment that I need to just shovel it all into my mouth, and choke it down painfully, as fast as humanly possible.

And so I do that.

And again.

And again.

Until my lips and chin are slathered in grease, tears streaming down my face. I close my eyes as nauseating visions of consumption flood my mind and make my stomach churn—crows gorging on blood-splattered roadkill swarmed with blowflies and maggots, jackals tearing at the emaciated corpses of diseased cattle rotting in the sweltering heat, people drinking sloshing bucketloads of offal and feces, fresh from the abattoir floor—forcing me to keep them open and fully witness the ritual before me.

Moans and gasps erupt from the shadows around me, and while I can't see the family, there is fevered activity out of the corners of my eyes—people restraining and consoling each other, feet scuffling on the hardwood floor, a murmuring of prayers and curse words that is growing in volume.

On the bed, Pilip continues to shake, the incessant rattling of the metal bed frame drowning out everything but the sound of chewing inside my head. The last of his sheets drops to the floor, exposing the full length of his spasming cadaver for all to see, as thin lines of blood reveal themselves on his translucent flesh, seeping through the thin fabric of his pristine, light-blue pajamas. Across his neck and face, down the length of his exposed forearms and feet, I see the crimson lesions spreading across his skin, like incisions from the inside out, his very body coming apart at the seams.

I keep eating, impulsively, uncontrollably, in a frenzy of sheer terror and disgust; and as a woman screams from somewhere behind me, the fireplace roars to life, flames erupting across the room, sending shards of burning wood exploding outward as the logs crack in half, swirling sparks engulfing the entire tableau of spectators, igniting small fires on the fine rugs beneath their feet.

For every forkful of the meat, there is a violent movement from the bed; for every bite I shove into my mouth, there are teeth marks blossoming on his flesh; for every chew of rancid steak, there is a crackle of his bones breaking; and with every insufferable morsel, his body disconnects a little further from itself.

An IV stand crashes to the hardwood, dragging the monitor and ventilator down with it in an implosion of glass and plastic, prompting a shriek from the gallery as someone rattles the handle at the exit door, unable to escape. I shove my head down and eat faster, struggling to finish this meal, the cacophony of the family rising now—shouts and screams from the shadows, doors slamming open and shut, glass breaking, bringing a great rush of cold air whirling through the suffocating heat of the room. A gunshot rings out, sparking on impact with the fireplace stones; then another shot, splintering something wooden across the room.

I keep cutting, and biting, and swallowing, moldy gelatin sliding down my throat, maggots writhing between my teeth in the broken-down fibers as I force it all down my gullet.

And on the bed, the skin of his face sloughing off, his limbs separate—fingers from hands, hands from arms, arms from torso, head from body—pulling apart under its own weight like so much meat in a slow-cooked roast. His blood releases onto the floor in a wave of violence, in a great *slushing* sound like the breaking of an amniotic sac, his body parts slumping to the floor, scattered across the ground, his mattress soaked red with blood turning to black.

I chew frantically on the last taste of the seemingly endless meal as the fireplace unleashes one final deluge of sparks and flames, catching the cascading curtains across the room ablaze. More bullets fly around me, desperate screams and howling fill the room, my ears flooded with the sounds inside my own mouth, while a high-pitched wailing screeches through my mind.

I swallow.

The meal is done.

What I thought were bullets meant for me were the men shooting at each other. In the haze of the smoke-filled room, as the fire spreads to every combustible object, and chaos unfolds all around me, I see his family and his henchmen tearing each other apart like a pack of savage dogs, drunken with the scent of blood, fists punching, hair being torn out by the roots, teeth gnashing and biting, gunshots, screams, and heavy thuds as flaming bodies collapse, grappling each other to the floor.

The bones and flesh in front of me have coalesced into a formless black mound, its outer surface hardening into an armor that suddenly sprouts legs, antennae, and chittering mandibles. An army of ants and beetles and cockroaches and earwigs and spiders and ticks and fleas swarm over every surface in the room, blanketing the writhing bodies of Pilip's family and his men, until there is nothing left but death.

I collapse to my knees, untouched by the swarming insects, terrified to release what is inside me, but there is no holding this back any longer. As my jaw stretches wider than I ever thought possible, and my eyes bulge to the point of bursting, my body locks in a convulsive rigor, and I release a torrent of white feathers into the room.

On my walk down the hill, the flames of the mansion stretch upward into the night sky, black smoke blotting out even the brightest of stars. I reach up and touch my slick face, coated in a layer of blood, my chin glistening with rendered fat, hearing a steady thrum of wings beating in the air above me, as I raise my head to see a single white dove illuminated by the house fire, circling ever higher into the darkness, before disappearing into the night.

I guess there was some goodness in him after all.

When I cast my gaze down toward the water, there is no rip, no tear, no shimmer of gold parting to reveal some other horrific landscape. There is only silence. I am empty, gutted, and stumbling forward, my torso coated with a sheen of sweat beneath my clothes, that is quickly turning to ice, and a faint aura of light surrounds my body, warm steam rising gently into the cold, cold night.

I am frozen to the bone, and yet I am burning with heat.

I am rippling with disgust, and yet coated in peace.

He has not been absolved.

He has been recognized, and taken.

Lumbering in the woods to my left is a peculiar presence, surrounded by glowing eyes, snorting in the darkness as it stomps through the undergrowth, snow burying everything around it. And as a glint of moonlight slips out from behind the looming clouds, it is gone.

I have kept my word, and so has he.

What comes next, I honestly don't know.

# EPILOGUE

In a small town surrounded by a tangle of rivers, a community rallies to raise a barn, a church gathers to sing praises into the sunlit day, a family has a picnic in a grassy park where birds chirp, dogs bark, and music fills the air. But in the shadows, when the night descends, a man smokes a cigarette in an alley, muttering under his breath, cursing everything he doesn't understand, every belief that didn't jive with his own. And a rip begins to tear at the far end of this dirty, stinking alley, milk rotting, chicken carcasses festering, urine staining the brick walls, as he exhales, trembling with rage. He is not alone, not in this world, not in this country, not in this state, and not in this town. Hell, he's not alone in the one hundred feet around him—others of a similar nature wandering in the night as they clench and unclench their fists, spitting anger to the sidewalks, putting fists through walls, looking for something beautiful to destroy.

Several miles away, a young girl awakens and has a vision. She sees the ripple, the tear in reality, and beyond it, a cornucopia of beasts. Some are peaceful, quiet, and content, while others roam the dunes looking for vengeance, their manifested sins complete in form—hard scaly armor, sharp piercing quills, dull penetrating horns. She has received the calling now, as others have across the globe, and in time, she will pack a bag and head out into the world, leaving behind her family and friends to combat the horrors that long to push through from the other side, as well as the dangers that linger here, just around the corner, creating this violation, this stain, and rippling menace. She will do this because she has lived many lives, evolved to a state beyond need of absolution, reborn into this very moment in order to combat this hate. This is her fate, her destiny, and she will carry out these duties in order to make this world a better place. It's not a futile battle, this war she wages, just one that seems never-ending.

The wolf that survives? It's the one you feed.

# ACKNOWLEDGMENTS

First and foremost I have to thank my family for their love and support. I never could have done any of this without you. So, thank you Lisa, Ricky, and Tyler. I want to thank my agent, Paula Munier, at Talcott Notch for continuing to believe in my work—it always matters. I have to thank Repo Kempt—my arctic advisor—for helping me to make this book really shine. The details, the authority, the expertise—you were an invaluable asset to this project, and a great friend, too. I want to thank my students, peers, and fellow authors for listening to me as I tried to figure this novel out, for helping me to go deeper, wider, and weirder, for pushing me to go beyond what is expected, to strive for greatness, to push until I was uncomfortable, vulnerable, and spent. I value your opinions and input, and appreciate your kindness and generosity along the way. Finally, I want to thank you, the reader, for being here. When I sit down to write anything—short story, novella, novel, whatever—I always think of you first. I want to make sure that the journey is worth it, that I appeal to all of your senses—body, mind, and soul—in ways that entertain you, move you, and (if I'm lucky) blow your mind. If this is your first time reading my work, thank you for taking a chance on me. If you've come back for more, know that I'm grateful. As writers, we often do this alone—and that's not easy. They say that when we die, we have two deaths—the first is when our body expires, and the second is the last time somebody says your name out loud. My hope for us all is that we may we live forever.

## ABOUT THE AUTHOR

Richard Thomas is the award-winning author of nine books. These include the novels *Incarnate, Disintegration, Breaker,* and *Transubstantiate*; the collections *Spontaneous Human Combustion, Tribulations, Staring into the Abyss,* and *Herniated Roots*; and a novella, collected in *The Soul Standard*. Thomas has been nominated for Bram Stoker, Shirley Jackson, ITW Thriller, and Audie awards. He has more than 175 stories in print.

# DISCOVER
# *STORIES UNBOUND*

PodiumAudio.com

www.ingramcontent.com/pod-product-compliance
Lightning Source LLC
Jackson TN
JSHW020920020125
76325JS00016B/86

\* 9 7 8 1 0 3 9 4 5 3 2 0 3 \*